Chapter 1

LaShaun savored the taste of her last homemade boudin ball dipped in Creole mustard sauce. Both based on Monmon Odette's recipe. She'd gotten a warm feeling of nostalgia reading her grandmother's flowing handwriting. Suddenly, she opened her eyes. Chase, Ellie, and even their dog Beau sat staring at her.

"Um, babe, you really hungry, huh?" Chase's dark eyes twinkled. He reached beneath the table to squeeze one of her thighs.

"Yeah, Mama. Hungry." Ellie blinked at LaShaun, then glanced down at her mother's empty plate.

"I wouldn't mind another girl," Chase murmured and ate another forkful of jambalaya.

"I want a little brother!" Ellie chirped. She clapped her hands and started to sing. "Baby brother, baby brother."

Beau woofed his two cents happily, though his vote was unintelligible.

Ellie leaned toward him and nodded eagerly. "Maybe both. Twins. Jared and Janeen are twins in my class. They're a lot of fun! Baby sister and baby bro—"

"Stop!" LaShaun wiped her mouth and tried to get over the shock. "You two have jumped way too high into those assumptions. I had a real busy day is all, and... and I missed lunch. Oh, and I had hardly any breakfast since someone was almost late for school after staying up way past her bedtime. Reading when she was supposed to be sleeping."

"Miss Valerie told us to read about the history of Mardi Gras. I wanted ideas on a costume for the school parade," Ellie piped up, throwing in her teacher's name for added credibility.

"So you were doing homework." Chase winked at Ellie, who nodded with vigor and grinned back.

LaShaun heaved a sigh at the conspirators. Classic. "You were reading one of Daddy's old comic books."

"Um, there was a Mardi Gras parade in it," Ellie mumbled. She tucked her head down when LaShaun cocked an eyebrow at her.

"Speaking of bedtime," Chase broke in before LaShaun could speak. "You've got thirty minutes before you take a bath and get ready to turn in. I put your notebook out so you can do your math assignment."

"Thank you." Ellie stuffed the last piece of a hush puppy into her mouth. Still chewing with gusto, she

Devil's Swamp

Lynn Emery

Lazy River Publishing

Lynn Emery/Lazy River Publishing
P.O. Box 74833
Baton Rouge, LA 70807
www.lazyriverpublishing.com

Publisher's Note: This is a work of fiction. Names, characters, places, and incidents are a product of the author's imagination. Locales and public names are sometimes used for atmospheric purposes. Any resemblance to actual people, living or dead, or to businesses, companies, events, institutions, or locales is completely coincidental.

Book Layout & Design ©2013 - BookDesignTemplates.com

Devil's Swamp/ Lynn Emery. -- 1st ed.
ISBN 978-0-9997628-5-1

“Va te faire foutre”

(Go to the devil)

hopped from her chair. "I bet Taylor I'd get a better score on the pop quiz Thursday."

"Be sure to wash your hands," LaShaun called out as Ellie sprinted down the hallway. "We don't want you handing in greasy paper."

Ellie stuck her head around the corner. "Mama, we don't hand in homework like you did in the old days. I scan it in and email it to Miss Valerie." Then she vanished.

"Excuse me for living in the olden days," LaShaun retorted. "I'm checking your work in another twenty minutes, so don't get distracted with more comic books."

"She's gone, hon. Hey, you were the one who insisted she attend that fancy school. And I don't want her having an email account," Chase added with a frown.

LaShaun didn't have to ask. She knew he was thinking of child predators online. "Relax. Red Oaks Academy has its own server. She only uses her student email in class. I think it's great they're learning to use technology."

"Yeah, well. I'm on a wait-and-see basis with that place. Don't know how the Louisiana version of a wizardry school got approved. She better not come home with a flying broomstick is all I know. Or start practicing spells to change Beau into a rabbit or something."

Beau's large head lifted at the mention of his name. He let out a sharp bark before trotting off. LaShaun knew he was going to Ellie's bedroom. Maybe to check his human sister wasn't up to magic that involved him.

"Now you've got our poor dog worried. He'll be watching Ellie out of the corner of his eye for days now," LaShaun said with a giggle.

"Seriously, though. Are you sure it's legal for a shadowy outfit like the Third Eye Association to fund a magnet school?"

"They're not a 'shadowy outfit.' I'm beyond happy TEA helped build a charter school nearby. Kids with special needs like Ellie can learn without feeling like they're freaks."

LaShaun knew she'd have to keep selling Chase on the idea of Ellie's special schooling. The Third Eye Association, an organization founded over one-hundred-fifty years ago, conducted research on paranormal phenomena. TEA also gave people with psychic ability a safe haven to be with those who were like them. The supportive environment meant a lot to its members.

"Regular children attend as well, and most of the teachers are regular too," LaShaun continued in a patient tone as she cleared the table.

"Yeah, yeah. Next you'll pat me on the head and say, 'Bless your regular-guy heart,' " Chase said.

He packed a helping of leftover jambalaya in a container for his work lunch. Then he filled the farmhouse sink with hot, soapy water. He washed and rinsed while LaShaun dried. Their dishwasher only got a workout when they had company over. They preferred spending time chatting over kitchen cleanup each day. They took every opportunity to have alone time as a couple. Chase frequently worked long hours heading up the Vermilion Parish sheriff's criminal investigation section. LaShaun split her hours each day between mommy duty and her own business. Between select paranormal investigations and managing assets left to her by her grandmother, LaShaun kept just as busy. But being a mother and wife always came before "ghostbusting," as Chase insisted on calling it.

LaShaun put away her grandmother's cast iron skillet with care. Then she turned to him and took the wet dishcloth from his hand. She pulled his tall frame against her body and kissed him. "There is nothing regular about you, Chase Broussard."

"Your sweet talk always wears me down," Chase said, putting his arms around her.

"Still can't resist me, huh?" LaShaun grinned up at him.

Chase gave her butt a playful squeeze before he pulled away, his work cell phone buzzing in a demand for attention. "Duty calls."

"Way to spoil the mood, officer." LaShaun pouted at him.

"Being so sexy is what got you knocked up with another little Broussard," Chase joked. He laughed while dodging the wet kitchen towels she lobbed at his head.

"I'm not—" LaShaun felt a twinge of nausea. She placed a hand on her stomach. "I just ate too much, that's all," she muttered to herself.

Chase's full attention was already on his phone call. LaShaun shook her head as she wiped the kitchen table and counter tops. The Broussard clan would just have to be content with their only-child status. That included their dog, Beau. LaShaun's OB-GYN doc had assured her that a second pregnancy was unlikely. The unusual shape of her uterus affected fertility. Still, she didn't remind Chase of the long shot. He got such a happy twinkle in his dark Cajun eyes when he dropped a baby hint.

"Gotta go in," Chase announced. He started to say more but glanced over his shoulder first.

LaShaun knew he was checking to make sure Ellie hadn't returned. He wanted to protect her from the grim facts of his job. "Bad?"

"Body found near the docks," Chase said low even though they were alone. "So make sure you—"

"Double-check the locks and set the alarm. Yes, sir." LaShaun gave him an affectionate peck on the cheek. "We'll be fine."

"Good. I guess I'll keep you and the kid," Chase replied with a smile. A distant bark sounded. "I mean you three. Is that dog really psychic, too? Never mind, don't remind me."

LaShaun laughed but then grew serious as she watched him prepare to leave. "You be careful."

"My middle name."

Chase marched to their mudroom off the kitchen to put on his work boots. Moments later, the door bumped shut as he left. Locks clicked. Then the rumble of his truck engine signaled he was on his way. LaShaun was about to put the plates in the cabinet when their landline phone rang. The caller ID told her it was Cee-Cee.

"Hey girl," LaShaun said in her cheerful tone. Her friend's somber greeting killed her hope that this was a social call.

****

Chase came home around two o'clock the next morning. The distant pinging from their alarm system signaled the back door had opened. LaShaun's eyes fluttered open at the quiet sounds of him trying not to make too much noise.

"Sorry to wake you," Chase said, his voice muffled because he stood in the walk-in closet of their master suite.

"It's okay. I was half awake anyway." LaShaun pushed back the comforter and sat up. She fluffed the pillows for back support.

"Still sick?" Chase stepped from the closet; his handsome brow creased with a concerned frown.

"No, that's not it. Cee-Cee called. There's a problem at TEA. Two top officials have died in the past three months. One of a massive heart attack. The other had a stroke."

"Humph, natural causes. Why's that a problem?" Chase padded into their bathroom.

LaShaun flipped back the covers and followed him. "Leadership vacuum. These two, one man and woman, were in charge of the two largest divisions at TEA. Plus, they were on opposite sides of political infighting over the direction of TEA as a whole."

Cee-Cee Cuevas had risen to the rank of Regional Operations Manager. She relished the increase in pay and perks. Still, she'd often complained to LaShaun about the administrative side of her job. Cee-Cee missed the action of fieldwork.

"Don't get involved," Chase said around a mouthful of toothpaste. He rinsed, then turned from the vanity mirror to point his toothbrush at her. "Not *your* fight."

"Cee-Cee didn't call me about the politics, but about the *deaths*. I mean, isn't it strange that two top leaders die within weeks of each other? Their aides say they'd begun peace efforts between the sides, tamping down the rhetoric." LaShaun leaned against the counter. She admired her husband's taut muscles as he stripped.

Chase stepped into the spacious walk-in shower. As was his habit, he stood under the initial cold blast of water from the jet when he turned the handle. The glass enclosure slowly fogged up. "Babe, people die every day because of health reasons. People in top jobs have even more stress. Don't I know it. How old were those folks?"

"Late fifties, early sixties." LaShaun started to say more, but decided to let him lather and rinse in peace. His way of winding down was even more important after a homicide.

"There you go. Probably had pre-existing conditions," Chase said.

"I'll tell you the rest later." LaShaun left and climbed back into bed. She thought over Cee-Cee's facts, laid out in a compelling step-by-step, logical way.

Chase appeared ten minutes later. He wore some of his comfy pajama pants. Water droplets beaded on the dark waves of his hair. He sat down on the floor, then handed LaShaun the cordless hair dryer and a brush. She continued to mull over the TEA drama as she worked. Five minutes later, his thick hair was almost dry. LaShaun turned the dryer off, took the tools back to their bathroom, then returned to join him in bed.

"So, what else did Cee-Cee have to say?" Chase pulled her close.

"You go to sleep. We'll talk about it in the morning," LaShaun said, and snuggled against his chest. She wanted to help banish the grimness of what he'd dealt with at the crime scene.

"It is morning, darlin'. C'mon," Chase replied and then yawned. "We both know you want to tell me now."

"You're right. Could just be natural causes, but..." LaShaun let her voice trail away. "Cee-Cee has probably just gotten overly cautious in her old age," she joked.

"She's what, twenty-six, twenty-seven? If she's old, then we're ancient."

"Responsibility can age you, not to mention long hours. And like you said, stress. Gone is the carefree Gen Y-er we knew," LaShaun said with a chuckle.

"Yeah, well, if she's got to deal with a crew like Jonah, I totally get it." Chase gave a grunt.

Jonah Parker had been with Ellie through a trying time. They'd connected since both were kids with paranormal abilities. He'd become her self-appointed big brother. He'd also been hired as a field operator for TEA. His ability to amplify the psionic skills of others had made him a valued addition.

"Jonah isn't that bad. Remember, he's your adopted son." LaShaun laughed again at the moan her comment brought. "Ellie adores him. You have to admit, he's had a positive effect on her."

"Yeah, well. Whatever. Postmortems done?"

"Confirmed heart attack and stroke as the causes," LaShaun replied.

"There you go. I don't see why Cee-Cee is worked up about it." Chase yawned again as he shifted to his side. He patted LaShaun on the butt until she moved to spoon against him.

"She suspects foul play, as they say in your profession."

"Tox screens results?" Chase swung into lawman mode.

"Initial tests came back with no drugs that would cause death," LaShaun said.

"There you go. I admire her caution, but I'd say in my professional opinion that Cee-Cee should move on. I would close that kind of case based on those facts." Chase kissed the back of LaShaun's neck. "Night."

LaShaun frowned at the memory of how tense Cee-Cee sounded. Her friend might have been more carefree in the past, but she'd also always had a laser-like focus when it came to her work. If Cee-Cee smelled a rat, it was time to set out traps.

"You'd also trust your instincts if something didn't sit right with you. TEA is full of people with extraordinary abilities." LaShaun was thinking out loud rather than making a point to him.

"You mean they can kill people with their minds? Please tell me you're kidding. I have enough on my hands with normal killers running loose," Chase retorted.

"You won't have to worry about getting a call. TEA has a criminal investigation section." LaShaun patted his thigh with one hand.

"Great. Just what we need. A secret wizard police force," Chase muttered, his voice muted by the pillow.

"I have more good news. Jonah is a CI cop."

"Lord help us all. Ellie's big bro better not be talking to her about that stuff. If he is, I'll have a heart-to-heart with him."

LaShaun tucked closer against his firm torso. "Of course he doesn't. They have normal discussions about school and the latest toys."

"Good. By the way, don't think you're off the hook."

"What are you talking about?"

Chase cupped a hand over LaShaun's belly. "Go see Dr. Hollensworth. Let her tell you what me and Ellie already know."

"Tell you what, Papa Broussard. *You* carry a kicking, squirming little human inside you for nine months," LaShaun wisecracked.

"I'd do it for you, sweetness," Chase mumbled. His words trailed off into a soft snore.

"Yeah, I just bet you..." LaShaun didn't bother to finish. His regular breathing and slack body told her the discussion was over. She'd already scheduled her appointment anyway.

****

Three days later LaShaun sat on the examining table in her OB-GYN doctor's office. A nurse's aide had instructed her to get undressed to wait for the doctor. Minutes later the door opened again. A young woman with caramel skin and dyed red hair came in.

"Good morning. I'm N'Keisha." She tapped the plastic name tab on her chest. "I'm your nurse today. "How are we doing?"

N'Keisha cheerily bustled around, taking LaShaun's blood pressure first, then her temperature. The routine list of questions followed. When LaShaun answered why she'd come in, the nurse congratulated her with a wide grin. Dr. Hollensworth, tall with blond hair mixed with gray, came in wearing a smile. After washing her hands, she got right to work. She kept up a steady stream of chitchat, asking about her family and commenting on news accounts about LaShaun's last investigation.

"That was wild about that guy searching for buried treasure. Ghosts and all," Dr. Hollensworth said. The nurse nodded agreement. The doctor finished up her examination. "You can sit up now."

LaShaun took the nurse's hand as she helped her. "Yeah, crazy. So, I've got a stomach virus or something?"

"Did you do a home pregnancy test?" N'Keisha replied with a grin.

"Um, no. I was pretty sure I wasn't, so.... I came to satisfy my husband." LaShaun shrugged. "I've had the flu before. This felt just like it. I usually feel fine after a few days."

"You'll get over this in about eight months." Dr. Hollensworth beamed at her like a proud aunt.

"I'll get samples of prenatal vitamins to get you started," N'Keisha announced and left.

LaShaun blinked hard at the news. She'd thought more about Ellie's after-school gym and dance classes, Chase's new murder case, and Cee-Cee's call than a baby. "But I thought..."

"I said getting pregnant again would be difficult. I never said it was impossible." Dr. Hollensworth gave her right knee an encouraging pat. "The shape and tilt of your uterus does make it harder. But don't you worry. Last time you had few issues, as I recall. You're still young and healthy. These few months will fly by. We're going to take good care of you, Mama."

LaShaun shook her head to clear out the haze her diagnosis had brought on. The nurse joked about a psychic not knowing she was pregnant. LaShaun tried to explain that psychics didn't see their own future. N'Keisha, a woman of hard science, it seemed, gave her an indulgent smile.

"Here are your supplements. I've printed out how often you take them." N'Keisha went on to give LaShaun more medical instructions.

Fifteen minutes later LaShaun sat in her Subaru Forrester in the clinic parking lot. A pink and blue bag the nurse had given her to carry everything home lay in her lap. Bright February sunshine warmed the interior of the SUV while people wore coats against the chilly temperature outside.

"You will have children." Monmon Odette's voice floated around LaShaun, her soft Creole accent so clear.

"Well, Monmon, you were right. I wish you were here to babysit," LaShaun sad. She teared up at the image of Monmon Odette playing with her great-grandchildren. She still missed her. The passage of time dulled the pain, but hadn't filled the void left by her transition to the next life. Then, as if a recording button had been pressed, she heard Monmon Odette's other words.

"They will need protection."

LaShaun made the sign of the cross and whispered one of the prayers her grandmother had taught her. She started the SUV to head for home. Sunshine, a blue sky, and the lovely landscape helped push aside gloomy thoughts of unseen danger. The stretch of Highway 82 curved gently with prairies on one side and sugar cane fields on the other. A mix of '90s R&B and zydeco on her radio finished the job of lightening LaShaun's mood. Chase and Ellie would be over the moon. Then something caught her eye when she turned on Highway 693 going west. A figure stood next to a small, red truck at the intersection of the highway and Trahan Road. He waved her over. LaShaun reached for her cell phone, ready to call road assistance for a stranded driver. As she slowed the SUV, a sharp tingle spread down her arms and up her spine. The man, handsome in his own unique way, strode forward. His brown hair curled to the edge of his checked shirt collar. Faded blue jeans hugged his slim hips. He took off his sunglasses. Emanuel "Manny" Young grinned at her.

"As I live and breathe. Ain't this a lucky break for me. LaShaun Rousselle Broussard, of all people, coming to my rescue."

"What in hell are you doing here?" LaShaun blurted. "You're supposed to be in Lafayette at your job or the halfway house."

"Oh, right. We haven't kept in touch," Manny replied, his smile fading. He sighed. "And after all we've been through together."

"We're not friends, Manny. Not even close." LaShaun glanced around and looked back at him.

"I'm sure not your enemy," Manny said with a hint of melancholy in his tone. He expression brightened again. "Anyway, I've been doin' so well, got me a one-bedroom apartment. My social worker says I'm one of his star clients."

Almost two years before, Manny had been paroled from prison despite being an alleged serial killer. She'd uncovered evidence that threw doubt on his guilt. Many in Beau Chene blamed LaShaun for his release. Her investigation pointed to other possible suspects, including Manny's father.

"I thought you weren't supposed to go more than fifty miles outside of Lafayette," LaShaun said.

"Nah. Now I can't leave the state. My lawyer is working on a request for clemency. That would shorten my parole time by ten years. Ain't that grand?" Manny rested both hands on his narrow waist.

"For who, I wonder," LaShaun muttered with a frown at him. She gritted her teeth when Manny chuckled in response. "Well? I assume you arranged this little meet-up for a reason."

"You don't believe in coincidences? Maybe I was out for a pleasant ride to enjoy this pretty weather. Then my little truck, Susie-Q, let me down."

"Bullshit." LaShaun muttered more profanity when he laughed.

"Straight up, no chaser—like always. I can't help but like you, even though you try hard not to like me back."

"It's not hard. At all," LaShaun replied. "Let's review. A serial killer connected to a string of bloody crimes with psychic powers. Nope. Not on my friends list."

"*Alleged* serial killer."

"Which doesn't make anyone feel safer," she shot back.

LaShaun looked around once more. No one was nearby. Not a car or truck was in sight. She wondered if Manny had somehow managed to keep people away. Then dismissed her own thought as irrational.

Manny pointed to an almost flat tire and small car jack on the ground next to it. "There you go."

"Looks like you got it under control then. Bye." LaShaun revved the engine.

"Okay, okay. I'll tell you the truth," Manny said, a palm up as a request that she not pull off.

"I don't think that's a skill set you ever developed, Manny," LaShaun shot back. Still, she could not resist the tingle of curiosity he stirred. "But give it a try."

"I didn't want to get you in trouble by asking you to be seen with me in Lafayette. So I was gonna drive to Alcide and ask you to meet me there. Little chance of some nosy reporter spotting us there," Manny said, referring to a small, unincorporated community between Abbeville and Beau Chene.

"I'll bet at least one reporter has an informant to snitch about where you are all the time." LaShaun looked around yet again at the mention of news media.

"Had, past-tense. Sadly, Nola, the halfway house employee in question, is no longer with us. I mean she got fired is all," Manny added when LaShaun gasped.

"Meeting over. Not interested." She tapped the accelerator.

"I need to you to help solve my murder," Manny yelled.

Her tires squealed when she jammed the brakes.

Chapter 2

Fifteen minutes later LaShaun sat on a wood picnic bench in the village of Maurice just outside of Abbeville. She'd followed Manny to a tiny country store. Two gasoline pumps and a garage were the other half of the business. An attendant had set about repairing the small hole that caused a slow leak in Manny's truck tire.

LaShaun accepted the paper cup of coffee Manny handed her before he sat down. "My husband knows where I am."

"And who you're with?" Manny grunted. "I'll bet he not too happy with you right about now. You shouldn't have told. Woulda been less trouble."

"We don't keep secrets."

"Everybody has secrets," Manny said with a brooding expression.

"We don't share every minute detail of our pasts or even everyday life. But there are certain things, important facts, you don't keep hidden," LaShaun replied.

"Well, I can't talk about what makes a marriage work since I ain't been in one. Not likely to at this rate," Manny added with a laugh tinged with bitterness. "Don't even know if I can ever have a normal relationship. Ain't never been close to one."

LaShaun's prescient tingle shot through her body, a sort of electric itch. Images of Manny walking into a rundown motel with a prostitute flashed in her head. Then scenes of his abusive and dysfunctional early family life. The story of twelve-year-old Manny watching Orin beat his older brother to a pulp played like a scratching recording. Manny never saw Ethan again after that brutal clash. He assumed his brother had ended up buried in the woods or had been thrown in a swamp to be eaten by gators. She even saw the malevolent face of his dead father, Orin. LaShaun winced at the bile that rose at the back of her throat. She swallowed hard, took in deep breaths, and let them out.

Manny stood over her with a taller paper cup. He put it on the table in front of her. "Sip this."

LaShaun hadn't even realized Manny had left. She drank deeply without asking. It took a few seconds, but the lemon-lime soft drink settled her stomach. "Thanks."

"Sorry I triggered some badass visions. Didn't mean to..." Manny rubbed his face hard with one hand. He looked off into the distance. "Sorry for a lot of shit."

LaShaun didn't bother asking how he knew what was wrong or how she was feeling. One of Manny's paranormal abilities was projecting images. Most people weren't affected. Because LaShaun was clairvoyant, his skill could have an intense effect on her. Yet he'd revealed something. At times Manny had no control over his extrasensory faculties. Maybe this made him even more dangerous.

She drained the rest of the cup. They sat in silence as five more minutes ticked by. Manny seemed content to give LaShaun time to recover. Light traffic came and went as a few customers stopped for lunch. The small store had a deli section in the back. The smell of fried chicken and hamburgers wafted on the air.

"You okay?" Manny said, referring to the possible effect of food scents on her upset stomach.

"Yeah, I'm fine. Really." LaShaun steeled herself to sever whatever telepathic connection they'd developed. She was suddenly alarmed at Manny knowing too much about her, especially that she was pregnant.

He nodded, gave a sharp sigh, and then sat down across from her once more. "Good."

"Back to the reason you interrupted my day," LaShaun said in an abrupt tone. She almost mentioned having to meet Ellie's school bus, but stopped in time. *Keep references to your personal life to yourself*, she thought.

"I'm serious," Manny replied evenly. They both knew he didn't need to repeat his shocking request.

"You're going to be murdered. You've seen this as a dream, or a waking visualization of some sort?"

Manny blinked at her in genuine confusion for a few seconds. He shook his head as if to clear away his tangled thoughts. Then he laughed. The short, sharp sound sent another set of chills through her. Here she sat with a serial killer who could laugh about blood being shed, including his own.

"Alleged serial killer," Manny reminded her once more. "No, I mean the murders I'm supposed to have committed."

"You want me to find the real killer," LaShaun said, enunciating each word as if testing out the sound of what he wanted.

"I already suspect I'm the real killer," Manny said quietly.

LaShaun leaned away from him in reflex. "Then why ask?"

Manny's pensive expression stayed in place another few beats. "Not sure I am, but I want to separate my father's crimes from my own, if I have any."

"And if you did kill those people, what are you going to do about it?"

"Not sure of that either. Well? You gonna help me?" Manny avoided looking at LaShaun. He rubbed his hands together in a nervous motion, realized it, and stopped.

She should have said "Hell no." But the possibilities intrigued her. Unanswered questions surrounding the Blood River Ripper case flooded her brain like a drug. One no psychic investigator worth her salt could resist.

****

Later that afternoon, Ellie and Beau bounced around in celebration of their new sibling. Chase had come home earlier than usual to join in, but his mood was decidedly less lighthearted. He and LaShaun relaxed on the sofa in the family room adjacent to the kitchen. Outside in the backyard, Ellie squealed as she threw a ball to Beau. The Great Weimar mostly ignored it in favor of bounding into the woods that edged their neat lawn.

"I didn't set up a meeting with Manny, Chase," LaShaun said for the second time.

"Okay. But you should have hit the gas and gone right by him. I mean, you're pregnant, for God's sake." Chase put a large, protective hand on her belly.

LaShaun felt a spike of irritation, which seemed to cause a flutter. The baby was already responding? LaShaun would ask Miss Rose, her friend and fellow psychic, what that might mean so early.

She pushed up from the sofa and walked to the kitchen. Remains of Ellie's after-school snack still lay on the kitchen island. "Don't be silly. I'm not helpless just because I'm pregnant."

"No one was around. That stretch of highway is isolated and..." Chase held up both palms when she turned to face him.

"How many times do I have to show you I can take care of myself? Besides, Manny doesn't scare me even if he does try." LaShaun ate a chunk of apple and a grape Ellie had left in her bowl. She also eyed the piece of cheese.

"He tried what?" Chase stood and strode toward her with a frown.

"Calm down. He didn't lay a hand on me. Manny knows better." LaShaun decided on the cheese. She also poured apple juice into a glass. Then she reached for the cookie jar.

"That's your second round of munching. You were the one complaining with Ellie about your out-of-control appetite."

"Don't talk to me in that tone, Chase Broussard. I'm not one of your junior deputies. My weight is just fine, thank you very much," she snapped.

"I didn't say anything about your figure. Now who should calm down?" Chase raised an eyebrow.

"And my hormones are *not* making me grouchy." LaShaun pushed away the cookie jar. To distract herself from more food, she washed Ellie's dirty plate by hand instead of stacking it in the dishwasher. Then she scrubbed the kitchen table. Next, she straightened already-neat canisters on the counter.

Chase let out a soft chuckle as he put a bag of grapes back into the fridge. "Yes, dear."

LaShaun swallowed the tart words on the tip of her tongue. No need to prove the point for him. She breathed in and out to settle her jangled nerves. "Back to Manny. Aren't you the least bit curious to know if there's another killer out there?"

"I don't care what the judge said. Manny is dangerous. He may have been the leader, or he could have followed Orin. Or his older brother. I hear he was a nasty chip off the old block, too. Doesn't matter. Three people ended up dead. Probably more," Chase said, referring to the forensics tied to Manny. "Other murders fit the pattern, but there wasn't enough evidence to be definitive.

"He admitted having sex with the two women. He partied with the male victim. And Orin Young—"

"Yeah, yeah. I heard all the reasons he got cut loose. Doesn't mean he's not a serial killer. Sure as hell didn't inspire public confidence in the criminal justice system either," Chase complained.

Before LaShaun could reply, the phone rang. She picked it up without looking at the Caller ID display. The deep voice at the other end startled her. "Yes sir. Eight is too early. I have to get my daughter off to school. That should be fine. You're welcome."

"Now what?" Chase put both hands on his waist.

"That was Zachary Desmond, TEA secretary-general in charge of strategy and field operations in North America. He and Cee-Cee want to meet with me Monday. They had me on speakerphone with two other bigwigs in the organization. Which means... I'm not sure what it means." LaShaun puzzled over the call. What Desmond didn't say seemed more important.

"They want you to help look into the deaths. That psychic stuff must be catching," Chase quipped.

"Funny," LaShaun wisecracked. "He didn't mention the deaths specifically, only said it was very important. Monday afternoon at five o'clock in New Iberia. I'll call my cousin Azalei to babysit."

Chase's expression grew solemn. "Look, I know you believe in second chances and not judging folks based on their past."

"This doesn't have anything to do with my… exploits back in the day," LaShaun broke in. She was still living down her legendary wild years. Many in Beau Chene hadn't forgotten.

"A crusade to clear the Blood River Ripper is taking this 'fight for the underdog' thing way too far," Chase pushed on.

LaShaun sighed. His point hit home even if she couldn't admit it out loud. She'd been suspected of a lot of awful things in the past, including murder. Truth be told she made mistakes, big ones. The consequences still haunted her at times, especially during nights when she couldn't sleep.

"I won't let sympathy about Manny's horrible childhood cloud my judgement," LaShaun said.

"You'll be busy with getting ready for the baby and helping TEA track down clues on these deaths. Can't believe I'm actually glad you're getting involved in one of their 'projects.' " Chase walked over and put his arms around her. "So, that's it. Let Manny use some of Orin's money to hire a private detective."

"Hmm." LaShaun gave him a vague smile.

He kissed her forehead and stepped away. "I'm going to start clearing out our spare room. I can donate some of that stuff to St. Augustine for their annual spring garage sale. The ladies' auxiliary will be thrilled. A lot of the toys and Ellie's clothes are in great shape. Won't need them since we're having a boy."

LaShaun blinked back from her thoughts. "Hey, you don't know that. We're going to be surprised. Like with Ellie. No gender reveal."

"Don't need to. Remember, psychic. Catching." Chase tapped his temple, grinned, and winked at her.

He strode off, whistling as he went down the hall that led to their bedrooms. Chase assumed she was already distracted by the bright shiny new TEA puzzle. But LaShaun could multitask.

****

LaShaun spent the next few days in her role of work-at-home mama. Cee-Cee e-mailed LaShaun TEA documents about the two officials who had died. Secretary General Desmond sent more documents about the inner workings of TEA. LaShaun read up on the murder cases against Manny Young.

Ellie got over the new baby excitement fast. She settled back into the world of her friends and what happened at school. Chase spent evenings clearing out the extra bedroom. He had begun to draw up plans for the nursery, consulting with LaShaun on wall paint, furniture, and helpful gadgets for parents of newborns. LaShaun welcomed his intense focus on the new project

Sunday, they had a rare quiet evening ahead of the regular work week. Not that Chase's schedule had ever been Monday through Friday, nine-to-five. They lingered over a simple Sunday dinner of baked chicken, sweet potatoes, and green beans. Early that morning, Chase's parents had brought over one of the elder Mrs. Broussard's specialties, a pecan pie. Two subtle hints; the younger Broussard family should attend mass and visit more often.

"We can go to your parents for their usual big Sunday dinner next week," LaShaun said.

Ellie paused in the act of eating pie. "Yay, I'll play Hide-the-Rabbit with Melanie and Bubba."

"His name is Kristopher, Ellie. You know his mama and your grandmother don't like that nickname," LaShaun said, then added quietly, "We don't need to give Elizabeth more reasons to blackball us."

"Granny Liz doesn't like me much anyway, so it doesn't matter," Ellie said with a matter-of-fact shrug.

Chase's head came up with a jerk. "Your grandmother loves you like all of her grandchildren."

Ellie shook her head. "Nuh-uh. She told Jessi, Mel, and Bubba to be careful around me. And to let her know if I do anything to hurt them. I never would. I don't even use my superpowers to beat them at kickball or Hide-the-Rabbit."

"They're not 'superpowers.' That's just a term we used when you were a little kid," LaShaun said quickly. "You have highly developed senses, like Mama, that most folks don't have."

"Saying superpowers is more fun." Ellie ate more pie.

Chase leaned toward Ellie, an arm on the back of her chair. "When did my mama say that?"

"I don't know. Troy told me," Ellie replied, referring to a sixteen-year-old cousin. "I asked Melanie and she said yeah. I told them they were safe from my superpowers. We all laughed. They didn't take Granny Liz serious. Troy can be kind of mean sometimes."

"I'll have a talk with him and his daddy." Chase's dark eyes sparkled with anger.

"He's just being a typical annoying teenager, honey. He likes to tease the younger kids a lot—right, Ellie?" LaShaun tried to head off the potential family storm she saw brewing.

"Yeah. He's always pushing Bubba, I mean Kris, around. Sometimes I make him stop," Ellie added casually. She wiped her mouth with a paper napkin and hopped from her chair. "I'll wash out Beau's food and water bowls."

"Okay," LaShaun called after her. "Then—"

"Get ready for bath time and bed. I know," Ellie called back without looking at her mother or father. Beau's barks of affection added to her little girl voice talking to him.

Chase tapped a fist on the table top rhythmically for a few seconds. LaShaun cleared her throat as she began to stack now-empty dinner plates. Happy sounds of Ellie and Beau in the background didn't lighten the dark cloud that lingered. LaShaun left the table to load the dishwasher.

"I'm sure your mother..." LaShaun searched for the right words to defend her mother-in-law. Her strained relationship with Elizabeth Broussard didn't help.

"Even I can't come up with an excuse for her this time," Chase blurted.

LaShaun jumped when he slapped the oak surface hard. "Most people have a hard time dealing with people like us. She's just protective of her family."

"Ellie's a baby," Chase went on as though LaShaun hadn't spoken.

"Better not let Ellie hear you say that. Since she's 'getting closer to ten years old every day', In Ellie's mind she's practically old enough to drive."

"Mama should know better, damn it. I don't want my little girl growing up feeling like a freak or monster." Chase shoved his chair as he stood.

"Whoa, whoa. Maybe take a few deep, cleansing breaths before you get on the phone." LaShaun blocked his path to the cordless land-line phone.

"Phone, hell. I'm going over there," Chase huffed. "I've been playing nice, being diplomatic. Well, not anymore. We have another baby coming. If he's gifted—"

LaShaun placed a palm on his broad chest. "It's almost eight o'clock. Ellie always expects you to read her a bedtime Bible story, remember? Neither of you start the week off feeling right when you miss it."

"Bet my mother would be shocked to hear we read the Bible in this house," Chase hissed. Then he looked at LaShaun. "I *will* have that talk with Mama."

"Okay. Did you notice Ellie didn't seem upset? Sounds like she just takes it in stride, another weird grown-up."

Chase's furious frown eased a bit. "But I don't want her thinking Mama doesn't like her. That's bound to make Ellie feel bad."

"Which is a great point to make when you *calm down* and discuss the subject with your parents."

LaShaun intended to let her father-in-law know what was coming. She had a warm, affectionate relationship with Bruce Sr. He and Elizabeth seemed to have polar opposite temperaments. Yet they'd made their marriage work for almost forty-two years.

"Yeah." Chase let out a deep sigh.

For the next hour or so he worked around the house in a solemn, pensive way. He'd gotten Ellie ready for bed. LaShaun shamelessly listened at Ellie's closed bedroom door. Chase's deep voice rumbled, and Ellie's lighter voice answered. She didn't have to guess the subject of their exchange. She knocked and entered.

"Hey you two. Everybody all right?" LaShaun gave them both a bright grin.

Ellie nodded. "Daddy read the story about Deborah. She could see things other people couldn't. And she was a fighter against evil, like you, Mama."

"Well, let's not plan any battles right now. Lights-out time." LaShaun went to Ellie and kissed her soft cheek.

"Oh, and I need to bring cupcakes to school tomorrow. I forgot the note from Miss Simpson in my backpack." Ellie yawned as Chase smoothed the purple and pink bedspread around her.

"Ellie!" LaShaun went to her backpack and pulled out the sheet of paper. She read and sucked in a breath. "By nine in the morning. The bakery opens at eight."

"We like homemade fresh ones best, Mama," Ellie protested sleepily.

👁

"Do you now? So, we get to be choosy cupcakes snobs with last-minute requests? I don't think so, young lady." LaShaun finished reading the printed instructions.

"Love you, Mama and Daddy." Ellie's eyes were closed.

"Love you too, princess," Chase said. He kissed the top of her thick, dark curls. Then he followed LaShaun out into the hall. "Guess I know what you'll be doing at the crack of dawn. Don't worry. I'll help you measure out the ingredients tonight. We'll get all set up."

"Uh-huh. In other words, you'll sleep in while I'm slaving over a hot oven," LaShaun retorted.

They went to their master suite. Less than an hour later, they'd showered and changed. LaShaun wore an oversized t-shirt over matching yoga-styled pants. Chase wore sweat pants and a muscle shirt. True to his word, he helped her set up for baking the next morning.

"I have two cans of vanilla frosting. I hope it's enough," LaShaun said as she pulled them out of the pantry. Then LaShaun had another thought. She went to the fridge. "Wait a minute. Food coloring, check. I'll make the frosting with the colors of Mardi Gras."

"The kids will love that." Chase measured out flour, then baking powder. He put them in small bowls LaShaun used for ingredients. They worked in silence for a few minutes.

"Listen, darlin'. Don't be too hard on your mother. She's done better since Ellie was born." LaShaun rested a hand on his shoulder after a while.

"Yeah, well she's gonna do great once I talk to her." Chase slapped his hands over the kitchen sink to get flour off of them. He leaned against the counter and wiped his hands with the paper towel LaShaun handed him. He sighed. "But like you said, Ellie doesn't seem to be preoccupied with Mama. Thinking about the families of murder victims puts drama in perspective, though."

"Your latest homicide case?" LaShaun arranged her baking station in one corner of the kitchen counter.

Chase nodded. "I don't know what's worse, getting the news your loved one is dead or not knowing what happened to them."

"I don't understand."

"He's still a John Doe at this point. No wallet, no keys to anything. Hell, even the labels were removed from his clothes. Very odd," Chase said.

"If he was a transient that might explain it. His clothes might have come from thrift shop or a church with a free clothes closet. Check with the local congregations. They might recognize him from a picture."

"Maybe, but his clothes weren't worn out. And he was too clean to have been living on the streets. He just didn't look like the typical street guy." Chase frowned as he rubbed his chin.

"You really are psychic," LaShaun teased.

Chase's frown melted into a half-smile. "Some criminals might think we are, but no. Just training combined with years of experience. There's something not right about this one."

"Other than the poor man being dead. That's definitely not right." LaShaun turned somber as she thought of the victim. All alone in life and now in death.

"Yeah, but you know what I mean." Chase's expression grew pensive again.

"Well, you said he had no wallet. I'm assuming no watch, no cell phone. Maybe he was robbed of the few possessions he had." LaShaun crossed her arms.

"A likely explanation. Anyway, Dave approved us releasing his photo to the local media. Someone will recognize him, I guess. It's past your bedtime, young lady." Chase crossed to LaShaun and took her hand. When she stood, he placed a hand on her tummy. "Both or maybe the three of you?"

"Don't even," LaShaun said with a pretend scowl and playfully slapped his hand away. "The doctor didn't mention anything about twins, thank you Lord."

"Hey, you never know." Chase gave a hopeful sigh as he followed her to their bedroom. He rubbed her butt. "Papa's got the power."

"Oh, c'mon." LaShaun hooted with laughter when he strutted with his chest out.

They exchanged taunts and teases for a few minutes. The jokes turned into serious foreplay. Later they fell asleep after lovemaking that warmed LaShaun to the core. The shadow her critical mother-in-law or sad thoughts of an anonymous murder victim faded. At least for a time. Chase's regular breathing next to her helped lull LaShaun toward slumber as well. Then her eyes blinked open. Traces of a dream, or maybe an image, drifted at the edges of her consciousness. She tried to sift through which it was, a premonition or simply a fantasy conjured by her drowsy mind. No matter which, it left her with an anxious feeling that echoed Chase's words. Something wasn't right.

The next morning LaShaun made her best effort to be cheerful. What could be happier than baking Mardi Gras cupcakes for a group of six- and seven-year-olds? Ellie hopped out of bed early at the smell of baking. She was definitely in the most buoyant mood of all three. Chase smiled at his daughter as she chattered with excitement about her day. The first blush of morning sunshine completed the carefree family tableau. Still, the reality of death waited for Chase and LaShaun just outside their door.

"Everybody loves Mama's cupcakes. Taylor is gonna be so jealous when she sees Mardi Gras frosting. Her mama always brings cookies from the grocery store." Ellie wrinkled her nose.

"You're spoiled, huh?" Chase teased.

"Well, you can taste the difference, all those preserves in 'em," Ellie said with a sniff.

"You mean preservatives," LaShaun corrected and suppressed a smile. "Where'd you learn about them?"

"Cousin Azalei is into a wholesome diet. She says eating fresh isn't new. Our ancestors didn't put all kinds arta..." Ellie squinted as she stumbled over the word.

"Artificial ingredients?" LaShaun said.

"Yeah, that, in our food."

"Azalei strikes again," Chase muttered low. He covered his sarcasm by bringing his large coffee mug to his mouth.

"She's being a good influence. You can't argue with healthy eating advice," LaShaun replied. She grinned when Chase rolled his eyes.

"I better get going. I have a conference call with the state police lab folks." Chase headed for their mudroom.

"You have to talk about the man with the red stain on his blue shirt," Ellie piped up. "I'll see you later, Daddy. Cousin Azalei is gonna pick me up from school. She'll bring me home after Mama's meeting."

Chase stopped short and looked at Ellie. "Who told you about the man?"

"You're worried about finding out who he is. I could tell," Ellie said, choosing her words with care.

"Honey, we talked about looking into other people's heads." LaShaun kept her voice even as she crossed to Ellie, who sat eating the last of her toast.

"I don't do it on purpose. But when Daddy is thinking hard and something is bothering him, it just happens. I'm practicing not to, though." Ellie licked apple jelly from her fingers, jumped from her chair, and went to Chase. She took his hand. "Don't be mad at me like Granny Liz, Daddy."

The mention of his mother melted the crease on Chase's brow. "I'm not mad at you. Not a bit, pumpkin. Now finish your juice so you can get ready. You don't wanna be late for the bus. Miz Trina doesn't like waiting more than a minute, you know."

"She likes me, though, so she gives me wiggle room." Ellie beamed at the mention of the bus driver. She raced off with Beau right behind.

"What the hell?" Chase said low, a glance over his shoulder.

"She could have seen something on the television, a news bulletin. Or heard something at school. Beau Chene is a small town with a very effective informal news channel," LaShaun said and rubbed his arm.

"We didn't release details about his appearance, including his clothes. Or how he died."

"Whatever small bits she picked up on weren't enough to scare her." LaShaun knew Chase fretted that Ellie's paranormal abilities would traumatize her. So far, his grim fear hadn't come true.

"I'll talk to her TEA tutor about her exercises on control." LaShaun rubbed one of his muscular biceps. Ellie's chipper dialog with Beau floated down the hall. "See? She's fine."

"Yeah. Okay." Chase blinked in the direction of the sounds. He kissed LaShaun on the cheek. "See you later."

LaShaun smiled at him, waved, and followed him to the backdoor. She waved again when he glanced at her standing in the window. Once Chase's Ram truck turned onto the road from their driveway, LaShaun headed to Ellie's bedroom. She was going to have a talk with her little psychic about a few things.

Chapter 3

"Well, this this is not my favorite way to start a week. Mondays are always crappy, but today..." The man with iron-gray hair grimaced as he brought a mug of coffee to his lips.

"Your sunny disposition is a big help," Cee-Cee retorted under her breath.

"He's going to hear you," LaShaun whispered aside to her friend.

"Too late," the man said. He tapped one ear with a forefinger. "Just because I'm old doesn't mean I can't hear, Ms. Cuevas." He raised an eyebrow as he gazed at Cee-Cee.

"Yes, sir. Sorry, sir. Like you said, shitty Monday." Cee-Cee cleared her throat.

A young black woman stuck her head in the door. "Phone call for you, Mr. Miles."

"Humph. Figures." He pushed his chair back from the large oval conference table and marched out.

Cee-Cee let out a breath. "Forgot that guy can hear like a dog."

"Hey, that's not a very nice thing to say," LaShaun replied.

"It's true though. He can hear frequencies and sounds at least six times better than average."

"He's chief of operations for North and South America, and a member of the TEA High Protectorate Council. And you just called him a grumpy cat." LaShaun shook her head.

"Yeah, well... At least it wasn't General Soames. She's fanatical about protocol and respect for those in command."

"Lucky for you she's not in this meeting then." LaShaun jabbed her friend in the side with an elbow. "Don't push it, though. Desmond doesn't strike me as a man with a sense of humor either."

LaShaun poured herself of cup of coffee from a carafe on the table. A plate of sliced king cake sat on a covered platter. Three top TEA officials had checked into the DoubleTree Hotel in Lafayette. They'd reserved a conference room for the meeting. The door swung open, and Frank Miles returned. Zachary Desmond, one of three secretary-generals of the council, followed him. They were soon joined by two more women. LaShaun grinned when Jonah sauntered in last, looking as relaxed and confidant as always. His blue eyes sparkled with energy. His brunette hair was cut short with a shock of silver on one side. She left her chair to give him a hug.

"Ellie will be thrilled to have a visit from her big brother." LaShaun gave his cheek a maternal pat.

Jonah blushed at the attention. "Hey, *Mom*," he replied, continuing their joke about him being part of the family.

LaShaun had met Jonah during a previous TEA investigation. Then, he'd been a defiant teenager with rich, emotionally cold parents. Jonah's father treated his paranormal gifts as a kind of deformity. He and Ellie bonded over being kids who were different. He'd finally found acceptance and warmth with Ellie, LaShaun, and TEA. And Chase, though he was loath to admit he'd taken a liking to the mouthy youngster who didn't like rules.

"What have you done to your hair?" LaShaun ran her fingers through his thick locks.

Jonah's expression darkened. "Last operation was intense."

Before LaShaun could question him, the others made noises that signaled the meeting was about to begin. Zachary Desmond strode to the head of the table. He seemed determined to stretch to his full lanky height. His blond hair, mixed with gray, was tousled, as though he'd been raking his long fingers through it. Lines etched into his forty-something face gave him a grim expression. Everyone followed his cue and took seats.

"First, introductions. Ms. Rousselle, this is Zenia Bauer with our Canada division. Dimitrova Wagner is based in Costa Rica. She's with our intelligence section. You know Jonah, of course. I see you've kept in touch." Desmond glanced from LaShaun to Jonah and back.

"Yes," was all LaShaun chose to say. She could tell Desmond wasn't sure he liked the idea yet. Jonah squirmed in his chair between Cee-Cee and LaShaun.

"Let's get started then." Desmond nodded to Zenia Bauer.

She set up a tablet computer and synced it with a large-screen television on the wall. The others murmured among themselves as she worked.

"Zenia was my boss on the last two cases I worked. Operations coordinator. Desk job, mostly," Jonah whispered to LaShaun.

"I see."

She didn't though, not yet. LaShaun studied his face for a few seconds. His tone suggested she should remember those facts. Cee-Cee cleared her throat loudly and drank from a glass of water. A hint they should knock off the side conversation. Frank Miles stared at them. He sat to the right of the secretary-general. Seconds later he leaned close to Desmond. They had a quiet exchange, but neither looked at LaShaun or Jonah.

"Ready," Zenia Bauer said. She resumed her seat but held a remote.

Desmond nodded at her again, and an image appeared on the television screen. "Ms. Cuevas has given you a short summary about the inquiry we're opening. But I'll do a quick review and provide updates none of you have."

The last sentence caused the other TEA officials to murmur to each other. LaShaun noticed everyone seemed surprised except Dimitrova Wagner. Jonah sat forward. He looked at the intelligence commander and then at Desmond.

"Dianne Kirk and Alberto Ricci died of natural causes. On the surface. Dianne was our recently appointed global director of investigations. She'd earned the position based on twenty-years of experience in Europe and the Middle East. Alberto had been the chief of historical research in Europe and Asia since nineteen eighty-nine. Two fine people. They'll be sorely missed." Desmond paused in respectful silence for a few seconds. The other TEA members nodded with solemn faces.

"Indeed," Miles murmured.

"They were also both former intelligence operatives who still kept ties with that section," Desmond said.

Frank shot forward in his chair. "What?"

"Brenda worked in the forensic labs examining documents and historical artifacts," Zenia blurted out.

"Ties. You mean they were plants to spy on their own," Jonah said.

"Unbelievable." Zenia looked at Commander Wagner. The intelligence official's impassive expression did not change. She continued to gaze at Desmond.

"This is outrageous. If this gets out it will completely undermine the trust of every member. We'll all be looking at our colleagues with suspicion."

"It won't. You were invited to this meeting because I was assured you would not talk," Commander Wagner said and looked around the table at her colleagues. The steel in her steady, ice-cold gaze held a warning.

"Are you implying I would..." Miles sputtered.

Desmond rapped his knuckles on the table hard to restore order. "Enough. We had to root out a band of infiltrators two years ago. A fact you well know, Frank."

"I certainly didn't," Zenia complained.

"You weren't promoted to your current position at that time," Commander Wagner said in her heavy accent. "You did not have clearance to such information."

"Once the intelligence division made sure the threat had been removed, the spying should have stopped." Miles scowled at her.

"I assure you there is no threat to the integrity of TEA at this time. Settle down, Frank," Desmond said.

Miles snapped his mouth shut. He huffed a silence for a few beats. "Having intelligence focus on TEA members throws a different light on our problem."

"How's that?" Desmond steepled his hands as he sat back.

Miles leaned forward, both elbows on the table. "If we go with the theory that Dianne and Alberto didn't die natural deaths—"

"No evidence of such," Zenia broke in. Then she winced when the secretary-general cut a sharp look her way. "Sorry, sir."

LaShaun felt the tension go up a few notches. She gazed at Zenia until a prickle up both arms made her rub them. Jonah glanced at her sideways. He recognized the signs of her "reading" someone. Zenia had directed the investigation into both deaths. No wonder she was prickly about the results.

"Diane and Alberto were on opposite sides of changes to the mission of TEA. Their deaths have resulted in a hardening of positions of both factions. What's worse, accusations about murder have been tossed back and forth," Miles continued.

"Exactly the kind of rumors and suspicion we don't need," Miles muttered with a side glance at Commander Wagner.

"Pardon me, sir," Cee-Cee said. "But if either one had died, the vacuum in leadership would benefit the other side. I don't understand the purpose of both dying."

"I don't have all the threads pulled together yet," Miles said with a sigh. He ruffled his hair with one hand as though that would help him think.

"Hmm, indeed." Wagner gave Miles a dismissive glance before she turned to Desmond. "Sir, this theory is not supported by facts."

"The criminal division—" Miles waved a finger at her.

"Is not equipped to investigate on multiple levels. You lack manpower and our resources," Wagner added when both Cee-Cee and Zenia started to comment.

"I agree," Desmond replied without hesitation.

"So much for no more spying on fellow members," Miles retorted with a glare at the secretary-general.

Desmond didn't rise to the bait. His smooth, reasonable expression remained. "The intelligence division will coordinate with the criminal division." Everyone except LaShaun started talking at once.

"Those guys hate sharing information," Cee-Cee blurted out. "The last time I worked with one of their units they kept secrets from us."

Wagner bristled. "My team members are highly trained. I see no need for—"

"That's an order," Miles snapped. "Directly from President Truman as recommended by the North American Sub-Council." Silence fell under the weight of his words.

Wagner alone seemed not to be affected. "I only meant to offer relief to the already overburdened Criminal Division, sir."

"Gee, thanks for the love," Jonah said.

Desmond squinted at him, but spoke to Wagner instead. "You don't need to worry, Commander Wagner. We're calling in extra help. A class of ten trainees are only a week away from assignment. They'll be sent to Chief Officer Cuevas and her team. She'll act as field director since she's worked in both sections."

LaShaun blinked in surprise. Cee-Cee hadn't mentioned being a criminal investigator and in intelligence before. But now it made sense why she'd been at such a young age. His news seemed not to sit well with either Zenia or Wagner.

"Yes, sir," they said at the same time.

"Which brings us to Ms. Rousselle-Broussard and why she's here." Wagner aimed her intense blue-gray gaze at LaShaun.

"I appreciate being included, but I agree with Commander Wagner," LaShaun said, addressing Wagner's implied objection to her presence. Wagner's nostrils quivered at being read. "I don't see how or why any of the political or criminal matters of TEA affect *me*."

"You're a member of TEA. Everything that happens to us and within the organization affects you," Wagner replied in a flat tone.

LaShaun sensed the woman's intense dedication to TEA. No personal life, all focus on work. "Then anyone around the world who's a member could be pulled in."

Desmond looked at Wagner. The commander pressed her lips together. "Three reasons. First, there's a Louisiana connection. Officer Parker and Chief Officer Cuevas have worked here before, which is why they were pulled in. Dianne Kirk had notes in a file referencing the state."

"That's kind of vague," LaShaun said with a frown.

"Second, our Criminal Division is barely one year old. As Commander Wagner pointed out, we're not fully staffed up yet." Desmond nodded at LaShaun.

"And the last reason?" LaShaun felt that insistent tingle along her arms.

"Not only do you have experience, but your husband is considered a top homicide detective. And your daughter is one of the most advanced natural—"

"Hold it right there." LaShaun pushed back her chair and stood. "My little girl isn't going anywhere near a TEA operation."

Desmond stood as well. "Mrs. Broussard, please—"

"Thanks for the coffee and king cake." LaShaun picked up her crossbody bag to leave.

"Pardon me, but your husband has been part of TEA operations before. Joëlle Renée provided key psychic insights and interventions that led to positive conclusions on at least two." Commander Wagner remained seated, her expression blank. Yet her pointed comments caused the air to crackle.

LaShaun spun around to face her. "How do you know..."

"She needs much less babying than you might think," Wagner continued.

"I swear, if you've been monitoring my child or tinkering with her in any way," LaShaun shouted.

"Please, Mrs. Broussard. I can assure you we have not," Desmond said with force. He looked at Commander Wagner. "Thank you for the input, Commander. I think you've done enough for now."

As if on cue, the young black woman swung open the door. A young man who looked like a younger, less-congenial version of Dwayne "The Rock" Johnson was with her. He gestured to Commander Wagner.

"Commander, two members of your team have arrived for briefing," the young woman said.

Wagner's eyes flashed with rage. She stared at Desmond for several seconds. LaShaun expected an explosion in the already-volatile atmosphere. Cee-Cee and the others tensed up as if ready to react. Wagner stood and smoothed down the black suit jacket she wore over matching slacks.

"Thank you. I'll address this matter at a later time, Secretary-General." Wagner nodded to him and then the others before she strode out. The door banged shut behind her.

"Well, that was interesting," Jonah mumbled. He shrugged when Cee-Cee glared at him.

Cee-Cee stood and crossed to LaShaun. "I don't agree with her hammer approach, but Commander Wagner is right. Ellie will probably provide information even if you don't ask her to. Once you're involved, she'll pick up vibes."

"Just because someone at some time mentioned Louisiana—"

"Emmanuel Young has approached you for help. You'll need TEA resources at some point," Desmond put in.

"You've got spies following me? Miles is right to be pissed. I can't believe this." LaShaun looked at Desmond.

"No one is following you, Mrs. Broussard," Desmond said quietly.

LaShaun started to continue her rant, but stopped short. "You're following Manny."

"He'll soon be a suspect. Please sit down, Mrs. Broussard." Desmond pointed to her chair.

His words made Jonah and Cee-Cee gasp in unison. They looked at each other and then at LaShaun. Cee-Cee dropped into her chair hard, blinking rapidly.

◉

"We have at least three TEA members who can match your abilities. Though admittedly you're the most genetically advanced." Desmond gazed at LaShaun as if she was a specimen.

"Say what now?" Jonah looked from Desmond to LaShaun.

"We've talked about your family lineage before. Each generation mixed with other bloodlines seems to have only enhanced what nature provided," Miles put in.

"No, what God provided. He has blessed a precious few of us to see small insights," Desmond replied.

"Hold on a minute," LaShaun spoke up before the debate between science and spirituality took over. These were two sides of a debate that cause tension within TEA. "Let's get back to more bodies."

Desmond faced LaShaun again, his back to Miles. "Your husband's officers or possibly the Louisiana State Police will uncover more deaths. Our people couldn't see who, how many exactly, or any additional details. I would prefer you not mention it. Allow their natural investigative process to discover the link. We have no hard evidence he would accept."

"Are you insane? Manny is killing people, and I'm going to do everything I can to prevent more bloodshed," LaShaun said.

"Exactly what will your *normal* law enforcement people do?" Zenia Bauer cocked a shapely dark eyebrow. "They can't revoke his parole based on information from a psychic. Mr. Young will be on alert and more cautious."

"And more deadly," Jonah added with a frown.

"The secretary-general said he's going to be a suspect. Not that he did it." Zenia looked at her boss, and he nodded to her with a pleased half-smile.

LaShaun decided to take Desmond's advice and sit again. "Explain."

Desmond sighed and took his seat as well. "As you know, being psychic doesn't mean we have all the answers. Wouldn't it be nice, though?"

"No shit," Jonah wisecracked. He grinned when Cee-Cee and Zenia gave him twin frowns of disapproval.

The secretary-general gave a short laugh at the young operative's bluntness. "No, we think either you have another serial killer on the loose, or these murders aren't connected to Dianne and Alberto's deaths. But someone wants Emmanuel Young to be blamed for them. We'll do what we can to help law enforcement sort it out."

"Manny wants me to prove he not guilty of murder," LaShaun said. "Could this be the same killer?"

"Our PP & A team isn't sure." Desmond rubbed his jaw as he sat in thought.

"Who?" LaShaun glanced at Cee-Cee for answers.

"Predictive and Prognostication Analytics Division. Pretty small team, actually. They use a combination of statistical analysis, science, and telepathic data to detect trends," Cee-Cee said.

"Our forensic teams help. They've been invaluable in dozens of criminal investigations," Zenia added.

"Hard science is responsible for the most remarkable results," Miles put in. He looked at the secretary-general as if issuing a challenge.

"Frank is correct, though not in all cases," Desmond replied mildly. "As I said, we don't know all the answers."

"Right, I see." LaShaun drummed her fingertips on the table for a few seconds. "Actually, I don't."

Miles sat forward. "We want you on the team to help us figure out who killed our colleagues."

"If they were killed, you mean," Jonah put in. "Even PP & A and the forensic teams haven't figure it out yet."

"Agreed. And I'd like nothing better than to put the rumblings and rumors about murder to rest." Desmond rubbed his forehead. Lines in his face came from worry and fatigue more than age.

"You want someone from the outside, a fresh and objective view," LaShaun said.

"You've hit the target with your usual pinpoint accuracy." Desmond said with a tired smile.

"My division is fairly new, but we're hardly short on investigative and field experience, sir. Not that I'm bucking a direct order from top," Zenia added with a respectful nod.

LaShaun decided to head off any strain between them. Zenia Bauer relished approval from Desmond. She even had a crush on the older man. All this LaShaun saw in a flash, but she worked to keep it from showing in her expression.

"Which is why I'm happy to be working with them," LaShaun said. "Like you said, your resources can do a lot more than regular cops."

Zenia studied her for a few seconds. Then she nodded again. "Okay, then. Let's start."

For another two hours, they went over information gathered so far. LaShaun got a short course in TEA internal politics for context. From time to time she cast glances at Cee-Cee. By the time they wrapped up at nine o'clock, LaShaun's head buzzed with all of the details. Jonah and Cee-Cee walked along as she headed for her SUV in the parking lot.

"Won't somebody be suspicious so much of the top brass is in Lafayette, Louisiana, of all places?" LaShaun asked. She glanced around the busy lobby as they passed through it.

"Just so happens we're having a regional meeting here. A lot of members wanted to visit during Mardi Gras season," Jonah said with a grin.

LaShaun laughed. "I'd have thought you'd go for New Orleans."

"Yeah, well, the younger members will drive there. Those with kids prefer the more family-friendly versions. We got out-voted." Jonah gave a dramatic sigh.

"I'm sure it won't cramp your party-hard style," LaShaun retorted.

"We can have a great time here, then boogie down to 'Da Big Easy,' " he replied and did a few dance steps.

"You won't have time for anything but following leads, son. Believe *that*." Cee-Cee pointed a forefinger at him.

Jonah assumed a military, ramrod straight stance and saluted. "Yes, ma'am. Understood, ma'am!"

"See what I'm gonna have to deal with for weeks? I thought the Criminal Division and that assignment in Canada would straighten you out." Cee-Cee heaved a dramatic sigh.

"You missed me. Admit it." Jonah draped an arm around the senior officer's shoulders.

"Never in public," Cee-Cee shot back.

Jonah's playful grin faded. "What about in private?"

Cee-Cee brushed free of him. "Knock it off, junior. You've got your marching orders. Get to work."

"Okay, play hardball. And stop calling me 'son' and 'junior.' " Jonah studied Cee-Cee for a few moments until she squirmed. Then his dark eyes sparkled with mirth. "You can't resist the legendary Jonah Parker charm forever. Tell her, LaShaun."

"He's certainly worked his magic in my house." LaShaun rolled her eyes. Jonah waved good-bye, laughing hard as he walked away.

"Kids." Cee-Cee shook her head while she watched him.

LaShaun cocked her head to one side. "He's right, you know. He's twenty-two, you're twenty-six—"

"Twenty-seven next month," Cee-Cee said.

"Then he'll turn twenty-three, and so forth and so on. Back when he was seventeen it made a difference," LaShaun pressed on.

"He's still growing up and doesn't know what he wants. I'm past the teenage 'Let's party!' stage. And..." Cee-Cee raised a forefinger. "Work romances are a seriously bad idea. Discussion over."

"I won't say another word." LaShaun held up a palm as if swearing an oath.

"I doubt that," Cee-Cee retorted. "What about this case?"

"Which one? We've got the TEA deaths, Manny's conviction for a murder he claims he didn't do, and two more bodies yet to be found. Oh, for the simple life of not being psychic."

"The 'simple life' ship sailed without us a long time ago," Cee-Cee replied with a snort.

Chapter 4

LaShaun went to Aunt Shirleen's house to pick up Ellie. Aunt Shirleen brought a drowsy Ellie from her own bedroom. Though she'd been somewhat afraid of her psychic niece for years, Aunt Shirleen doted on Ellie. That "her baby girl" might be like LaShaun didn't seem to bother Aunt Shirleen too much. As expected, LaShaun's cousin Azalei tried hard to pump LaShaun for information. Their aunt finally intervened.

"Leave the girl alone. She got to get home." Aunt Shirleen gave Azalei the mama look, which meant obey or suffer.

"Whatever. I'm gonna find out anyway. Everything you do hits the news like firecrackers going off." Azalei rubbed Ellie's back and brushed a light kiss on her cheek. "Bye, sweetness."

"Thanks for stepping up last minute. You're a lifesaver," LaShaun said. She reached for Ellie's backpack, but Azalei grabbed it.

"I'll walk you out," Azalei said with a grin.

"Uh-huh."

When they were at LaShaun's Subaru Forrester, Azalei looked over her shoulder. She waved to their aunt standing on her porch. Then she spoke in a conspiratorial whisper. "Listen, you better stay away from Manny Young. Folks are talking about how you must be helping him k-i-l-l people." Azalei glanced at Ellie, whose eyes were still closed.

"How did..."

"You know how it is around here. Sneeze behind closed doors in the morning, and folks will call offering chicken soup by lunchtime." Azalei looked back at their aunt again. "I'm saying, watch yourself. People get pretty worked up about you-know-who."

"Thanks, but I won't be seeing him anytime soon." LaShaun roused Ellie enough to put her in the rear seat and the seatbelt.

"So, you *did* hang out with him and had a drink. LaShaun!" Azalei's hazel eyes stretched wide. "Girl, what the hell? I've done some crazy shit in my time."

"Oh, a serious understatement," LaShaun retorted.

"But hanging out with a psycho serial killer ain't even on *my* rap sheet." Azalei blew out air. "Look, I'll back you up. Blood and all. But you gotta make better decisions."

"Advice on life decisions from you? That's a good one. Bye, Azalei." LaShaun got in the car. She gave one last wave to Aunt Shirleen, who still watched them from the front door.

"K-i-l-l spells kill," Ellie piped up from behind her. She yawned. "I'll back you up, too, Mama."

LaShaun glared at her cousin, who winced and shrugged an apology. "Don't worry about me, baby."

On the drive home LaShaun scanned the surrounding landscape. She kept anticipating seeing Manny's beat-up 1995 Toyota truck. By the time she pulled into their driveway, her arms and shoulders ached from tension. Ellie only perked up briefly when Beau barked in welcome. Chase strode outside, got Ellie from the backseat and carried her in. LaShaun put away their bags. Beau trotted by her side, sticking close to her. She looked down at him and patted his back.

"Did Azalei call ahead for you to keep an eye on me?"

Beau let out two short woofs in reply. Since Ellie wasn't around to translate, she'd take that as a no.

At two and half years old, the Great Weimar almost reached LaShaun's waist. He had the skill of sniffing out spirits. LaShaun got him from Mathieu Baptiste, a local TEA member who bred and sold dogs. Ellie needed an extraordinary pet. Chase was just satisfied that Beau behaved like a "normal" dog. He chased rabbits, played with chew toys, and adored Ellie.

"I love you, too, boy." LaShaun rubbed his smooth blue-gray coat. She went to the master suite to get settled for the night. Chase came in thirty minutes later.

"Ellie's in bed. I've had a long day. No shop talk." Chase covered her mouth with his as if to make sure.

LaShaun breathed out when they came up for air. "This is what got me into baby mode again."

Chase pulled the pajama top over her head, kissed her throat, and guided her to the bed. "Yeah, the deed is done. So, we might as well..."

LaShaun shivered as his touch made any remaining stress drain away. She let him apply his own special massage technique until thoughts of everything else disappeared.

****

The real problems lurking just beyond their door returned with the dawn. Tuesday morning was bright with sunshine, but very cold. LaShaun and Chase didn't discuss murders or TEA over breakfast. Mainly because Ellie bounced up early, full of energy. Her chatter about her best pals Taylor and Eric kept her parents smiling. Ellie was excited about science day when they did experiments. LaShaun was just happy Azalei's talk about serial killers hadn't lingered on Ellie's mind. It seemed she'd quite literally slept like a baby.

The landline phone rang, shattering the sunny domestic ambiance. LaShaun and Chase exchanged a glance. Then they heaved a sigh at the same time. Chase crossed to pick up the cordless handset.

"Morning, M.J.," Chase spoke into the phone while gazing at LaShaun. "Uh-huh. Wait a sec, let me check my notes. I haven't uploaded them to the system yet." He walked to their bedroom.

"Daddy is about to leave for work," Ellie said in a bright voice. "To catch some bad guy killing people."

When LaShaun spun around to question her, she discovered Ellie was talking to Beau. The dog woofed and accepted the forkful of scrambled eggs she offered. "Hey, cut that out."

"But he loves eggs," Ellie said as if that settled the matter. She patted his large head when he rested it in her tiny lap.

"Eat your breakfast." LaShaun took the fork away and gave her a clean one. Then she looked at Beau. "Don't play innocent. You've had breakfast—that pricey dog food. Time for your morning exercise."

Beau gave a good-natured woof and trotted to the kitchen door. He waited for LaShaun. He looked back as if to say, "Bye mom." LaShaun laughed before she could stop herself. She gave him a hug around the neck. He barked again, shook his head and trotted out of the large pet door.

"I ate most of my breakfast. See? I only gave Beau one tiny bit left," Ellie said to preempt their usual mealtime tug-of-war. She was a picky eater, and LaShaun worried over her appetite.

"You have to get enough nutrients, Ellie." LaShaun went to the table. She grabbed her third slice of toast and slathered grape jam on it. She also eyed the bacon left on the serving plate.

Ellie pushed it closer to her mother. "It's okay. You need to gain weight for him."

LaShaun froze. "Where are you getting all this stuff about a baby brother and advice for mommies?"

"Cousin Azalei says maybe if I wish for a brother hard enough that's what I'll get. And my friend Elliot says his mother ate piles of food when she had his little brother. So maybe lots of eating means a boy!" Ellie nodded with enthusiasm and pushed the plate toward LaShaun again.

"Can't argue with that logic," LaShaun said around a chunk of toast. She grabbed Chase's abandoned mug of coffee and washed it down. "But honey, I had a healthy appetite with you."

"Oh." Ellie looked deflated, but only for a second. Then she smiled again, springing back as quickly. "But it's going to be a boy. I just know it."

"Ellie, I... Never mind. We'll talk about the baby and what happens in a mommy's stomach later."

"My friend Elliot's grandmother knew they were having a boy. She said it was because his mama was carrying the baby low. Everybody teases us about being twins. You know—Ellie and Elliot—but he's shorter than me and he's got red hair and freckles. He's white, well, really pink. And I'm brown and—"

"Ellie," LaShaun said fast. Her head was swimming from the rapid-fire information dump. Her little girl had covered gender, race, and old wives' tales about pregnancy in seconds. Ellie paused, sipped apple juice, and waited.

"Yes, Mama?"

"You said something about Daddy catching a man who kills people," LaShaun kept her voice low. She glanced toward the hallway.

"I think he's got more work," Ellie whispered, taking her cue. "But I won't tell Daddy. He gets upset."

"You mean..." LaShaun didn't want to put words in her mouth.

"I think it's a lady this time. Not sure. I was trying not to hear." Ellie put a finger to her lips.

Chase strode in. He kissed LaShaun's cheek and the top of Ellie's head. "Good thing I'm through with breakfast. Time to get on the move. Have a great day, princess."

"Thanks, Daddy. You, too." Ellie gave LaShaun a look full of meaning.

"Um, anything pressing? I mean, since M.J. called," LaShaun added.

"Another day at the office. Hey, you two have enough to think about. I might be able to take Friday off. We could go to the first Mardi Gras parade in Lafayette. Get you a mask and everything. What do you say?" Chase ruffled Ellie's mass of tight curls.

"Yaay, I want to catch lots of beads!" Ellie bounced in her chair.

"Go wash your hands and get ready. I'll be there in a minute," LaShaun said.

"Okay." Ellie hugged Chase's knees before she raced out.

"Slow down," Chase called after her. A chuckled rumbled deep in his chest. "That kid is better for my mood than anything."

"Yeah." LaShaun studied him for a few seconds. "So, what did M.J. say?"

"Meet me at the station. Say around ten-thirty. Got a briefing with the state police and the Department of WildlLife and Fisheries first thing," Chase said, his voice low even though they were alone.

"WildlLife and Fisheries?" LaShaun blinked at him.

Before he could reply, Ellie rushed back into the kitchen. She wore her school uniform and sneakers. "I'm ready. Except I need my snacks and lunch."

"Good girl." Chase's frown lines melted away as he grinned at her.

For the next thirty minutes they went into a whirl of activity. LaShaun placed Ellie's food for the day in her backpack. Chase said his final good-byes before heading off. Beau bounded in when Chase opened the door to leave. He accepted a pat from Chase. As his human family talked, Beau circled among them as if part of the conversation. Finally, Chase's truck pulled off, Ellie's bus arrived, and LaShaun was alone with Beau.

"You stay here and hold down the fort. Okay?" LaShaun rubbed one of his haunches and got a woof of agreement in return.

LaShaun cleaned up for another hour. Then she read through the TEA materials Cee-Cee had emailed her. Some parts were missing. A text exchange with Cee-Cee revealed some information was on the TEA secure server. She would have to get clearance for LaShaun to get a password. That set in motion, LaShaun got dressed in her favorite corduroy jeans and heavy flannel shirt jacket to keep away the cold.

She ran several routine errands. Then it was time to meet Chase.

She arrived at the main Vermilion Parish Sheriff's Office in Abbeville just before ten thirty. As she parked her SUV, she spotted Detective Mark Anderson striding down the sidewalk, badge clipped to his belt. His crisp, light-blue dress shirt and navy pants gave the plainclothes detective an air of authority. Not that he tried to hide it. LaShaun knew from Chase that exuding the right attitude helped cops. Those in crisis got reassurance from their composure. Witnesses could be more willing to talk. And perps would be suitably intimated.

"Morning, ma'am," Anderson said.

"How are you, detective?" LaShaun pasted on a polite smile. Detective Anderson had made his disapproval of her clear in the past.

"Fine. Fine. Hope everything is okay at home and you're not here on business." He gave her the appraising gaze of an investigator.

"Pardon?" LaShaun squinted at him.

"I mean no crime to report on the Rousselle property," Anderson said in a mild tone.

LaShaun didn't answer him right away. Instead, she gave him a deliberate head-to-toe glance. Then smiled. "Detective Anderson, you have enough unsolved crimes on your patch. I wouldn't dream of adding to the stack."

Anderson's smug expression slipped into a tight mask. "Have nice day, *ma'am.*" He made a circle around her and walked away.

"Same to you," LaShaun called after him. She grinned at the thought Anderson strewing over the dig for hours.

Pushing through the glass doors into the sheriff's main office, LaShaun went through security. She greeted several civilian employees as she headed to Chase's office. Once there, he waved her in while still talking on the phone. He hung up just as M.J. Arceneaux, chief deputy and the head of property crimes division, joined them.

M.J. extended a mug with the sheriff's department logo on it. "Morning. I figure if Chase invited you, we'd all need some strong coffee."

"Happy to be of assistance, though I wouldn't mention it to Detective Anderson. I met that welcoming ray of sunshine on my way in." LaShaun accepted the mug and sat down in one of two visitor chairs.

"Humph. Not great with people, but he's a solid cop. His days of judging you may be over soon. At least in this office," M.J. said.

"Oh?" LaShaun sipped coffee and winced. She looked in the mug for the first time. "Haven't you learned yet I don't take sugar or cream?"

"Hey, it's not my job to know that stuff. I'll let your husband fix you up next time," M.J. retorted.

"No hospitality award for you either," LaShaun wisecracked. "So, y'all finally giving Mark the boot? He must have insulted somebody important."

"Nah, he's a shoo-in to become the Abbeville Chief of Police. His stepping stone to get a top job with the Louisiana State Police. At least that's his goal."

"I can't believe he's sharing his hopes and dreams with you of all people," LaShaun said to Chase.

"Not exactly a secret he feels like his talents are wasted on us," Chase said with a snort. "Anyway, I made sure he wasn't assigned to liaison with the state police on this second body found."

"Two suspicious murders, two bodies in the space of two weeks. Dave is already squirming about the optics," M.J. said, referring their boss, Sheriff Dave Godchaux. "Election is next year, you know."

"Oh, we'll wrap this up long before then." LaShaun winked at them and laughed when both groaned. "What?"

"Not you, honey. You know how long memories are around here." Chase glanced at M.J., who grimaced, and took a deep breath. "We needed to tell you about the second victim."

"Okay. Wait a minute." LaShaun's heart skipped. "It's not—"

"What... oh no. Not a member of your family," Chase said quickly.

LaShaun let out a long, shaky breath. "Thank the Lord. Not that I'd wish death on another family."

"But it is someone you know. Mathieu Baptiste, the guy who sold us Beau," Chase said. "Sorry, hon. I wanted you to hear it before we released it to the public."

LaShaun made the sign of the cross. "May he rest in heaven. Such a kind, gentle soul."

"That's what a couple of people interviewed said so far. Still early in the investigation," M.J. replied with a frown.

"I only met him a couple of times. Once when we picked out Beau. Or really Ellie and Beau picked each other. I didn't pay him, by the way. Remember, Beau was meant for Ellie." LaShaun felt sadness like a lump in her chest.

"Meant for Ellie? He was a present?" M.J. looked at LaShaun.

"Hmm, not quite. Beau comes from a very special bloodline."

"I'm not sure I really want to know."

Wrapped in her own thoughts, LaShaun went on. "Back to Cain and Abel, the first known pet dog. According to a Jewish legend, he protected Abel's body from scavengers after his brother Cain murdered him. Until Adam could find him, I mean, and give him a proper burial."

"Abel, as in son of Adam and Eve. Ooo-kay. So, this isn't going to be a normal murder case." M.J. gulped coffee.

"Mr. Baptiste could have had enemies, someone with a grudge. Maybe somebody felt like he cheated them over a dog sale," Chase replied. He shrugged when M.J. cocked her head with a skeptical expression.

"And yet you called LaShaun." M.J. waved at hand at his wife as if she was exhibit A.

"Nothing looked out of the ordinary," Chase began.

"Well that's a relief." M.J. put down her coffee mug when Chase grimaced. "Spill it all, then."

"That was Dr. Amory on the phone when y'all came in." Audrey Amory acted as the parish coroner. If a death investigation got too complicated, she got help from the Lafayette Parish coroner.

"Here we go." M.J. heaved a deep sigh.

"He had tattoos carved into his torso." Chase gazed at LaShaun.

M.J. looked at them both. "We get victims with tattoos all the time."

"They were fresh," Chase said.

"Again, no big deal. Just happens he got new tattoos that day. Sounds like a good lead to follow up on to me," M.J. said. She looked relieved for a few seconds. Then she noticed Chase's grim expression hadn't changed. "But there's more."

"Doc's opinion is someone took time to do those tattoos close to the time of death. Real close. He could have lay dying while they did it." Chase transferred his steady gaze to M.J.

"Hell. You mean fresh as in..." M.J.'s eyes went wide.

"The killer took great care with the victim."

Chase started to continue when a series of chimes came from his work cell phone. He picked it up, tapped the screen, and swiped. He held it up for them both to see.

"What the..." M.J. blinked at the image.

"Yeah." Chase's jaw clenched.

LaShaun took the phone from his hand to study the symbols. She gazed at the swirls. "Some kind of language maybe. Nothing obvious that crackpot cults use, like a pentagram. But that… looks like the Eye of Horus."

"Yeah. Of course it is," M.J. muttered. "Who the hell is Horus?"

"The ancient Egyptian sky God. This symbolizes power, royal authority, but it can also mean a curse." LaShaun tilted her head to one side and straightened again. "Hmm, a dragon symbolizes power, too."

M.J. shook her head. "Let's not get ahead of ourselves. Dr. Amory can't say for certain when those were done."

"I'll print these out for distribution. Anderson and another deputy can visit local tattoo artists. Could be just a coincidence that he got 'em recently." Chase's tone sounded encouraged.

LaShaun knew he and M.J. preferred normal, everyday crimes. She doubted this was one but didn't dash their hopes. "Forward the images to me. Can't hurt to do my own research."

"Because he bred and sold supernatural pets? Seriously? I've been around Beau plenty of times. He barks, plays fetch, and likes belly rubs like any other dog." M.J. looked from Chase to LaShaun.

"He's our second child, that's for sure," LaShaun replied with a grin.

"Hey, speaking of, congratulations. I'll bet Ellie is happy," M.J. said.

"Already planning for a baby brother. How she got that into her head, I don't know." LaShaun eyed Chase, who was distracted. He entered the latest information on Mr. Baptiste's murder into the online case file.

"Okay. We've got things lined up. Mrs. Baptiste and their oldest son will give witness statements. Anderson and Tate will run down the tattoo lead. And Dave is having a press conference to release a photo of the other dead guy." Chase stood and looked at the clock on his cell phone.

"You have a busy day ahead. I'll pick up lunch for you and bring it back." LaShaun stood and pecked his cheek.

"Could you, babe? That would be a big help. I need to be here for meetings or else I'd be doing some leg work myself." Chase gave her backside a pat.

"No problem. What about you?" LaShaun said to M.J.

She shook her head. "No thanks. I brought a healthy lunch. Part of my plan to build muscles."

"Our chief deputy is into cross-fitness and power-lifting these days." Chase nodded at his colleague with a grin.

"Sitting at a desk for hours is the downside of my promotion. Protein and resistance training will make me fit." M.J. hefted both arms like a bodybuilder.

LaShaun laughed. "M.J., you're not exactly out of shape. But I'll know who to call in a fight."

"Hey, you stay out of trouble. I better get going or Dave will be..." M.J. stopped when her cell phone buzzed. She looked at the screen. "And here he is. The mayor is probably wringing his hands. Two murders, not good for Mardi Gras tourism."

"Yeah, how inconsiderate of those guys to not postpone getting killed," Chase drawled. "Better you than me. Whiny politicians give me a rash."

"Thanks for the support." M.J. strode off while looking at her phone again.

"Savoie's deli has shrimp and corn soup. I'll also get you a sandwich to go with it." LaShaun picked up her crossbody bag.

"Whoa, I wanna stay fit, too," Chase teased.

"So, a kale shake with a seaweed side salad from the new health food shop downtown?"

"Soup and a roast beef sandwich is fine," Chase said. "I can eat the sandwich later if the soup fills me up. Oh, and a cream soda."

"Thought so," LaShaun said with a laugh as she left.

She made the short drive to the deli inside Savoie's grocery store. By the time she made it back to the station, Chase was in a conference. She put his lunch in the compact fridge in his office and headed out. Her first stop would be to see her friend, Rose Fontenot. The older woman had become one of her closest friends. Miss Rose, as she was called, had known LaShaun's grandmother. A retired teacher, LaShaun's mother, Francine, had been one of her students back in the day. Miss Rose had also been a card-carrying member of The Third Eye Association for years. Miss Rose had the gift of seeing the past, especially when she studied historical facts or handled artifacts.

LaShaun wanted to tell Miss Rose about her friend Matthieu before the news came out. They'd known each other for years. She kept glancing at the digital clock as she drove to Mouton Cove, the tiny community where Miss Rose and her husband, Pierre, lived. M.J. said Dave would release limited details to the press at one o'clock. Which left LaShaun about an hour, plenty of time. She pulled into Miss Rose's driveway at twelve. The older woman stood at the front door as if expecting her. She leaned on a cane, something new. Even at seventy-four, Miss Rose had always been physically active.

"Hey, are you okay?" LaShaun exited the SUV with a frown. Her concern for her friend made her forget the usual southern chitchat.

"Arthritis got me down, girl. Cold weather doesn't help. You come to tell me about Matthieu, didn't ya?" Miss Rose accepted a hug when LaShaun reached her.

"Yes, ma'am," LaShaun said in a gentle tone. She took Miss Rose's free arm. They walked through her neat living room to the heart of her house, the cozy kitchen.

"His wife, Estelle, called me. Lord, I can't believe anybody would hurt him. But that's the world we live in." Miss Rose sounded tired from a place deep in her soul. She let out a long exhale as she sat in a comfy chair at the breakfast table.

LaShaun squeezed her shoulder. Then she made them both chamomile tea with lemon and honey. She knew her way around Miss Rose's kitchen, having been there so many times. "I hope Mrs. Baptiste has someone with her."

"Her daughter-in-law took her home with them. And her youngest grandson will tend to the dogs. You know, I don't think she'll want to stay at the house alone. They were going to celebrate their fifty-sixth anniversary in June." Miss Rose's voice shook as she spoke.

"Such a loss, such a waste."

LaShaun continued to prepare the tea. She hoped the domestic sounds of her puttering would help comfort Miss Rose. The rituals of grieving in the Deep South always involved remembrances and food. So she let her talk.

"They got married two years before Pierre and me. Mathieu went into the Army. Served in Vietnam before the war really escalated. He didn't suffer the way a lot of soldiers did. But he didn't like to talk about it either. Estelle worked as a nurse, you know. Mathieu came home, went back to school on the G.I. Bill. Got a degree in agriculture and animal husbandry. Raised three fine sons and two daughters."

LaShaun brought a tray with a pot and matching cups to the table. "They made a good life. She'll have happy memories."

"She should have her husband, and Mathieu should have his life." Miss Rose hissed out the words as if fire would jet from the tip of her tongue.

LaShaun gasped at the fierceness in her tone. The refined older woman seemed to transform into a female Dahomey warrior. Miss Rose appeared to be dressed for battle, a sword in one hand. She wore the traditional dress of the tribe, a beaded band around her thick hair. LaShaun blinked and the vision was gone.

Mr. Pierre enter the kitchen, his truck keys still jingling in one hand. He laid them on the table and put a hand on Miss Rose's back. "I just heard the news. You all right, baby? This got anything to do with..."

"LaShaun didn't come here just to comfort me." Miss Rose let out a slow breath. She leaned into her husband. The couple gazed at her, waiting.

LaShaun took her out her cell phone and showed them the photos. "There's more that you won't hear on the news."

Chapter 5

Two days later, Thursday, Cee-Cee arrived with Jonah. They'd checked into a hotel in Lafayette to avoid chatter in Beau Chene. They'd been in Vermilion Parish before on a case. Although that was a little over a year ago, it had generated a lot of news. LaShaun smiled as their rented Land Rover pulled into the driveway.

"Morning," Jonah called out with his usual raring-to-go energy. He hopped from the vehicle and turned in a circle. "Ah, this brings back memories."

Beau bounded out and went to Jonah, his tail wagging. The two seemed to exchange a heartfelt greeting. Beau barked with enthusiasm when Jonah talked to him as if he expected a reply.

"Good morning. Those two are happy to see each other." Cee-Cee smiled as Jonah walked toward the Rousselle woods with Beau at his heels.

"I swear, you'd think Jonah grew up here. Except for his Yankee accent," LaShaun joked.

"Hey, where's my baby sis?" Jonah yelled. He threw one of Beau's balls he'd found on the ground. Beau chased it. He ran a wide circle with the ball in his mouth.

"In school, where she should be. I made the mistake of telling her y'all were coming. Getting Ellie on the bus took quite a while. But I have to give her credit. She came up with really inventive reasons to stay home." LaShaun shook her head as she led the way inside.

Cee-Cee swung her backpack from her shoulder. She set it on the bench in the mudroom and followed LaShaun into the spacious kitchen. "Love what you've done with the place."

"Yeah, we redecorated last year. Nothing big. New granite for the countertops." LaShaun ran her hand over the smooth stone. She loved the rich earth tones of brown.

"Getting ready for the babies?" Cee-Cee's dark eyes sparkled with mischief.

"Don't you start, too." LaShaun stabbed a forefinger at Cee-Cee's chest. "Come on. I've got coffee and beignets."

Jonah and Beau came in, both breathing hard from exertion. "I need a dog like Beau. I travel a lot for work, so not practical."

LaShaun's smile faded. "Mr. Baptiste could have given you the perfect one. I don't know that his son has his...skill."

Cee-Cee grew serious as well. "We heard, a news update from TEA. Any good leads?"

"Yeah, I was gonna ask." Jonah went to the coffeepot. He poured them all a cup and then set the cups on the table.

They all sat down. Beau settled on his haunches nearby as if waiting to hear as well. They drank in silence for a few moments. All digested what they knew. For them, conversation was sometimes not necessary.

"I haven't heard back from Dr. Bakir," LaShaun said. She'd emailed the professor images of the tattoos. Dr. Farrah Bakir, a TEA member, was an internationally known archaeologist. She was also an expert on ancient languages and palaeography, ancient handwriting.

"Burglary gone wrong?" Jonah chose a beignet and popped it into his mouth.

"The family says two valuable pups are missing, a Pharaoh Hound and a Tibetan Mastiff," LaShaun said.

"Maybe they ran off into the woods. If they're our special breeds, we could learn something if we find 'em," Jonah said between chews.

"Cause of death?" Cee-Cee asked.

"Blunt-force trauma. He put up quite a fight though." LaShaun drank a sip of coffee, hoping to wash the bitter taste of violent death from her mouth.

"Those dogs alone are worth thousands, even tens of thousands depending on the bloodline. Money is the most common motive," Jonah said.

"Yeah." LaShaun studied Beau for a few seconds. She turned to Jonah. "You make a great point. If we could find those dogs..."

"And who better than my good buddy over there," Jonah said with wink at Beau. His grin widened when Beau barked in response.

"We're here to talk about the TEA investigation of two deaths. Top officials keeled over within weeks of one another? Whiffs of something rotten going on? We can't get sidetracked," Cee-Cee said firmly.

Jonah looked at his senior. "But if we have extra time—"

"We won't," Cee-Cee clipped. "We don't have authorization to begin another field op. Let the local normal cops do their job. I'm sure Chase and M.J. would agree."

"Fine." Jonah gave Beau a side glance.

Cee-Cee sighed. "If you do, don't make it obvious. I'm not covering for you again. Dimitrova Wagner is not the one you want pissed off."

"Stealth is my middle name," Jonah replied.

"No, aggravation is your middle name," Cee-Cee countered.

"I'll keep him out of trouble," LaShaun said.

"You're kidding, right?" Cee-Cee said and snorted. "Back on task."

"What if they're connected?" Jonah piped up. He looked from Cee-Cee to LaShaun.

"Oh!" LaShaun blinked at him, her mouth open.

"Wait, what?" Cee-Cee looked at him.

"Dr. Dougherty's favorite saying is the first part of any investigation is to be suspicious of coincidences," Jonah said.

LaShaun glanced at Cee-Cee. "Who?"

"He's one of the professors at the TEA University in Vancouver," Cee-Cee explained.

Jonah ticked off his points on the fingers of his right hand. "Dianne Kirk has notes on contacting a TEA operative based in Louisiana. We think she discussed whatever her concerns were or something she found out with Ricci. They end up dead. Mr. Baptiste is murdered. They're all TEA members. One connection. They're interested in something going on in Louisiana. Mr. Baptiste lives—well, lived—in Louisiana,"

Cee-Cee crossed her arms. "Okay, I'll play. We have to establish that Commanders Kirk or Ricci even knew Mathieu Baptiste or talked to him. There's still no evidence they were murdered."

"He could have been their operative, or at least a source of information," LaShaun offered. Jonah snapped his fingers and nodded.

"But *what* were they investigating? And why would it get them killed?" Cee-Cee argued. "Nah, too shaky. But I've got your girlfriend digging. If anyone can grab a loose end and tie it up, it's her."

"What's this about a girlfriend?" LaShaun raised an eyebrow at Jonah.

"Brianna. She followed him from his assignment in Canada," Cee-Cee stage-whispered.

"Which I didn't ask her to do," Jonah blurted out. "C'mon. You know the deal."

Cee-Cee laughed when he fidgeted. "How many times has she texted you today?"

"Twice." Jonah groaned when his phone trilled.

"I'm guessing that makes three. And it's not noon yet," Cee-Cee said.

"Wrong. It's the Dallas office. They're forwarding the results of their phone records search. Give me a minute." Jonah went to the kitchen table. He pulled a slim tablet computer from his backpack. Then he attached a Bluetooth keyboard and started to work.

"You two," LaShaun said to her friend and shook her head.

"What? Just having fun." Cee-Cee glanced at Jonah and giggled.

Jonah looked up at them. "There are numbers with Louisiana area codes on Kirk's record of calls, incoming and outgoing. Now we need to find out if any were to Mr. Baptiste." His fingers flew over the keyboard.

"I'll have more coffee and another beignet." Cee-Cee went to the counter and poured herself a cup.

Cee-Cee wandered over to the family room. Moments later she turned on the television with the remote. A recap of the morning news played. LaShaun joined her when she heard Mr. Baptiste's name.

"No arrest has been made in the murder of a beloved retired farmer and dog breeder. Mathieu Baptiste, known to close family and friends as Papa Bowwow, was brutally killed two days ago. Sheriff Godchaux says they are following several promising leads," the pretty blonde female news anchor said with a solemn expression.

"That's cop talk for 'We got diddly squat so far,' " Cee-Cee quipped.

"Chase will tell me if they do," LaShaun replied. She frowned at the TV.

"He hates it when TEA cases get hooked to his," Cee-Cee retorted. "He'll shut down the info pipeline even to you."

"Not for long though. He can't resist my womanly charms," LaShaun joked.

"Yeah, that's obvious since more little Broussards are on the way," Cee-Cee shot back.

"Only one," LaShaun protested.

Jonah joined them holding his tablet. "None of the three Louisiana phone numbers are listed to Mr. Baptiste, or even one of his relatives. At least not with his last name. Six calls to the Horizon House in Lafayette. Transitional housing for released inmates."

"Wait a minute. Let me see that." LaShaun snatched the tablet from him before he answered.

"Sheesh." Jonah wandered back to the coffee cop to refill his mug.

"That's where Manny Young was until recently. He's moved to his own apartment. But he's still being on forensic parole supervision," LaShaun explained.

"Hmm. Another one to a Khalid Bell, LCSW," Jonah said from across the room. He savored his third beignet. "You know, you could sell tons of these. So good."

"LCSW, licensed clinical social worker," LaShaun said.

"TEA is keeping an eye on Manny Young for sure. I mean, they feel responsible since they helped get him out," Cee-Cee said.

"Say what?" LaShaun gaped at her.

"I couldn't share everything with you, but since you're in on this inquiry..." Cee-Cee muted the television and sat down. She licked powdered sugar from her thumb before she continued. "Okay. So, TEA initially paid for his defense attorney. Turns out Manny inherited money from his grandfather slash father, the pervert. I need a shower thinking about the guy."

"TEA funded Manny's release." LaShaun sat down hard on the leather sofa next to Cee-Cee.

"There were more than a few who didn't think he was guilty, not directly. It's clear he might have been present for some of the murders he was tried for. But even TEA experts think he's dangerous," Cee-Cee said.

"They get him out, but watch him," LaShaun replied.

"More than just watch. I'm not authorized to say more," Cee-Cee said. She grinned at LaShaun over the mug as she sipped more coffee.

"Don't give me that crap. You're on my home ground, asking for help. I flushed out Orin Young, and I know Manny better than any of the TEA bosses. And by the way—"

"I'm just messin' with ya, girl. You know I'm selective about which orders I follow," Cee-Cee said.

Jonah joined them again. "Don't get the pregnant lady upset."

"I can still whip both of you and clean up before Ellie gets home from school." LaShaun scowled at them.

"Calm down, little mother. We hear you loud and clear," Jonah said in a gentle tone as he patted her shoulder.

"You..." LaShaun pointed a forefinger at him.

"All right, all right. Everybody cool it," Cee-Cee said with a wave of one hand at them. Her expression turned serious again. "Manny has a parole officer and a forensic social worker assigned."

"Let me guess. One works for TEA," LaShaun said.

"His parole officer is a fully trained operative. I only found out the day before we came," Cee-Cee added when LaShaun's eyes narrowed.

"He's got the all-seeing eye on him for sure," Jonah quipped, referring to TEA's official logo.

"Yeah, but Manny has a special talent for getting around restrictions and locks," LaShaun replied.

"You mean he seems able to teleport or execute astral projection," Jonah said.

"So, our next stop is to meet with the parole officer and this social worker. Find out why Commander Kirk called them. She wasn't part of the team assigned to analyze and support Young." Cee-Cee took out her smartphone. She tapped the screen and scrolled through messages.

"Humph. The High Protectorate Council isn't happy. Rumors are flying back and forth. Word's gotten out that we're investigating the deaths. Both factions are accusing each other of assassination. A member in Ghana claims someone tried to kill him on a trip to London recently," Cee-Cee said, scrolling down to summarize TEA internal news.

Jonah pulled a hand over his face. "Whew! Shit just got real."

Cee-Cee nodded. "Which means I'll be getting a call to kick our investigation into high gear. As in, 'We want the results yesterday.' "

"I'll call in reinforcements. Del should go to New Orleans, save us a trip. She has contacts there and can check local resources." Jonah took out his cell phone and tapped the screen. Del St. Denis was another operative originally from Louisiana.

"But that'll take time," LaShaun said.

"Nope. Her brothers are super rich. Some start-up that took off. She has access to their private plane. Hey, Del." Jonah walked off as he talked.

"Isn't that..." LaShaun looked at him.

"Yeah, another ex-lover. Fortunately, she's over the Jonah Parker magic. Not that Brianna believes it." Cee-Cee shook her head.

"Hope they save some of that energy for fighting evil," LaShaun wisecracked.

Cee-Cee sighed, eyes still on the cell phone screen. "And we'll need every ounce of it."

"Bad, huh?" LaShaun craned her neck to peek over Cee-Cee's shoulder. "That the new TEA news network? It's mostly been reports on archaeological digs and theological research. Dry stuff."

"TEA-NN, or TEA Network News, has a twenty-eight-year-old director now. He's hired a whole crew of young folks, another source of controversy. They don't stick to the dry stuff as you call it." Cee-Cee's gaze remained glued to the content.

"I'm gonna start making time then. I hardly ever log onto the TEA secure net."

"Yeah, well, him and the reporters have stirred the pot to boiling on a lot of issues. It doesn't help that Miller is an outspoken science over spirituality advocate."

"Which means the news is slanted to favor that viewpoint."

"Some think so. But he does have spirituality supporters provide commentary and present their views. From what I can see, he presents both sides. Most of the time." Cee-Cee looked at LaShaun. "But I can't get distracted by drama. Our focus is on figuring out what the hell Kirk and Ricci were doing, if it got them killed, and then..."

"And?"

"Commander Wagner and the Criminal Division can take it from there. Hell, I'm starting to feel like a cop," Cee-Cee grumbled.

"You're a top operative, a regional manager. Guess that's why you were assigned." LaShaun dumped out her now-cold coffee.

"No, I was assigned as cover. They didn't want a full-scale and obvious criminal team mobilized. That would have definitely attracted unwanted attention." Cee-Cee texted at high speed as she spoke.

"We see how well it worked."

"I tried to tell Frank and Secretary Desmond it wouldn't stay secret for long. They were hoping to keep it under wraps at least until the big meeting."

Cee-Cee read an answer to her last text. "Okay. We're on to meet Young's parole officer and social worker. Hey, Jonah, let's go."

Jonah strode back into the kitchen, phone still to his ear. He nodded to her, but kept talking. "Yeah. Del, cut it out and get to work. Damn."

"Let me guess. She's going to make sure Brianna knows she's coming to Louisiana, implying y'all will be together." Cee-Cee's face tightened into an angry frown.

"She likes the idea of keeping her trip a secret even more. Women." Jonah laughed as he shook his head. "Anyway, she's been reading the news, along with everybody else in TEA."

"So far. the news folks haven't mentioned Louisiana. We've got breathing space to get in and get out." Cee-Cee pulled out the Land Rover keys.

"Don't leave without telling me what you found out," LaShaun said as she walked them out to the SUV.

"Talk later," Cee-Cee called back.

LaShaun watched as the Land Rover drove away. Jonah gave her a wave as Cee-Cee turned onto the road from the driveway. The ringing phone pulled LaShaun away from enjoying the bright sunshine. Once inside, she hurried to pick of the cordless before the call went to voice mail. A quick scan of the caller ID showed it was from Ellie's school.

"Hello. Yes. Ten is fine." LaShaun hit the button ending the call. "Damn."

****

That afternoon Chase took a break from work to come home for a family meeting. The brightness of early afternoon light made for a cheerful backdrop. They sat around the kitchen island. Ellie pouted, her little face set in a mask of rebellion. She had a hand on Beau's head as he sat next to her. He stood as if in support of his human sister. LaShaun squinted at Ellie. She could almost hear Monmon Odette chuckling from the other side. Her grandmother would take great delight in the spunk of her great-grandchild. Except she didn't have to deal with the complications.

"Ellie, you know we talked about using your... skills on other people, especially kids," Chase said, his voice tight with self-control. He rarely got angry with his baby girl, but when he did it was epic.

"I'm not bullying anybody. Taylor, Hina, and me were not bothering those girls. They made fun of Hina's mom because she has an accent. Then they started in on other stuff. We're not a gang either. I heard what Kayley's mommy said." Ellie glared at them.

LaShaun refrained from blurting out what she thought of the woman. She could still see the redhead, her pale cheeks flushed with outrage. "I'll be talking to the principal again. But in the meantime—"

"Mrs. Rouzan thinks Kayley and Melodie shouldn't have said those things to Hina," Ellie blurted out, offering proof she was right since the school principal was on her side.

"That's not the point," Chase snapped. "Did you make Kayley trip and fall into dog poop, and then put a snake in her backpack?"

"It was just a baby garden snake! Papa Bruce says they don't bite and they're good for the garden." Ellie's face relaxed into the hint of a grin. "I thought she'd like a new pet."

"Not funny." LaShaun's expression and tone had the desired effect.

Ellie's eyes widened, and the mirth left her small face. "I told her sorry."

"After you got caught and the teacher made you," LaShaun pointed out.

Chase let out a noisy sigh as he rubbed his forehead. "Look, sweetie. You had the best of intentions defending another kid—"

"I don't like it when somebody gets pushed around. Hina's family may be different, but that's not a reason to call her names," Ellie said in a rush, her defiant stance back in full force.

"Different?" Chase looked to LaShaun.

"They're Pakistani immigrants. Her father teaches at the community college satellite campuses in Lafayette and Abbeville. Agricultural mechanics technology. Her mother's a nurse." LaShaun shrugged when Chase blinked at her wealth of knowledge. "The principal introduced us. We had a chance to chat."

"Now we're friends," Ellie added.

"And I'm proud of you for looking out when she was treated bad. *But*..." Chase held up a finger. "Hurting people is not the way to go. You tell the teacher or some other adult."

"Yes, Daddy. Though Kayley wasn't hurt. She did squeal real loud at the baby snake though." Ellie pursed her cute little mouth. She gave her mother a sideways glance.

"You meant to scare her, and that's kind of like hurting her because it doesn't feel good," Chase explained with patience.

LaShaun clicked her tongue at his soft approach. "Chase..."

"You're right, Daddy. I'm going to make a nice card for Kayley and Melodie to say I'm sorry," Ellie put in fast.

"That's my girl." Chase tugged her thick ponytail with a smile of approval.

"And?" LaShaun prompted with a look at him.

Chase looked at LaShaun for a few seconds. Then he turned to Ellie again. "No play date this weekend with your cousins."

"Yes, Daddy. I'll go make the cards now and then do my homework. I'll feed Beau, and then I'll pull weeds up in Monmon Odette's flower bed. To get ready when Mama plants new flowers in the spring." Ellie's tiny sneakers slapped on the kitchen tile floor as she jumped from her chair. "I better get to work."

She gave LaShaun and Chase a peck on the cheek in turn. Then she bounced off with Beau on her heels. The dog paused to glance back at the adults and then left to follow her. LaShaun heaved a sigh and stared at her husband.

"I think we made ourselves clear how wrong she was," Chase said.

"Oh sure. You put the fear of God into her. She's shaken to the core." LaShaun jerked a thumb in the direction Ellie had gone. Her girlish voice singing a popular kid's song floated down the hall.

"Discipline is not about frightening a child, but teaching them a lesson."

"She didn't care about playing with her cousins this weekend. Or did you already know that?" LaShaun eyed him with suspicion.

He avoided her gaze and took out his work cell phone. "You know I've been working crazy hours. Two murders, remember?"

"Uh-huh."

Chase looked up from the phone. "The important thing is we took action. Not to mention she was in time-out at school. I think she's been punished appropriately."

"Next time I'll take the lead on giving her consequences." LaShaun patted his chest and went to the counter. She started prepping for their dinner.

"Don't be going gangsta mom on my baby," Chase teased and went back to looking at his phone. He held up a hand when his phone buzzed. "Sorry, hon. I gotta take this."

While Chase was handling one more call from the department, LaShaun checked on Ellie. Then she returned to the kitchen. She was about to start dinner, but instead picked up her tablet. She scrolled through emails. Nothing from Cee-Cee, Jonah, or Dr. Bakir. Then she opened what looked like an ad for a palm reading, with the words *Devil's Swamp*, along with an animated image of oaks trees, water, and Spanish moss swaying in a breeze.

"Damn it, Manny," LaShaun murmured.

Chapter 6

"Looking at cartoons to relax?" Chase said at her shoulder. He chuckled when LaShaun jumped away from him, the tablet pressed to her chest. "Caught ya. Now I know you watch cat videos all day."

"Yeah, well…" LaShaun blinked at him. Affecting a guilty smile wasn't hard, considering. "A girl has to have a hobby, other than chasing ghosts, demons, and evil sorcerers. You hungry?"

"I will be starving by the time we get dinner on the table. I took Ellie a snack. She's being a good girl and straightening her room. See? No need to drop the hammer on her." Chase went to the fridge. He found the bag of fresh green beans ready to be cooked.

LaShaun was grateful he hadn't noticed anything unusual. "Thanks. Put them over there."

She took out a mixing bowl. She had smaller ones with seasonings for marinade. While LaShaun moved around the kitchen, Chase kept getting interrupted with more messages from his deputies. LaShaun turned to him.

"Ellie has gifts to not only read other people but… she can influence them. Direct their actions. I know what it's like to get drunk on the power of having extra-normal abilities."

"Scared she's gonna be as bad as you were, huh?" Chase looked up at her.

He grunted a chuckle when LaShaun winced. The reference to her wild childhood and adolescence sent shivers of dread up her spine. She whispered one more of many apologies to the spirit of Monmon Odette. Some of LaShaun's antics had even given her indulgent grandmother sleepless nights. Monmon Odette had remarkable paranormal gifts herself and reasons to dislike local folks. The Rousselle family had never been warmly regarded. From the time they'd arrived in Vermilion Parish, they'd wielded their powers. Still, Monmon Odette had more than a few challenges reigning in her willful granddaughter.

"Ellie has structure and more sources of guidance, especially from a wonderful father," LaShaun added with a smile to herself. She continued mixing ingredients.

"One thing about it, my girls know how to make me feel good." Chase put his phone down on the counter and placed his hands on her hips.

"You've caused enough trouble, Officer Broussard. Now you're getting sassy again." LaShaun rubbed her rear end against his groin.

"You're an accomplice, though." Chase nuzzled her neck. He placed one hand over her tummy. "You two take it easy. Don't let Cee-Cee and Jonah pull you into any kind of craziness."

"You talk like the baby is gonna be on the case solving clues." LaShaun laughed.

"Considering what Ellie's been able to do since she was two, I wouldn't be a bit surprised. Speaking of TEA drama, what's the latest?" Chase gave her butt a final, affectionate pat and sat down on a bar stool at the island.

"They're still trying to figure out the Louisiana connection. Cee-Cee and Jonah are meeting with Manny's minders today."

"Oh hell. Not him again. Did you tell them he tried to hire you as his private detective?" Chase said.

LaShaun nodded. "They know."

"They've been watching him," Chase said before she went on.

"One of the dead TEA commanders was in touch with someone in Louisiana. Manny's parole officer is a TEA member."

"You know, I'm starting to wonder if they got somebody embedded in the sheriff's department." Chase eyed LaShaun. "You'd tell me, right?"

"Of course, If I knew. I'm not sure TEA would tell *me* though. And what does it matter? They're on the side of goodness and justice," LaShaun replied.

"Except they're at each other's throats and may have murdered two of their own," Chase shot back.

"Well, if you're going to get picky about details," LaShaun said with a grin. Then she let out a harsh sigh. "I'm concerned, to be honest. I mean, what's happening with the operations all over? Like the old saying goes, the devil is busy. If they're fighting each other..."

"Then they can't fight the forces of evil and defend the innocent," Chase intoned, pitching his voice deep.

LaShaun slapped his muscular bicep. "Ha-ha. You know what I mean."

"Yeah, I hear ya."

"I mean, your boss is a stickler for team effort for a reason. May not be a bad thing Mark Anderson is leaving," LaShaun said.

"It ain't a done deal just yet. There's a plot twist. The mayor asked M.J. if she'd consider the job with a healthy pay increase. Seems he's already counting the money two new businesses will bring in."

"Really? I hadn't heard anything."

LaShaun began preparing their evening meal. She mixed up the marinade in a bowl. She placed chicken thighs in it and set them in the fridge. Chase got out her favorite cast iron skillet without needing to ask.

"A new sugar cane mill and a mining operation near Devil's Swamp. A big company thinks there's minerals worth something in there. Anyway, being Beau Chene and Vermilion Parish, word got out that the mayor talked to M.J."

"Uh-oh. Detective Anderson probably didn't like that one bit."

"No, he didn't. But one thing about it, Mayor Savoie is not somebody you can push around. Mark made the mistake of hinting at an ultimatum. Mayor

Savoie and Dave set him straight. Now maybe he'll track down the info on Mathieu Baptiste I asked for two damn days ago."

"You mean the tattoos?" LaShaun paused in her meal preparations.

Chase nodded. "So far, nothing."

"You think M.J. is considering the offer?" LaShaun sautéed mushrooms, onions, and minced garlic in the skillet.

"Nah, she's content where she is. If anything, she'd take a job with the state police. But not before her son graduates from high school. She doesn't want to uproot Tony."

"Hmm, good. He's only fourteen." LaShaun smiled to herself.

"And you get to keep your friend close by for a few more years."

"Hey, I don't have many, and I don't make 'em easy. The whole voodoo witch thing tends to make other housewives nervous," LaShaun joked.

"Speaking of witches, sorcerers, and stuff, any news from your TEA pals on the symbols?" Chase smirked when LaShaun turned to him.

She took the skillet off the fire. When she pointed, Chase handed her a baking dish. "Dr. Bakir is still working on it."

"Mrs. Baptiste confirmed that her husband didn't have those tattoos before. She was shaken up when I showed her the pictures." Chase frowned at the memory. "Poor lady. I'll try to make it as easy on her as possible."

"Miss Rose and me are going to visit her. We're taking her food so she won't have to cook for a few days."

"That's good. Hmm, I like the way that smells. What are we having?" Chase said as took out his cell phone again.

"Baked chicken with rice and mushrooms." LaShaun poured a broth mixture into a ceramic dish. She added rice and the marinated chicken pieces, then placed it in the oven. "We'll eat in another hour and a half. Give you time to check in at work."

"I'm going back to the station after I eat. Sorry, babe," Chase added when LaShaun groaned a complaint. "We still have an unidentified body on our hands. You know how Dave is."

"Yes, I do. He's on a mission." LaShaun continued cooking.

Sheriff Dave Godchaux was seen by some as more of a posturing politician than lawman, but it wasn't true. He felt keenly about victims with no names. Being religious, he took the duty to find and comfort families very seriously. Not to mention not knowing the deceased's connections made catching the killer almost impossible.

"Which is why he lit into Mark about concentrating on the job he has now." Chase chuckled and put away his cell phone. "I even felt a little sorry for the guy."

"So, you have no clue who the other guy is." LaShaun stirred the pot of green beans she was preparing. Then she covered it and lowered the heat. "Chase, did that person have any tattoos?"

"A skull on one arm but nothing like Mr. Baptiste."

LaShaun wiped the counters where she'd worked. She went through the motions of washing up, a habit she'd learned from Monmon Odette. She cleaned up as she cooked. Yet her thoughts were far away.

"All the same, I'd like to see pictures of them."

"I guess it can't hurt. We released his description to the public anyway, including about the tattoos. His weren't done locally either. We checked." Chase's cell phone played a tune and he groaned. "At least let me get a plate of food. It smells so damn good."

He answered the call and walked away, which meant it was serious business. LaShaun checked on Ellie. True to her word, Ellie sat at the small table in her room doing homework. LaShaun knew she'd finish fast. Beau sat next to Ellie as if checking she was right. His head was cocked to one side.

"I'll be through in a minute, Mama. Then I'll go outside and let Beau get some exercise while I pull weeds." Ellie spoke without looking away from her notepaper. Beau woofed as if to confirm their plans.

Once again LaShaun felt a tingle at the rapport between them. She thought of Mr. Baptiste, and how he'd brought them together. Ellie had been only a toddler when they'd gone to his kennel. Mr. Baptiste had been certain that Ellie would know which puppy to choose. He was right. When Beau and Ellie spotted each other their connection seemed instant. Somehow, Ellie had even known his name before being told. LaShaun felt a catch in her throat at the memory of Mr. Baptiste's kind smile. She could hear the soft burr of his Creole accent, and his infectious, pleased laughter at seeing Ellie and Beau take to each other.

"I'll find who took you away from us," LaShaun whispered.

The ringing of their landline phone tugged her attention away. She went down the hall. The cordless handset sat on an antique phone table. LaShaun's ancestor, her great-great grandfather, had been among the first blacks in Vermilion Parish to have phone service in the 1920s. She glanced at the display. No I.D. LaShaun picked up anyway.

"We need to talk." Manny sounded breathless, as though he were being pursued. "You got my message?"

LaShaun looked over one shoulder to make sure Chase wasn't around. "How the hell did you get my—"

"Wasn't hard. Just used your name and one of the two local internet companies. Anyway, I'm guessing you don't have long to chat. I need to show you something. Tomorrow, Route 333. Near Little White Lake."

"Devil's Swamp? You've lost your mind. I'm not meeting you—"

"We don't have time to debate. Meet you at eleven in the morning. Unless you're not interested in why two top TEA officials are dead."

LaShaun sucked in a sharp breath. She was hooked, and he knew it. "Fine. But no more games."

"Believe me. Nobody is playing around."

LaShaun started to ask a question, but Chase's voice pulled her back from curiosity. She muttered a string of expletives as she eased the handset back onto its base. First order of business was to change their phone number and her email address.

"Hey, I thought we were going to get something to eat in this house. Guess I better play chef then. I'm gonna put the dinner rolls in the oven," Chase said.

"Okay, I'm just... I'll be there in a minute," LaShaun yelled back. She turned around to find Ellie standing next to her.

"I finished my homework. Then I fed Beau. He's outside playing." Ellie looked up at LaShaun and then at the phone.

"Uh, that's good. I thought you were going to stay outside with him though?"

"I heard the phone ring. It wasn't a wrong number," Ellie added when LaShaun started to reply.

LaShaun knelt down to her. "You know we don't keep secrets from Daddy."

Ellie wore a serious expression that made her look older than her six years, seven months. She nodded. "Right. We trust each other."

"Exactly. Sometimes, though, I wait until I have all the facts first. So he won't worry for nothing."

"I understand." Ellie nodded. Then her expression brightened and she was a first grader again. "You'll be okay, Mama."

Before LaShaun could answer, Ellie skipped away down the hall. Her thick curly twin ponytails bounced with each hop. LaShaun joined Chase in the kitchen. They fixed dinner side by side. Chase and Ellie kept up a steady stream of chatter. Beau came through the electronic dog door and added his own occasional woofs. She tried to put thoughts of Manny, Devil's Swamp, and murder aside for the time being.

****

Manny had been right. He'd picked the perfect time, close to the middle of the day on a Wednesday. Most local folks were at work. LaShaun passed only three other vehicles as she drove down Highway 82. She'd seen only one pickup truck once she turned onto Highway 333. The day had clouded over. A fine mist of rain fell. The intermittent whisk of her windshield wipers was the only sound that kept her company as she drove. LaShaun preferred her beloved Louisiana bathed in sunshine. The overcast sky, the color of iron in some places, did nothing to assure her. She was going to meet a serial killer in a remote place. Near Devil's Swamp.

"Alleged serial killer," LaShaun mumbled to herself, echoing Manny's only half-serious retort to the label. Adding *alleged* didn't make it sound better.

"In a quarter of a mile turn right onto Cow Road," the friendly mechanical voice of her GPS system announced. "Your destination is on the left."

Manny had given her an actual address. LaShaun was expecting a small grocery store or lonely gas station. Instead, she saw an overgrown gravel driveway. A black mailbox on a post listed to one side like a drunk man. The house at the end of the driveway was raised on cinderblocks, probably to save it from high water. Manny's truck was parked underneath. The crunch of gravel and white shells announced LaShaun's arrival. Manny, leaning against the Toyota Tacoma, stood straight. He waved to her as the SUV pulled to a stop.

"Glad you could make it," Manny called out. "How's it goin'?"

"Not sure yet." LaShaun pulled up the hood on her rain jacket. She gave him a stony look.

"Rough start to your day, huh? This gloomy weather don't help, that's for sure. Well, come on in. I fixed some coffee. Got some sandwiches from Anna Mae's Café over in Mulatto Bend. Is it me, or is it getting chilly out here?" Manny turned to see LaShaun hadn't moved. "What?"

"I'm not here for a damn tea party," LaShaun retorted.

"Good, cause like I said, I fixed coffee. Good, strong dark roast. Anna Mae's makes the best grilled shrimp sandwiches I ever tasted. I got a couple chicken salad just in case. I mean, who don't like shrimp? But you never know."

"Manny, quit messin' around. This ain't Devil's Swamp."

LaShaun glanced around. The house looked old but not completely abandoned. Neglected, maybe. Someone had made recent efforts to cut back the wild shrubs and weeds.

"We're not far. Come on. Don't want the bread to get all soggy, and us neither," Manny quipped.

A steady downpour replaced the fine mist as if cued to reinforce his argument. LaShaun walked under the house to get out of the rain as it got harder. "Whose place is this anyway?"

"Orin owned property around the parish. My grandmama made my aunt hold onto this place for me. She never gave up hope I'd get out. She rented it out—my aunt, I mean. The lady who was living here died last year." Manny looked around as he talked.

"Humph." LaShaun didn't move.

Manny spun to face her. "Oh, not here. She got sick with cancer, died in a hospice care home in New Iberia. No ghosts." He smiled and spread his arms out.

"I feel positively cozy then," LaShaun retorted.

"We both know you're armed, and I'm guessing you could hold your own in a fight. So..." Manny shrugged. He gazed at her rain jacket.

LaShaun resisted the urge to place a hand on the pocket that held her knife. Her great-grandfather's antique derringer was in another slot in the denim jacket sleeve she wore underneath. Or was it her great-great grandmother? Manny startled her when he closed his eyes.

"It was your great-great aunt. She gave it to her sister, your great-great grandmother, as a gift." Manny opened his eyes. "Those were some badass women, so you got it honest. I have no reason to hurt you."

His ability to call up a vision set tingles through her body until she felt on fire. Yet she managed to keep her voice steady. "I'm not here for family gossip or lunch."

"But lunch is so damn good. I'm telling you, Annie Mae's got the best—"

"I'm not hungry," LaShaun clipped. Her stomach rumbled, a reminder she'd skipped breakfast.

Manny barked a laugh. He turned for a set of steps under the eaves that led to the porch. "No need to suffer. Besides, we can't go see what I have to show you yet. Raining too hard. But we can't leave it too long."

LaShaun stood as the sound of his boots clumped up the treads. "What are you talking about?"

His footsteps stopped, replaced by the unmistakable jingle of keys. "Devil's Swamp. Over coffee and food, I'll tell you an interesting tale."

"Damn you," LaShaun muttered low. She wasn't sure if she was angry at Manny or herself for taking the bait.

A squeak signaled he'd pushed open the door. After another, more colorful curse word, she climbed the steps behind him. LaShaun stopped short as if ready for an ambush. What she got startled her even more. The warmth of the room she'd entered didn't only come from a heating system. Soft beiges, browns, and dark reds of the attractive décor made the open floor plan inviting indeed.

"Your late tenant had a great eye for interior design."

The living room had long windows that gave a view of open prairies outside. An oak dining table acted as a divider between it and the kitchen. An archway led to a hall, which she guessed would in turn lead to bedrooms.

"This is all me. Poor Mrs. Landrieu was a hoarder. The place was a mess. Cat shit everywhere. Piles of magazines, some back to the eighties. Took me months to get the place fit to even redecorate." Manny threw the keys down and crossed to the kitchen.

LaShaun's mouth hung open for a few seconds before she recovered speech. "You did all this?"

Manny stood at a kitchen island. He pointed to bags of food. He put an already-unwrapped sandwich on a paper plate for himself. A fancy coffeemaker sat to one side. "Help yourself. I picked out the furniture. My aunt hired a decorator. Parole conditions and being watched limited how much I could do."

"You're not supposed to leave Lafayette Parish without permission," LaShaun said, quoting one condition of his parole.

He sipped coffee and frowned, but not at the taste. "Speaking of being watched, your TEA friends are back in town. And talking to my handlers."

"And you?"

Manny shook his head. "But then they don't have to since they've got spies on me. What's that about?"

LaShaun's stomach complained again at the smell of the food. She took off her rain jacket and draped it over a stool. Then she grabbed one of the wrapped sandwiches. I didn't drive out here to answer *your* questions."

Without replying, Manny grinned at her. He put his sandwich down, wiped his mouth, and went to the stainless steel refrigerator. He took out a pitcher of sweet tea, found a glass, rinsed it, and poured. Then with a flourish, he set the glass down on the counter in front of her.

"Let me guess. One or maybe both of those dead TEA commanders has been in touch with my parole officer. Or maybe it was my social worker." Manny took his seat again. He appeared relaxed, as if this was a normal lunch between friends.

"Damn, you're a regular host with the most. Better prepared than one of those celebrity chefs on The Food Network," LaShaun joked in a dry voice. She sat on the edge of a stool opposite him.

"Thanks, and you're dodging the subject. Never mind. They won't find a link to me. I can't leave Lafayette Parish, remember? Let alone travel to Canada and Portugal, which is where they died. I don't need you to confirm that, by the way." Manny took a bite of his sandwich. He pointed to her still-untouched lunch.

LaShaun sighed. She broke off a small section and ate. "The story you wanted me to hear?"

"Was I right? Is that not the best-tasting sandwich?" Manny started to say more, but stopped when LaShaun cocked her head to one side. "Okay, okay, okay."

"I'm gonna take my food to go if you don't stop messin' with me." LaShaun's eyes narrowed to slits.

"Ever heard of TCM, Inc.? I'm not teasing out info to irritate you," Manny added fast when LaShaun's scowl deepened. "So, you don't know about them. Terra Core, Incorporated is a mining company. They've applied for permits to dredge and mine Devil's Swamp. Gravel and sand, valuable as precious metals."

"The company our mayor is so happy about." LaShaun ate more of the sandwich and sipped sweet tea. She wasn't going to admit how good the food tasted, but the way she dug in did it for her.

Manny wore a pleased smile as he gazed at her. When she gestured at him with impatience to keep talking, he seemed to take it in stride. "The real value isn't in rocks or sand. They're after rare earth minerals, some used in high tech and even space exploration instruments."

LaShaun had, to her own surprise, polished off the grilled shrimp sandwich. She drank half of the tea in her glass. "I know you didn't bring me out here to talk crap about rocks—"

"Rare earth minerals," Manny cut in. His dark eyes held a gleam of excitement. Ever heard of monazite?"

LaShaun slapped a hand on the granite top of the island. "Manny, I swear..."

"Okay, I'm getting there." Manny sighed, giving LaShaun a look of reapproval. "Monazite is one of several rare earth minerals. Mining them is big business, as in big money. They're used in computers, to strengthen steel, make really powerful magnets, you name it. Terra Core Mining digs up the stuff. It's a global operation."

"Uh-huh." LaShaun drummed her fingers. "And?"

"Terra Core was founded by a family with TEA ties. I won't go into the history since you're so impatient," Manny said, one eyebrow raised.

"You got that right." LaShaun glanced at the time display on her cell phone, and then back at him.

"Sweet how well-funded TEA is. Anyway, to shorten this story—"

"Please," LaShaun said through clenched teeth.

"Monazite isn't just used in all kinds of normal electronic equipment and such. It can be used in certain specialized TEA instruments. A company scientist stumbled on that fact. Each of the major opposing factions within TEA are battling to run Terra Core. Whoever controls the company not only has billions in potential funding, but..." Manny sat back like a teacher waiting for a student to get his lesson.

LaShaun frowned. "They'll have the finances to take over TEA."

"Think of the manpower and tech you could develop with that kind of cash flow. But the real deal is this—monazite can be used in a modified device to ramp up magnetic fields from the brain, or something. I don't understand it all, but monazite can make super-psychics. You know what that means, right?" Manny's dark eyes lit up again. He stood and paced, rubbing his hands together.

"Enhance the abilities of people with psychic gifts to..."

LaShaun blinked hard as she stared through the window. A fine mist had returned to replace steady rain. The gray weather matched the train of her thoughts. Manny seemed energized about the potential use of a substance he'd never heard of before, and barely understood. Which didn't reassure LaShaun. At all.

"You and I could boost our powers, find out who killed those two girls, and clear my good name. Well, if I'd had a good name to begin with. But this could be a new start in life for me."

LaShaun stood. "Manny, someone could use this stuff to become powerful, maybe try to rule the world."

Manny stood still and waved a hand. "Oh yeah. That too."

Chapter 7

The rumble and hum of big machinery filled the air as LaShaun pulled her Forrester off the road. She found a makeshift parking lot, grass beaten down by vehicles coming and going. A group of pickup trucks, SUVs, and a few cars were scattered about. No doubt they belonged to company employees. Manny arrived seconds behind her. He eased his truck next to a gray Chevy Tahoe and got out.

Devil's Swamp looked grim. Tall trees and waist-high shrubs stripped of their leaves by winter didn't help. The sun tried to break through clouds, which might have brightened the place. Brief shafts of pale yellow only heightened the contrast. Devil's Swamp seemed to push back. Clouds closed over a spot of blue sky. Skeletal branches rattled in the wind, as if applauding the victory of gloom over radiance.

"Big-time operation for a podunk middle-of-nowhere place, huh? The stuff comes from the rocks and little bugs or something. Sounds nuts to me, but whatever."

"Over millions of years, dead plants and animals fossilize and become minerals. But swamps don't have a lot of minerals. Not enough to make the effort of digging 'em out worthwhile," LaShaun replied. A huge dredging machine sat on pontoons. LaShaun searched her memory for the name of the muddy body of water before them.

"Blood Bayou," Manny breathed close to her ear. He grinned when LaShaun jumped.

"Cut that out." LaShaun pushed him back.

"I think of you as my baby sister. So, don't get your hopes up," Manny joked. He strode ahead without waiting for an answer.

"I'm an only child," LaShaun snapped.

Noise drowned out her retort. She grumbled to herself as she followed in his footsteps. The ground had soft spots. LaShaun planted her boots in the prints Manny left behind. She didn't want to end up knee-deep in a sinkhole. A husky man in a hard hat approached. After a short exchange, he and Manny both nodded. Manny turned around and walked back to LaShaun. The noise level dropped as one machine gradually shut down.

"He says we can't get too close for safety reasons. Recent reports have brought out a lot of curious folks. Don't mind us looking, even taking pictures. But we gotta move back." Manny nodded toward their vehicles.

Once they got back to the parking area, LaShaun leaned against her SUV. She watched a few men pile into a large truck with an extended cab. Manny pulled a tangerine from his pocket and started to peel it.

"Dessert," Manny said when LaShaun arched her eyebrows at him.

"Good thing the guy thinks we're nosy neighbors." LaShaun studied the operation, not that she knew what she was looking at.

"Not unless one of these guys recognizes the voodoo queen of Vermilion Parish." Manny winked at her before he popped a section of the fruit in his mouth.

"Or the infamous Blood River Killer," LaShaun shot back, her gaze still on the bayou.

"Alleged," Manny replied in a mild tone around the pulpy mouthful.

"Humph. How do you know about Terra Core and monazite?"

"I might have picked up a few tidbits here and there in Dallas at the TEA neuro-psych clinic." Manny ate more of the tangerine.

"You know a hell of a lot more than *tidbits*, Manny."

LaShaun stared at him hard, but it had no effect. She didn't expect it would. Maybe if Ellie were here... LaShaun kicked the idea from her head. Where the hell did it come from? Miss Rose would say it was Satan's temptation stirred by the infamous Devil's Swamp.

"Hey, if they gonna poke around inside and outside of me, I got a right to know about *them*," Manny muttered. He threw a piece of tangerine rind to the ground.

"I'll accept that for now. But I'm keeping my eyes on you." LaShaun made a note to ask Cee-Cee if Manny had access to a computer.

"You and everybody else. Only place I don't feel like I'm in a fish bowl is out here." Manny sighed. "Look, it's possible I didn't kill anybody. Not that I'm a saint."

"That's too easy, so I'm gonna restrain myself." LaShaun continued to stare at the activity around. Most of the crew had left, probably to get lunch.

"Yeah, there's a grocery store that serves plate lunches about three miles that way. Close to Pecan Island," Manny said.

"Stop it," LaShaun hissed.

"Just using intuition and observation." Manny crossed his arms. "Just tell your little friends I didn't have anything to do with those TEA murders."

LaShaun faced him. "Medical evidence says they died of natural causes."

"You'll find out different soon. I made new friends who like to gossip," Manny said with a grin. "But only with a few trusted people who don't blab."

"And *you're* one of those trusted people?"

"Who knows how to keep a secret better than a serial killer?" Manny joked.

"You mean alleged," LaShaun replied in a dry tone.

"So, you finally accept the possibility I'm innocent. That's a start."

"Think again." LaShaun walked a few yards toward the bayou.

Manny jogged to catch up with her. "You had a psychic vision; saw me hurt somebody?"

"Nope. Intuition and observation," LaShaun said over her shoulder. She went back to staring at the pontoon floating on murky waters.

"I know I'm... different, and I've done things that—"

"Save it for therapy," LaShaun broke in. She raised her cell phone and started recording video. "Notice anything unusual?"

Manny strode a few steps past her. He stared for several minutes, and then shook his head. "I don't know..."

"The guy standing at the end there. He's moving his hands, but he's not using any equipment."

LaShaun concentrated. Tingling snaked up her arms, the usual signal her paranormal senses had kicked in. Minutes ticked by. She ignored Manny's aggravated pacing as best she could. Even taking time to tell him to keep still would break her flow. Then she saw it. Familiar symbols glowed a faint greenish-blue, visible in the air. They wisped away only seconds after they appeared. At least that's what it looked like to her. Then the figure on the pontoon paused and turned to face them. LaShaun grunted when a sharp pressure thumped into her chest. She dropped the cell phone in the mud. Manny came to a stop, retrieved it, and handed to LaShaun.

"What the...?" Manny shut up when LaShaun grabbed his arm in a tight grip.

"We better get the hell out of here," LaShaun breathed.

****

LaShaun made it home in plenty of time before Ellie's school bus would drop her off. She ordered her thoughts as she went about doing routine tasks. She folded laundry and put another load in the washer. With the sound of the first cycle, LaShaun sat down to pay bills online.

Her finally chore was preparing Ellie's snack. She cut up apple slices, spritzing them with lemon juice so won't they wouldn't turn brown. Ellie would declare them "too yucky" to eat otherwise. Then she put a small cup of hazelnut and chocolate spread aside for dipping, an extra treat. Two short, distinctive horn blasts announced the bus had arrived. LaShaun left through the kitchen door and walked down their driveway. The bus driver gave her a friendly wave.

Ellie stood at the top step in the open bus door. "Bye Dawn, bye Taylor, bye Traneeshia."

"You gonna see these same children in the morning, baby. Now run along," the bus driver said, eager to finish her route.

"Tomorrow ain't promised, Miss Brown," Ellie replied. She giggled when the bus driver blinked at her.

Miss Brown shook her head. "That child been here before, I swear."

Ellie hopped down each step until her little sneakers touched the ground. She grinned up at LaShaun. "Hey, Mama."

"Hello, sweetie. Good day at school?" LaShaun kissed her forehead as the doors of the bus cranked shut with a squeak.

"It was okay." Ellie launched into a spirited hour-by-hour summary of her day.

Like most mothers, LaShaun let her chatter and gave a dropped a few perfunctory responses. LaShaun's main goal was to get Ellie settled in her room before Cee-Cee and Jonah arrived. If she was very lucky, Ellie might even take a short nap. That way they could talk. Thirty minutes later her strategy was almost defeated when they arrived.

Ellie squealed with delight the moment she spotted the Land Rover. She ran to him when he got out and wrapped both arms around his knees. "Jonah, I'm so glad to see you!"

"Hey, baby sis." Jonah beamed at the welcome.

"Hi, Ellie." Cee-Cee brushed a hand through Ellie's thick curls.

"Hi, Miss Cee-Cee. How are you?" Ellie still clung to Jonah even as she remembered her manners.

"I'm good." Cee-Cee grinned at LaShaun. "She thinks he walks on water."

"Yeah, but then we're not sure he can't." LaShaun laughed as she watched Jonah swing Ellie around.

Their reunion was brief but intense. Beau barked his own enthusiastic greeting. LaShaun had to give in to letting Jonah go with Ellie to her room. Meanwhile she and Cee-Cee settled down with refreshments. Coffee for LaShaun, tea for Cee-Cee.

"Couldn't get a babysitter?" Cee-Cee sipped the special blend LaShaun had made herself.

"Not last minute, but I had to talk to you. And not on the phone." LaShaun looked at her.

Cee-Cee stared back. "What?"

"With all this stuff going on inside TEA and what I found out today..." LaShaun heaved a sigh.

"Girl, don't get paranoid. My cell phone isn't monitored." Cee-Cee chuckled. She started to say more, but the grave expression on LaShaun's face seemed to stop her. "You better tell me then."

Jonah joined them at the kitchen island. "I finally got her settled and distracted so we can talk. Beau will make sure she stays put."

"Yeah, we'll see how well that works," LaShaun said with a snort. "Anyway, here's the deal. I met with Manny."

"He's got nothing to do with our case. So you have a legitimate reason to tell him to eff off," Cee-Cee said.

"And keep Chase from blowing like an IED," Jonah put in. When LaShaun squinted at him he added, "Improvised explosive device, it's—"

"I know what it is, thank you," LaShaun clipped and turned to Cee-Cee. "Manny claims he's never been farther than the regional TEA medical center in Dallas."

"What he's told you is true. The commanders asked for updates on his status. Since they were high up with clearance, the PO responded. Nothing confidential, mind. Just confirming he hadn't been anywhere else," Cee-Cee said.

"So, they were checking to make sure he'd stayed put. Apart from the clinic appointment, that is. But we can't figure out why they wanted to know." Jonah frowned as though annoyed at the puzzle.

"That's weird. What did they think Manny might have been up to?" LaShaun looked from Jonah to Cee-Cee.

Cee-Cee shrugged. "No clue."

"They thought Manny was involved in TEA political intrigue? That's crazy. Manny's never shown any interest in becoming a TEA activist. Or has he?" LaShaun directed her question to Cee-Cee since she was a rising star in the agency.

"Not that I know of, but here's another weird thing. He's got a few, I guess you could call them admirers. And one woman who seriously is crushing on him." Cee-Cee heaved a deep sigh. "You'd think she'd have better sense than to get the hots for a serial killer."

"Apparently having a sixth sense doesn't automatically come with *common sense*," LaShaun quipped. "Though it does add up. Manny told me about TCM."

"Who?" Cee-Cee and Jonah exchanged a puzzled look.

"Terra Core Mining. They're dredge-mining Devil's Swamp, about twenty-five miles southwest of here."

"Colorful name..." Cee-Cee gazed at LaShaun.

"You know there's a story behind it. I'll tell you about it later. Manny says the two major factions fighting over control of TEA both want TCM."

"TEA has bought commercial companies since, I don't know, the industrial age. Pretty handy having psychics predict the next big product," Cee-Cee said with a smile. "Why do you think we don't need membership fees?"

"Like hell we don't. I pay the office coffee fund in two damn locations. Just because I'm so good I was assigned to both. Haters gone hate," Jonah grumbled

"Grow up," Cee-Cee retorted.

"Profits aren't why they want control. Ever heard of rare earth minerals?" LaShaun asked.

"Used in a wide range of electronic products, to make magnets, and advanced medical equipment." Jonah reeled off the uses as if he could go on.

"Huge market potential," Cee-Cee put in.

"Monazite can also enhance psychic abilities."

"Okay." Cee-Cee's eyes widened after a few seconds.

"The faction that gets the company can outpower its opposition." LaShaun nodded as the implications seemed to be sinking in.

"And control a helluva lot more than just TEA," Cee-Cee said.

"Are we talking world domination?" Jonah gaped at them. When both women nodded, he let out a hoot. "Holy shit, that's what I'm talkin' about. I want in!"

Cee-Cee clamped a hand on his arm as if to restrain him. "That kind of power always leads to some pretty nasty consequences."

"TEA can't be effective fighting evil when the members are fighting each other," LaShaun added.

"But think of all the *good* we could do." Jonah looked at them, hands on his narrow waist.

"Said every dictator who ever walked the earth," Cee-Cee shot back with heat.

"And I saw someone with remarkable psi abilities at the TCM work site. He was... like writing on the air. The symbols didn't last long, but I think they were similar to the tattoos on Mr. Baptiste." LaShaun rubbed her forehead as she tried to picture them again. The images proved elusive.

"Casting a spell is seriously old-school," Cee-Cee said.

"Superstition," Jonah said. "Science explains it. Someone is able to focus EMF to help locate the minerals faster. Neural activity creates magnetic fields and..."

Cee-Cee put up a hand. "Let's not have the science versus religion debate now."

"I'm just sayin'." Jonah leaned against the island and drank more coffee.

"Here's another thought. I'm not sure anyone knows the possible side effects of using monazite or any other rare mineral on people. Has research been done? We need to find out," LaShaun said.

"I'll need probably need clearance to even ask questions. I'll give it a try though." Cee-Cee took out her phone. Her fingers flew as she tapped in messages over the secure TEA app.

"Manny's admirers might be loyal to one of the factions. Which is why he didn't tell me everything." LaShaun scowled.

"Manny had to know you'd figure it out. Even without training you're a fifth-level psychic." Jonah pulled out his large smartphone and unlocked it.

"What's this level you're talking about?"

"New classification developed by Research and Development. It's a rough description, more for academic and research purposes," Jonah said.

"For someone who hated school, you've become quite the student."

"Finally found subjects that didn't bore my nuts off. Pardon the expression," Jonah grunted. He continued swiping through screens. "Humph. I'm going to get info on Manny's girlfriend. See what she's been up to. If you're sure it's a she."

"Positive. Manny has a way with needy women." LaShaun gazed through the bay window facing them.

Jonah looked up. "Maybe we should take action in case she's in danger."

"I don't think so. At least not at the moment. She's got something he wants. He's convinced I can use the mineral to help clear him of the murders," LaShaun murmured, deep in thought about all she knew so far.

"I'll say this for him, he's a planner," Jonah said and went back to swiping. "I'd like to have a long talk with that guy."

"You will before we're done." LaShaun shook her head when Jonah glanced at her sharply again. "No psychic insight—just obvious he's part of the case."

"Yeah, and in a way we never saw coming," Jonah said.

"I've got a meeting with Frank Miles. I used Code Orange, which means a potential internal threat," Cee-Cee explained when LaShaun wore a puzzled frown.

"Also means it's just between them for now. Super-sensitive, not shared with any other operative," Jonah added.

LaShaun looked at Cee-Cee's troubled expression. "Because you don't know who to trust."

"Except me, of course. I'm always on the side of the righteous," Jonah joked, his youthful enthusiasm intact.

"Hmm," was Cee-Cee's only response as she arched an eyebrow at him.

"Meanwhile, I'll get Manny to find out more from his lady love," LaShaun said.

"I'm not authorizing we use Manny as a confidential informant. Hell, his membership in TEA is still being reviewed. With his track record, sounds like he's would be a better fit in Legion," Cee-Cee replied, referring to TEA's nemesis, a group they battled almost daily.

"C'mon, the guy seems to be trying. His social worker says he's kept a job since he got out. He's keeping his therapy appointments. Taking his meds," Jonah said.

"How many serial killers were described as a 'nice quiet fella'?" Cee-Cee argued.

"And he's helped me before. Though he wants something in return," LaShaun added.

"For you to prove he's innocent." Jonah gave a dramatic shudder. "I've read the clippings. Brutal killings. I'd fight to clear my name too."

"Isn't it even more dangerous that he doesn't remember what he's done? We don't know his role in those crimes." Cee-Cee crossed her arms. She stared from Jonah to LaShaun with a stern expression.

"We need to keep that in mind dealing with Manny," LaShaun said. "But don't alert the friends he's made at the Dallas clinic. We need to track how much they know and if they're involved."

"Crap, I think you're right." Cee-Cee chewed on her lower lip for a few seconds. "I'm not sure my boss will agree though."

"Don't tell Frank." Jonah shrugged when Cee-Cee gave him a sharp glance. "None of what we've found out connects Manny. At best it's a very thin thread. Sometimes it's better to ask forgiveness than permission."

"Your personal mantra," Cee-Cee clipped. She grunted when he lifted both hands.

"I'm with Jonah. Besides, I kind of think Manny is trying his own brand of rehabilitation," LaShaun said.

"By helping us, well *you*, really," Cee-Cee replied.

Ellie and Beau raced into the kitchen. They both slid to a stop. "We finished schoolwork. Is Jonah done talking?"

"She's asking if Jonah can come out to play. That's too cute." Cee-Cee's solemn expression melted as she laughed out loud.

"C'mon, pint-size. I've got a little time before we have to go."

Jonah took Ellie by one hand. He stuck his tongue out at Cee-Cee as they both left through the back door. Moments later they heard Ellie's shouts and Beau's enthusiastic barks. Jonah tossed a large colorful ball to Ellie as the dog bounded between them.

"He's still such a kid," Cee-Cee mused as she gazed at them through the bay window.

"Well—"

"Don't even," Cee-Cee broke in. "Jonah is not ready for a steady relationship with a grown-ass woman. I need more."

"I think you're selling him short. But that's all I'm gonna say. Subject closed," LaShaun said fast when Cee-Cee jabbed a forefinger at her.

"Speaking of relationships, talk to Chase about Manny soon. You really want to test his patience keeping secrets?"

"I'm not keeping secrets," LaShaun protested. "I'm... gathering all the information I can before sharing it."

"Very creative. One more cup of soothing tea for the road. With the way this case is headed, I have a feeling my nerves will need it." Cee-Cee scowled in contemplation of the tasks ahead.

"I'll fix you a few bags to take," LaShaun said. She figured they'd all need ways to de-stress in the days ahead.

At almost ten o'clock that night Chase strode in. He gave LaShaun a distracted kiss on his way to their master suite. She heard the shower come on moments later. She didn't need psychic powers to know what his routine would be. Chase would linger under the pulsation setting of the warm waterfall shower head. He'd plant both palms on the walls and let it massage his muscles. A shower was his way of washing away the grime of the terrible things he had to see, hear, and clean up. Once the shower stopped, he'd towel off, dress, and head to Ellie's room. Even if she was asleep, seeing her pretty little face would soothe his jangled nerves. No tea blend LaShaun's ancestors had concocted would work better. LaShaun placed a hand on her tummy. Soon he'd have another source of peace and contentment. She let out a long, happy sigh. Soft lighting in the kitchen, a gentle Cajun tune on the sound system, and a hot plate of food. Home.

Chase came in while she was still at the sink. He put his arms around her waist from behind. "We better talk."

"Your dinner..."

"Can wait a few minutes." Chase tugged her until she followed him to the family room. He pulled her down next to him on the sofa.

"You've found out something disturbing. About Mr. Baptiste's murder," LaShaun said, searching his face for clues.

"Both murders have the same MO as the Blood River crimes. Stay far away from Manny Young, LaShaun."

Chapter 8

The Friday-morning weather matched her mood as LaShaun drove to town. Gray skies and early-morning fog made trees, grass, everything look dreary. Reporters milled around outside the main Vermilion Parish Sheriff's Department station in Abbeville. LaShaun observed from a couple of blocks away. She'd managed to get a parking space when a car pulled out. The usually sedate small downtown area buzzed with activity. No wonder. The Blood River Ripper had been brought in for questioning. Wearing dark sunglasses and a knit hat, LaShaun didn't attract attention. A scarf around her neck kept out the chilly breeze and helped conceal her face. Everyone gawked at the area around the courthouse and sheriff's office. She went into a coffee shop inside a new boutique hotel. A long, high table with barstools faced the front floor-to-ceiling window. She had a view of the oak-lined street and sheriff's office. A middle-aged waitress with bright-red hair walked over to her.

"Ma'am, you got to order something. Can't just sit and watch the show," the woman said and popped the gum she chewed.

"I'll have a vanilla latte with whipped cream. Oh, and a cinnamon bun," LaShaun said. She hadn't felt hungry until that moment. The new baby seemed set on having her gain too much weight.

"Uh-huh." The waitress nodded to the scene across the street. "Lucky for you that mob hustled out a few minutes ago. They say Manny Young about to show up with his lawyer. The place been packed since we opened the doors at seven this morning."

"News got out fast. I just came to get my nails done down the street," LaShaun said. "Was wondering what was goin' on."

"You know who Manny Young is, don't ya? That serial killer, a real nutcase straight outta one of them horror movies," the woman went on before LaShaun could answer. "I can't believe they let him out. Folks startin' to turn up dead again. No surprise. What the hell did they think would happen?"

"Wilma, refills," a man yelled. He frowned at the woman and jerked a thumb at her.

"Okay," she yelled back and then lowered her voice. "Make some people assistant manager and they get uppity." She went to another table of customers.

LaShaun turned her attention back to the courthouse grounds. A tall, blond male reporter aimed a video camera to take in a panoramic view. "Hey, Miss—"

"Wilma's fine, honey. Your order will be here soon. I could get you some water or juice," the waitress called back.

"A small apple juice would be great. I'll be right back. I'm gonna leave this here so nobody takes my seat." LaShaun draped her scarf around the chair.

"No problem." Wilma waved a hand at her.

LaShaun walked the half block to approach the reporter. After a few minutes of adjustments to the tripod, the reporter smoothed the front of his jacket. Then he stood straight and gazed at the video camera with a solemn face.

"Once again, the people of this small town are on edge. Channel KATC was first to break the news that Emmanuel Young, aka Manny Young, aka the Blood River Ripper, is once again a murder suspect. Sources tell KATC news that the position of the bodies and wounds are eerily similar to the string of killings that led to his arrest and conviction. Mr. Young has been brought in for questioning. The first victim found has yet to be identified. Sheriff Godchaux released this sketch, asking anyone who might recognize this man to come forward. A second victim, Matthieu Baptiste, was found dead a week ago. Authorities quickly ruled out natural causes. We're told his body had strange markings, but law enforcement hasn't confirmed the details."

The reporter began a summary of a string of murders committed over fifteen years earlier. LaShaun blended into the knot of onlookers who had gathered around as the reporter talked. She crossed the street and went back into the coffee shop.

"It's a mess out there, ain't it?" The waitress served her order from a tray balanced on one hand. "Here ya go. Live reporting and everything. Breaking news."

"Yeah, I guess so, considering." LaShaun sipped her coffee and plotted her next move.

After a suitable period of looking like a normal customer and curiosity seeker, LaShaun walked to the sheriff's office. She almost made it.

"Ms. Rousselle, sorry Mrs. Broussard. Why am I not surprised to see you here?" a male voice asked.

LaShaun turned to face the source. She groaned when she recognized him. "I didn't speak of the devil, and yet here you are."

James Schaffer, host of a popular ghost hunter reality series, beamed at her as if they were old friends. His videographer hovered behind him. "Nice to see you again, too. Emmanuel Young is the gift that keeps on giving. In my case, reliable ratings."

"Anyone would start to think you're obsessed with Louisiana. Coming all the way from Los Angeles so often must be expensive. I'm sure are plenty of local stories to keep you at home."

"Relax, I'm not doing a story on *you*. This time."

"Gee, thanks," LaShaun snapped.

"Or at least I wasn't, but you showing up has me intrigued. Since you played a role in Young's release..."

"That's bull," LaShaun cut in.

"Maybe you're concerned that another miscarriage of justice is about to take place. Look, I'm a sympathetic journalist." Schaffer put on an earnest expression.

"I thought you were supposed to be objective," LaShaun retorted. She glanced around in hopes no one knew him or noticed them talking.

"You must not be paying attention, dear. The days of media pros droning on with dry facts and figures are long gone. Every reporter or news organization has an agenda." Schaffer pressed on despite LaShaun's snort of distaste. "I'm willing to give you and Manny a forum to make a case for his innocence. Together, we could help your friend."

"You're crazy if you think Manny Young is my pal or that I'd talk to you. Oh, and my husband works for the sheriff's office. Since you're so full of information, I'm sure you know that already. So, me showing up here isn't unusual at all. Now if you'll excuse me." LaShaun started to push past him, but he placed his tall, bulky frame in her path.

"We started off on the wrong foot." Schaffer spread his arms out.

"We?" LaShaun scowled at him.

"Mea culpa. I came off as a smug jerk. I'll make it up to you with lunch at Dupuy's," Schaffer said.

"During which you hope I'll spill some news you can use. No thanks." LaShaun was about to go on when Detective Mark Anderson strode up.

Anderson glared at them both. "I'll save you some time, Schaffer. No comment to every question you might have ever. Yeah, I know who you are and what you do."

"A free press—"

"You're an overrated hack pumping up phony stories for idiots dumb enough to believe you. Get lost," Anderson growled at him, drawing up to his full six feet.

"I'm on public property," Schaffer countered. "Now if you'll excuse me, I'm going to get an official statement."

Anderson clamped a meaty hand on his arm and yanked him back. "One more step, and I'll charge you with interfering with an active investigation."

"Hey, you can't do that!" The videographer spoke as he continued to film. "He's got no grounds to say we're obstructing justice."

"Oh, you a lawyer, too? We'll work it out while y'all sit in a jail cell," Anderson replied with an evil grin.

"We have every right to be here," Schaffer said.

"Yeah," his cameraman added.

I said move along." Anderson batted at the camera, which caused it to bump the man's forehead.

The videographer yelped and almost dropped it. "You'll end up the one charged, dude. With assault."

"Not very bright. Smile for our millions of viewers, Detective Anderson." Schaffer smirked at him.

Anderson's long arm shot out and knocked the camera to the sidewalk. Piece of it flew off into the grass. A crowd gathered as the videographer yelled at Anderson, who smiled with satisfaction at his handiwork. Then his mouth drooped when more reporters scurried over. LaShaun used the commotion to her advantage. She moved to the edge of the crowd while their attention was on Anderson. Then she headed for the sheriff's office. She almost made it inside when another gaggle of media people spotted Manny and another man coming out of the side entrance. LaShaun found herself caught between them.

"Tell them they've got it wrong, LaShaun," Manny yelled.

A male reporter spun to face LaShaun with a microphone extended. "Are you a witness in the case, ma'am? Can I get your name?"

"Are you a friend or family member?" A black female reporter with a shoulder-length braids took up the chorus.

"No to all three questions. My husband works here. I'm just visiting," LaShaun said. She stared hard at Manny in fury.

"She's LaShaun Rousselle, the psychic that's been used in other murder cases," a woman called out.

LaShaun recognized the shrill voice of her neighbor, Betty Marchand. An avid gossip and attention-seeker, it was no surprise Betty had come to town. LaShaun gritted her teeth and tried to push her way past the female reporter.

"Sheriff Godchaux is consulting a psychic in the recent murders?" The female reporter stepped in front of LaShaun. Her eyes widened at the dark glare LaShaun gave her.

"Don't be ridiculous," LaShaun hissed. "Now excuse me."

"Do you have any insight into the strange markings on the body of one victim? Sources say they're connected to satanism," another reporter called over the hubbub.

"There is no evidence linking my client to the recent crimes. He's fully cooperated and been released," the young black man next to Manny said, his deep voice cutting through the noise. More than one reporter asked for his name at the same time. He waved a hand to shush them. "I'm Michael Grover with the Tulane Justice Project. And I can assure you nothing discovered so far in either murder investigation implicates Mr. Young. Beyond that we have no more to say. Excuse us."

Naturally, the reporters continued to shout questions at the pair, some directed to Manny. LaShaun was relieved when two uniformed deputies came out to clear the reporters away. Chase appeared in the glass door of a side entrance. Gold letters on it said, "Authorized Personnel Only." Before LaShaun could take advantage of the second distraction, the reporter with braids blocked her way again.

"I promise fair reporting in exchange for an exclusive." The woman pushed a business card in LaShaun's face.

LaShaun didn't read the card or take it. "No. Now move. Please."

The woman blinked hard as she gazed at LaShaun, but finally backed up to let her pass. "You've only made me more curious, Mrs. Broussard. I'll have you and your husband's entire life story by lunchtime. Your daughter was part of a past case, too, wasn't she?"

"I very much doubt you'll have even a fraction of accurate information, lady." LaShaun spun to face her, a forefinger pointing at the woman's nose. "And if you print anything about my child—"

Chase pushed through the door with another deputy behind him. "The department will release a statement updating the status of our investigations shortly. Thank you, ma'am. This area is restricted."

"You're welcome to wait out front. I'll show you the way." The female deputy wore a congenial smile, yet she firmly herded the reporter ahead of her down the sidewalk.

"C'mon before I have to bail you out for slapping the woman." Chase grabbed LaShaun by one arm and pulled her inside.

"Did you hear—"

"Calm down. She can only rehash what's already public record. She was just pushing your buttons." Chase rested a hand on her waist as he led her deeper into the station.

M.J., dressed in a sharp black pantsuit with a crisp, light-gray shirt beneath, appeared in the hallway. "What a damn circus. Two reporters found their way inside the station somehow. You know how happy that makes our boss and the mayor."

"Mayor Savoie is chewing antacid pills like a kid eating Halloween candy," Chase joked. "All he can think about is how this might affect the Mardi Gras crowds."

"Well, two corpses don't exactly shout 'Laissez les bon temps rouler,' " M.J. retorted.

M.J. led them down the hall and up the stairs to her second-floor office. Though busy, it was noticeably quieter than the first floor where most of the uniformed deputies worked. Plainclothes detectives and administrative offices took up most of the second floor.

"Dave is furious with Mark for losing his cool out there." M.J. pushed through the door into her expansive office. She unbuttoned her jacket and leaned against her desk. "He doesn't know LaShaun stirred up more drama with her arrival. At least not yet."

"Hey, that wasn't my fault. I came to town to run an errand, maybe take Chase to lunch." LaShaun winced when Chase and M.J. gave her twin skeptical looks. "Okay, that was pretty pathetic. I didn't have time to come up with something better."

"For once you're not our biggest problem," M.J. said.

"How reassuring," LaShaun drawled as she squinted at her friend.

M.J. strode around to sit at her desk and picked up a report. "We found a cigarette butt with DNA on it near the body at the docks."

"Good." LaShaun took a seat. Chase sat next to her in a matching office chair.

"Water and a couple of warm humid days allowed fungi to grow, which means the DNA is degraded. It could match Manny, but..." M.J. heaved a frustrated sigh.

"It could also be a distant relative or even non-relative white male of European ancestry. The body had been in the marshy area for up to twenty-six days. Maybe a bit longer," Chase explained.

"Despite what the public thinks, the state has eyes on him pretty consistently. The staff at his prisoner rehab program, the social worker, and his parole officer. We can't see a window of opportunity for him to slip off and do a kill." M.J. looked at Chase.

"Or a motive. Manny didn't operate as a lone wolf, no pun intended," Chase added when LaShaun raised an eyebrow. Local rumors had it that he and his father were leaders of a loup garou pack, the Cajun version of werewolves.

"Right. His father would party with a group of his friends, and either he'd do the killing alone or they'd all do it together. We never confirmed which was which." M.J. propped her elbows on her desk.

"Both," LaShaun said firmly. "Sometimes he'd take part in a group kill that included torture. Other times he'd lure the victim away from the party and kill them. Based on the visions Manny showed me."

"Visions," M.J. echoed. "Do I really want to know what you're talking about?"

"When I first interviewed Manny at the secure forensic facility, he somehow shared a vision of one, maybe two murders. Like sending his memory to me. I can't explain it, and neither can TEA researchers yet. He's unique in his ability to project." LaShaun looked at Chase. "I could ask them for more information."

"Okay. The thing is... and I can't believe I'm saying this." Chase shook his head and gazed at M.J.

"What?" LaShaun leaned toward him. Her arms started to tingle at the shared mood between her husband and friend.

"We both have doubts that Manny is the killer this time or part of the crime," Chase said. "Dave or Mike would blow up if they heard me."

"I said it first, so if the shit hits the fan you can throw me under the bus," M.J. joked.

"Yeah, but we were both thinking it about the same time." Chase looked at LaShaun. "The cigarette butts could have easily been planted. Manny's movements are being closely monitored, at great expense I might add."

"Thank God not out of our budget," M.J. added.

"It's too neat. Like someone putting voodoo tattoos on Mr. Baptiste after he was dead or close to it," Chase said.

"Not voodoo symbols. Dr. Bakir is sure they're some kind of ancient written language. Which means the killer was sending a message. Or crafting a spell maybe. I'm still waiting to hear," LaShaun added when M.J. looked at her with a question in her dark-brown eyes.

"I'm told Mr. Baptiste was a superstitious guy. He believed some of his dogs could smell out ghosts and evil. Maybe those were his tattoos," M.J. looked from LaShaun to Chase.

"No more superstitious than the average person around here. By all accounts he was a good Catholic man, active in his church. Went to mass every Sunday," Chase said.

"Monmon Odette used to say the old religion's loas were spirits that took messages to God. The vodun from West Africa mixed with Catholicism several hundred years ago," LaShaun said in a distracted murmur as she thought over the new facts.

Chase shrugged. "He sold dozens of dogs over the years to folks around here, even out of the parish."

"Yes, but none of those folks are LaShaun Rousselle, a descendant of infamous voodoo queens and kings. And James Schaffer is in town," M.J. said.

"Ghost Team USA. Load of crap USA more like it. I can't believe he's still on the air," Chase said with a sour expression.

"Of course he is. Look at the rich material we keep giving him." M.J. leveled a steady gaze at LaShaun.

"None of this is my fault. All I did was get my kid a pet from a well-known dog breeder. Like a *lot* of people, I might add," LaShaun said.

M.J. cocked her head to one side. "Oh really? Loads of people get dogs who can hunt hobgoblins, I guess. My grandmother says his father had the same side business, besides farming. That he knew Monmon Odette."

"I didn't know about the family connection. Honest," LaShaun insisted.

"Except for getting Beau from him, LaShaun doesn't have any information material to the investigation," Chase put in to help her out.

"I believe you, but you can guess what folks will think if it gets out that you knew Mr. Baptiste. Let alone what that Schaffer character will have to say. But we don't have to deal with it now. Our pressing problem is a wave of vigilantism building against Manny."

"You're kidding." LaShaun looked at Chase, who shook his head, and then at M.J.

"I wish. Worse news, I think Mike Anderson is helping to whip it up. Not to encourage lawlessness, but to put on a strong law and order show."

"To get the job as police chief for Abbeville," LaShaun said with distaste.

"Especially since M.J. has changed her mind and might consider the job," Chase added in an accusing tone. His eyebrows scrunched together.

"No, you can't," LaShaun blurted out.

"My son needs more of my attention, and the money for college would be nice. A small police force with little or no crime in a limited jurisdiction. Mighty appealing after dealing with an entire parish and the Blood River Ripper." M.J. rocked back in the leather executive chair.

"But, but we need you." LaShaun blinked at her.

"I'll literally be across the street." M.J. laughed and pointed in the direction of the Abbeville PD police station. The one-story, white-brick building was two blocks away from the courthouse complex.

"Dave is sure to promote Chase to Chief Deputy. You might even run for the office one day." M.J. looked at him.

"No. Way. I'd prefer going to the Louisiana State Police if I move, which I'm not planning on. Believe it or not, I like working here." Chase patted one of LaShaun's thighs and smiled. "Anyway, M.J. hasn't decided yet."

"Back to our present complications, which seem to be reproducing like mosquitoes after a flood," M.J.

retorted. "We need to sort through this Manny Young mess."

"As in figuring out why someone would set him up." LaShaun frowned at no one in particular.

"Solve two murders, get him locked up again, and everybody around here would breathe a huge sight of relief," Chase replied.

"And not be fussy about whether he's actually innocent or not," M.J. added.

LaShaun blinked at her in surprise. "Are you admitting to the possibility Manny might not be a killer?"

"Hell no," M.J. said promptly. "He's a killer."

"But he's being framed for these latest two murders. Crazy." LaShaun looked from her husband to M.J.

"Or he's hooked up with a copycat killer. We're looking into if he has any groupies around here," M.J. said.

"Manny Young fans in Vermilion Parish." LaShaun shook her head. "I don't think so."

"Yeah, well, stranger things have happened." M.J. raised both eyebrows as she gazed at LaShaun.

"Why do you always look at *me* when you say stuff around here is strange?" LaShaun crossed her arms and stared back at her friend.

Chase looped an arm around LaShaun's shoulder. "Well, honey..."

"I'm not the trouble magnet y'all make me out to be," LaShaun protested. "In fact, I've helped this department solve a few cases. *You're welcome*."

M.J. looked serious for a few seconds before a grin cracked her face. "Just kidding. But you have to admit that you've been at the center of a lot of weirdness."

LaShaun tried to come up with a forceful argument against her statement and failed. "Yeah, well."

"And I am grateful you're around to help out when cases get tricky because of... you know." M.J. spread her arms out.

"The supernatural. Hard for practical Chief Deputy Arceneaux to say the word." LaShaun laughed when M.J. squirmed.

"I still say everything has a logical explanation," M.J. said and stood. "Now, you two get out of my office and get us some answers."

"You're officially appointing me to join the investigation? Cool." LaShaun stood at the same time as Chase.

"Of course not. But I can't stop you from doing what you do," M.J. replied.

"Which is?" LaShaun looked from M.J. to Chase.

"Ignoring our 'official' request that you not talk to people and nose around," Chase replied.

"Just let us know what you find out sooner, not later." M.J. gave LaShaun a pointed look of warning.

LaShaun stood at attention and saluted. "Yes, ma'am."

M.J. rolled her eyes but went on. "Chase told me your TEA pals showed up. Maybe between the three of you, you will get to the bottom of this mess."

"Yeah, actually there are more than three. Cee-Cee—"

"I don't want to know *why* they're here," M.J. broke in fast. "But if they have useful, actionable information I'll be a very happy cop."

"No mention of ghosts, demons, loup garou, and such," LaShaun said with a mischievous grin.

"Please and thank you," M.J. gestured at them to leave.

LaShaun walked close to Chase and stared up into his dark Cajun eyes. "And you don't mind that I might talk to the Blood River Ripper."

Chase winced at the sobriquet. "It's not like you'll listen if I ask you not to."

LaShaun smoothed down the front of his shirt and kissed his cheek. "You know me so well, lover."

Chapter 9

The weekend passed with nothing out of the ordinary happening. Chase's mood lightened as he enjoyed a normal home life. Ellie complained a few times about being grounded, but more as a matter of childish principle. She seemed content to do chores around the house instead of going on her play date. Chase put in a few hours on Saturday at work, but Sunday was all their day. The weather even cooperated with the gray, rainy, late February days clearing up. He was in such a good mood that Chase took them out to eat at their favorite seafood restaurant. Monday morning brought back the clouds. They seemed to be an omen.

They were in the kitchen getting ready for the day. Chase had gone to the bedroom to finish getting ready for work. LaShaun put a twist tie around Ellie's thick curls. She turned her around to examine the twin pigtails on either side of Ellie's cute face. Then she wrapped dark blue ribbons at the base of each. These matched the dark-blue plaid skirt of the school uniform.

"Now, you're going to have a good day at school. Right? No taking revenge on behalf of your friend. You'll tell your teacher and let her handle it."

"Uh-huh." Ellie stuffed colorful pencils into her backpack while LaShaun brushed stray hairs.

LaShaun didn't like the noncommittal tone of her reply. "You'll tell her first thing when you see someone being mean."

"Uh-huh." Ellie avoided looked back up at LaShaun. "Can I take my new paper tablet with the unicorn on it?"

"You still have plenty of paper in the old one. We don't waste. And don't change the subject. If someone is mean to Hina, Taylor, or anyone else you'll do what?"

"I'll tell Mrs. Simpson and not drop da hammer on them myself," Ellie said dutifully.

LaShaun gaped at her baby girl's gangsta statement. "Wait, what? Where did you get that from?"

"Daddy said I shouldn't drop the hammer cause it'll just get me in more trouble than the perp," Ellie replied with a shrug.

Chase walked in with his mug of coffee in one hand and stared at his cell phone in the other. His favorite cowboy-styled work boots made his steps echo on the tile floor. He wore Army-green pants and a crisp cream-colored dress shirt. Chase winked at Ellie and almost bumped into LaShaun. LaShaun stood to face him, hands on both hips.

He blinked at her with a puzzled expression. "What?"

"Your daughter was just telling me about your advice. You know, dropping the hammer on *perps*." LaShaun looked at Ellie and back at him.

"Oh, she took it to heart. Good girl." Chase winked at her and went back to staring at his work emails.

LaShaun turned to Ellie. "Your school mates aren't perps, Ellie."

"Okay. Is Daddy in trouble? Daddy's going to be in time-out?" Ellie's eyes sparkled as if the thought inspired gleeful anticipation.

LaShaun suppressed a frustrated groan. "Never mind. Tell me what you'll do if someone bullies your friend."

"I'll tell Mrs. Simpson and let her drop the hammer," Ellie said with a smirk.

"Ellie..." LaShaun sputtered for a few minutes and then sighed.

"Yes, Mama. But if Mrs. Simpson isn't around—"

"You'll find the closest adult," LaShaun cut her off. She wagged a finger at Ellie's little nose. "Mind what I say."

"Uh-huh. The bus is almost here." Ellie grabbed her backpack from the kitchen island.

"Looking for loopholes to do what she wants, giving vague answers to direct instructions. Apple didn't fall far from the tree," Chase murmured with a side-eye at LaShaun.

"Hardheaded like her daddy." LaShaun jabbed him in the side as she walked by.

"Owww-wee!" Chase doubled over in a comic act of being injured.

LaShaun rolled her eyes and kept going. She walked with Ellie to the bus stop. Though that was being generous. Ellie raced ahead of her, eager to avoid more promises she wouldn't keep. At least that's what LaShaun figured. The driver seemed to have coordinated a rescue. The familiar toot-toot of the bus sounded within seconds of them leaving the house. LaShaun could only wave good-bye as Ellie scampered up the steps.

She turned to see Chase standing farther up the driveway waving as well. When she reached him, LaShaun stuck two fingers in one of his belt loops and pulled him along. They played tug of war and traded jokes as they went back inside.

"Hey, thanks, babe." LaShaun grinned at the clean kitchen.

"I'm a renaissance man. I can fight crime and do the dishes." Chase winked at her. Beau endorsed his view with a bark and went back to eating his breakfast.

"Yeah, but did you mop and do the windows?" LaShaun picked up a dish towel he'd dropped in a heap on the kitchen island.

"Don't push it, woman. So, what you got on for today?" Chase slid his phone into a shirt pocket.

"You mean investigation-wise, I'm guessing, not laundry," LaShaun quipped. "I have to meet with Savannah to go over some legal stuff about Monmon Odette's assets." Savannah Honoré was a friend, but also her attorney.

"You mean *your* assets," Chase corrected.

"I still think of the stocks, bonds, and land as hers. She's such a strong presence." LaShaun could almost hear her grandmother's voice. Monmon Odette had been a force of nature each day of her seventy-nine years.

"I sure hope you don't mean she's literally hanging out with us," Chase joked.

"Ha-ha, you know what I mean. Anyway, it won't take long. Then I'll meet Manny. Cee-Cee and Jonah will be there," LaShaun added before Chase could ask.

Chase nodded for her to follow as he went to their bedroom, and LaShaun obliged. Once there he grabbed keys, wallet, and other items from a tray in preparation to leave.

"Where?"

LaShaun decided not to mention they were going to Manny's inherited property. "Not far from Devil's Swamp."

"Where they're mining vibranium like in Wakanda."

"Very funny."

Chase slid on his work wristwatch and faced her. "I'm not joking when I say be careful."

"Broad daylight, two TEA operatives trained in combat, and I'm no slouch. What could go wrong?" LaShaun kissed his cheek as he grunted but didn't answer.

By a quarter to noon, LaShaun left downtown Beau Chene and drove down Highway 14. She cut across to connect to the small, two-lane route to Manny's house. Scattered homes gave way to empty prairies or farm fields on either side. The sunshine from the previous day had been covered again by clouds. LaShaun was lost in thought. She turned over the issue of Ellie's growing up with supernatural abilities. Then her mind switched to TEA and the two mysterious deaths. R&B songs from the SUV's sound system played softly in the background. LaShaun absently brushed the prickle along one arm. She snapped out of her musings, blinking a few times.

A soft mist had rolled across Highway 333. As if in response to her finally noticing, it rose to envelope the Forrester. LaShaun's automatic headlights switched on. Glancing into her rearview mirror, LaShaun saw two circles of light from a vehicle behind her. Her heart sped up as she pressed the gas pedal. Then she had to jam the brakes. A dark shape loomed ahead blocking both lanes of the road. The mist had thickened so that she couldn't make it out. It could have been a semi-trailer truck or an RV. Yet the unmistakable figure of three people walking toward her SUV soon claimed her attention. The vehicle behind her had stopped. LaShaun concentrated until the image of a gray Ford Expedition formed in her head. The color blended so well with the fog it had almost disappeared. Pulse racing, all she could do was watch as the three figures fanned out. They halted a few yards from her SUV. Then one advanced slowly, arms up. A lithe black woman, hair pulled back in a bun, nodded to her.

"Let's talk," the woman said.

Her voice reverberated and seemed to penetrate the windshield. LaShaun gasped at the effect, then recovered. She slid her derringer from the center console, put it in her inside jacket pocket, then got out.

"You don't need the gun. I said talk, not fight. Besides, we could have picked you off a good twenty minutes ago, Mrs. LaShaun Rousselle Broussard." The woman lowered her arms. She clasped her hands in front of her and assumed a wide-legged stance.

"Blocking me on an isolated road with low visibility doesn't shout friendly chat," LaShaun barked.

"But you are curious," the woman said.

"I'm pissed is what I am," LaShaun countered. "What kind of game is Legion playing?"

The woman started at LaShaun's bold reference to the nefarious global network. Legion sponsored chaos, wars, and all manner of dangerous activities. Their demonic allegiance guided every evil plan. The Third Eye Association had effectively checked them for generations.

Then the woman seemed to recover her composure, "Stay away from Devil's Swamp. You might stumble on something more dangerous than an alligator."

"What have you got to do with a TEA mining operation?" LaShaun kept the SUV door open to use as a shield just in case.

"I'm trying to help you, sis," the woman said. "In case you hadn't noticed, TEA is in a bit of turmoil. You don't want to get smashed between the two factions."

LaShaun studied the woman in silence for a few beats. Then she glanced at her companions. To her left was a white woman with short, reddish-blond hair. A man with Asian features stood to her right.

"You should be tickled pink at the prospect of TEA tearing itself apart," LaShaun said. She turned her attention back to the woman taking the lead.

"You can benefit as well."

"How?" LaShaun shifted to make sure her left hand could easily retrieve the gun in her pocket.

"C'mon, sis. Focus on this valuable offer I'm about to make instead of planning how to shoot at us," the woman said in a mild tone.

"I can multi-task. Now get to the damn point," LaShaun clipped.

The woman gave a tolerant sigh. "Fine. We know they've recruited you to help them. Let TEA self-destruct. Then you can pick up the pieces, rise to the top. You and Mr. Young."

"What the—" LaShaun gripped the window frame of the driver's side door. "Manny is working with you?"

"TEA is a toothless dinosaur in a rapidly changing world, Mrs. Broussard," the woman said. "Their leadership is not just stagnant, they've become corrupt."

"Oh, I see. And you can offer me untold riches and power. You folks haven't changed your pitch for, what, thousands of years?" LaShaun saw movement to her right. She let her arms fall to her sides.

"Tens of thousands. No need to change what works so well." The leader bared her teeth in a smile.

LaShaun felt another chill. The woman's ruthless look marred an otherwise pretty brown face. More movement out of the corner of her vision made LaShaun pause. "Yeah, well."

"You can ensure a magnificent legacy for your children. Little Joelle has a rare gift. From what I hear, saying she could rule the world isn't hyperbole." The woman took a step forward. "Why she can do—"

"Keep my daughter's name out of your mouth," LaShaun broke in. "Tell your leaders, overseers, grand poobahs, or whatever you call them, to stay out of my way. And stay away from my child. Doing otherwise will be very unhealthy."

"She's foolishly clinging to a god that doesn't care about her," the blonde snapped. "Let's move on."

The black woman's gaze shifted to her companion. "We'll leave when I say."

Though she didn't raise her voice, the soft hiss of it sounded like the warning of a dangerous snake ready to strike. The blonde visibly flinched. LaShaun saw more movement to her left. Then she felt a flush of warmth, like she wasn't alone anymore. *Keep them talking*. The words appeared in her mind like captions on a video.

"I'm not sure who's in charge. Or which one of you to bargain with." LaShaun turned more toward the white woman.

"No bargaining. Yes or no," the white woman said crisply. "You're either in or out. Anything less means you're working an angle, less than committed."

"Oh, now that's hilarious. A cult made up of liars, thieves, and worse expects loyalty. And you call me foolish," LaShaun said.

"Self-interest is our common bond. We have ways of ensuring compliance once someone enters the fold." The blond woman's face twisted into a feral smile.

"So, if I refuse this so-called generous offer?"

The blonde's lips pulled back wider. "I'll volunteer to deal with you and the other losers. It won't be quick or merciful."

"Don't waste the scary act on me. I've slapped a few Legion idiots silly, and they were tougher than you," LaShaun said.

The blonde started for LaShaun, but the leader raised a hand and made a chopping motion. She looked off into the fog. "Tango, report."

Soft grunts and thumps made the black woman swung around in a circle, a Glock appearing in her left hand. The blond woman cursed as she made a beeline for LaShaun. She whipped past her leader in seconds. LaShaun made as if she would close the SUV door. Instead she slammed it open again. The edge clipped the blonde's right arm. She stumbled, but held onto her knife. Like a ninja, she hit the ground and rolled. Then she popped up again and raced toward LaShaun.

"Stop," the leader barked. "I said stop!"

The blonde skidded on the pavement. "We're under attack. I can take her out," she shouted.

"Hold her here. We need to find Tango," the woman said. When the blonde finally nodded with reluctance, the leader vanished into the fog.

LaShaun shut the SUV door and pretended to lean against it in a relaxed pose. "Whoever took care of your buddy Tango will probably take care of her, too."

"Bitch." The blond woman clenched both hands tight. She pointed the knife at LaShaun.

"You're not as articulate. She's not only smarter and more rational. Probably got more than one fancy degree. No wonder they put her in charge." LaShaun darted glances around as she talked.

"Shut up." The blonde's eyes narrowed to slits.

LaShaun had struck a raw nerve, it seemed. "Yeah, she's moving up to even bigger things. Which is why she's authorized to make big-time offers. You're just muscle. And not very impressive muscle at that."

Sure enough, the woman lost control. She growled, an announcement she would strike. LaShaun launched her body forward to meet her. In a smooth motion, LaShaun pulled out her gun and fired twice. The woman staggered. She grabbed her right thigh, teeth clenched, and pushed on toward LaShaun.

"If you come close, I'll press this gun into your gut and shoot," LaShaun said, her voice calm. "You prefer a knife, making your opponents bleed. Suffer. You rely on your two associates to carry firepower."

"You... you..." the woman spluttered in frustrated rage. "Tango! Makeela! What the hell is happening?"

LaShaun forced her eyes to remain open as images flooded her mind. She couldn't afford to close them during the vision. "Made up names for this operation. So corny."

"I don't understand," the woman huffed as if talking into the fog.

A rumble of thunder startled them both. Not thunder. The sound grew louder—an engine. As the fog cleared, a dark-brown recreational vehicle became visible as the object blocking both lanes ahead. Tires crunched through sugarcane stalks as the vehicle left the packed earth shoulder of Highway 333. The black woman, Makeela, appeared from the fog dragging a sack. LaShaun blinked when she realized it was a person. Makeela panted with the effort to support the man they called Tango.

"Get in the truck," she gasped to the blonde.

"This is crazy, we—"

"I'll leave you then," Makeela screamed.

She made a wide loop on the opposite side of LaShaun's SUV. She strained under the man's weight. He let out a pained yelp when she tripped on a pothole. She shifted his weight, but kept moving to the Ford Expedition.

"Damn you, Makeela! At least tell me what's going on," the blonde demanded. She made to turn her right leg but cried out.

"I don't think she's bluffing about leaving you." LaShaun held the derringer pointed down to the pavement. "I hope you're not a supernatural creature, or a hybrid. That bullet is silver."

"Shit." The blonde's breath hitched a few times.

"Oh-oh, I'm guessing the answer is yes. The burning sensation you feel will spread. Even a superficial wound could be fatal for you. Funny how the old folk tales about silver bullets turn out to be true." LaShaun watched as the woman's eyes widened in terror.

"I'm coming. Wait for me." The blonde hobbled away and dropped the knife in the process, but didn't appear to notice or care.

LaShaun spun when she heard footsteps. Manny emerged from the fog walking at a casual pace. He picked up the knife, examined it, and spoke over his shoulder.

"Another souvenir, kid." Manny continued to squint at the knife.

"Cool," Jonah said. His outline looked ghostly as he still stood in the sugarcane field some yards off.

Cee-Cee strode up to stand beside LaShaun. "They don't want to stay for coffee and cake, I guess."

Tires screeching on the pavement answered her question. The Legion crew peeled off down Highway 333 away from them. LaShaun inhaled and exhaled a few times. She raced over to the grass and threw up. Cee-Cee pulled a packet from a back pocket. The cool wet wipe felt soothing when Cee-Cee held it against LaShaun's throat.

"Here's another one," Cee-Cee said. She frowned at her. "The baby..."

"I'm okay. Morning sickness doesn't just happen in the morning," LaShaun said after a time.

Manny jogged over. "Morning sickness? You pregnant, girl? Damn, you shoulda said something. I wouldn't have had you running around Devil's Swamp. Look, you better get on home. I don't want my godchild to get hurt."

LaShaun let out a whoop. "What planet are you on?"

"He'll be my godchild in my mind," Manny said with a nod. He didn't appear the least bit offended by her reaction. "Just like Ellie. I'll have your back, and theirs."

"Comforting," was all LaShaun managed to get out. She felt queasy again, but not because of Manny. Chase would probably freak out, but she didn't feel threatened by him.

"You should have had a bland breakfast," Cee-Cee said.

"Nah, that's normal in the early stages. Plus, the stress of a fight might have triggered it." Jonah stood turning over the knife the Legion operative had dropped. He didn't notice all three of them staring at him.

"The expert." Cee-Cee shook her head.

"Our full-time housekeeper back at my dad's estate had four kids. I spent more time with her than my parents." Jonah held up the knife. Then he sniffed it. "Humph, titanium and... sulfur. Strange etchings on it."

"Play with your toys later," Cee-Cee drawled. "You sure you're okay?"

"Stop fussing. Nobody laid a hand on me." LaShaun stood straight and showed them her gun. "She didn't have a chance to get close."

"Good girl," Manny said with a laugh.

"Okay, now tell me how y'all ended up here?" LaShaun looked from one to the other in turn.

"Ellie called my cell phone, said I should 'follow Mama because bad people wanted to get her,'" Jonah said, as if it was the most normal thing.

"What?" LaShaun's mouth dropped open.

"Yeah, she's got my number in case she needs to talk. I know, I know. She doesn't have her own cell phone yet. But you should consider it because—"

"Bookmark that crazy idea. So, how did she call you?" LaShaun waved both arms.

"From the office at school. She told 'em there was a family emergency and she had to call home. And she called me. Aww, ain't she sweet." Jonah beamed with affection for his adopted sister.

"They let her use the phone. Unbelievable." LaShaun pressed a hand to her forehead.

"Yeah, then she told them everything was fine and let me talk to the assistant principal. Her *uncle* assured them she could return to class." Jonah made air quotes and grinned at them. "The youngest TEA operative in the history of the organization."

"Must have been about the time I got a vision that I should follow you," Manny put in. "I took a few back roads to get here, but they had already blocked you in."

"Manny called us, through his parole officer. We were on the way. Snuck up on 'em and pow! That guy knows a hybrid of hapkido that's damn good." Cee-Cee rubbed her right side. "His first kick almost brought me down. He dropped this, though." She held up a Browning Hi-Power semi-automatic pistol.

"I parked their mobile op vehicle on the side of the road. A local TEA team will process it. Forensics," Jonah said aside to Manny.

"We better not stick around. Those folks might try to come back. Losing valuable stuff won't make their bosses happy." Manny squinted into the distance.

"Our team's ETA is twenty minutes. They've been on alert since we got here. Coming from New Iberia," Jonah replied.

LaShaun reached out for the knife, and Jonah handed it over. She studied it with admiration. "TEA has operatives that close?"

"They came in posing as tourists to blend in with the Mardi Gras crowds." Cee-Cee pulled out her cell phone. She tapped the screen. "They're almost here."

Jonah left to meet the TEA team at the RV. Cee-Cee vetoed Manny going with him. So, Manny leaned against LaShaun's Forrester, grumbling about lack of trust.

"Good call. We're not sure exactly whose side he's on," LaShaun said low as she and Cee-Cee moved farther out of his earshot.

"Yeah. I don't like that some lovesick TEA staffer is feeding him information. Especially one with shady intentions. Using Manny as a 'double agent' could backfire. And if that's not bad enough, Commander Bauer says the Criminal Investigations Unit has reason to believe Legion planted at least one mole."

"Damn. I thought they'd rooted out the cell of infiltrators two years ago." LaShaun rubbed her tummy. The first flutters from their baby made her anxious. What was she bringing this new little one into?

Cee-Cee looked worried. "Maybe you should back out of this one. If anything happened to you or the baby—"

LaShaun put an arm around Cee-Cee's shoulders. "I'm touched that y'all are being so protective, but Ms. Rose and the twins both say this baby will be born."

LaShaun referred to the older women, all mediums, who were her mentors and friends. Rose Fontenot had been friends with Monmon Odette. They met when the now-retired teacher had taught LaShaun's mother, Francine. Justine and Pauline Dupart were fiftyish twins who combined their psychic skills when they weren't bickering.

"As if everything wasn't bad enough, Legion crawls from under their slimy rock. Feels like things are spinning out of control, and I hate it." Cee-Cee tapped a fist against one thigh.

LaShaun stepped away from her and handed the knife to Cee-Cee. "C'mon. You kicked ass and managed to grab what looks like some valuable equipment. Think of the intel you'll get. Your bosses will be ecstatic.

"There's that," Cee-Cee replied. She started to say more but paused when Jonah appeared.

"Team is on it. Now what?" Jonah rubbed his hands together. He looked energized by the action, while the others were coming down from frenetic events.

Cee-Cee turned to LaShaun. "We can meet tomorrow. Give you a chance to rest. Dr. Bakir's report can wait."

"She's got information on the symbols? No way. I'm in," LaShaun said.

"You've got to think of the baby, girl," Manny said.

"Pregnancy does not equal invalid." LaShaun looked at each of them in turn. "Those symbols on the knife blondie dropped? They match the ones that were tattooed on Mathieu Baptiste's corpse. Let's go."

Chapter 10

Cee-Cee took charge. She decided against meeting at Manny's property or going to Devil's Swamp. With Legion active in the area, Cee-Cee decided it was too risky. So, two hours later they were in a meeting room at the historic Essanee Theater. The performing arts center had become the heart of cultural events for the small town of New Iberia. A local group made up of theatrical directors and actors included several TEA associate members. They rehearsed downstairs. Sounds of stage directions and snatches of dialogue were faint background noises. Cee-Cee closed the door, giving them complete quiet. Manny remained standing while the others sat. He ran his fingertips along the polished wood of a vintage credenza along one wall. Then he walked to the oval conference table.

"Wow, they did a serious renovation of this old building. Right down to the antique furniture. This place was built in 1937. My grandfather used to bring his girlfriends here back when they showed movies. The owners finally closed it in 1980." Manny made a circle of the room to study old movie and theater posters.

"We'll get the historical tour and the happy childhood trip down memory lane later," Jonah joked.

"I don't have happy memories from my childhood, or any other time," Manny spat.

Jonah's expression grew solemn. He nodded and some unspoken message passed between them. Manny's tense posture relaxed the longer they gazed at each other.

LaShaun looked at Manny. "I'm not sentimental about this place either. Ironic that they're hosting Black History tributes. Segregation meant black residents couldn't come here for decades. Until they finally allowed them one section in the balcony. And only after the white patrons had bought tickets and been seated.

"Bet those old bigots are spinning in their graves. It's a wonder they don't show up to cause trouble," Jonah said. He glanced around as if expecting a ghostly reply.

"The place is said to be haunted," Manny said.

They all looked at Cee-Cee. Her paranormal skill was clairfactance, the ability to sense the supernatural through smell. She made a great show of sniffing the air.

"Lemon furniture polish. The only message I get is they take care of the place." Cee-Cee's witticism broke the bleak mood.

Jonah laughed and opened his laptop. "I'll get us connected to video conference in a sec."

Manny sat across from him. "My head almost explodes at all the tech stuff. No wires. Tablets that hold more stuff than old computers. So much changed while I was locked up."

"You might want to concentrate on following the conditions of your parole," LaShaun said.

"You're so suspicious. I'm not going to work some scam, not my style."

LaShaun suppressed the urge to clap back that murder and violence suited him more. Manny the chameleon had returned. When Manny gave LaShaun a crooked smile, she narrowed her eyes at him in warning. The gesture only seemed to amuse him more.

Cee-Cee looked up from her smartphone. "We're transporting the Legion RV to Dallas. The local forensic folks don't have the equipment to examine the gadgets inside the thing."

"And you sent a preliminary report, I'm guessing." LaShaun knew TEA field op procedure.

"Yep. Del is still in New Orleans. She's put together an ad hoc squad to flush out more Legion operatives in the area. I'd say within the next twenty-four to thirty-six hours we should be good."

"I messaged Dr. Bakir. She's in a student conference. She'll be ready in about twenty minutes," Jonah announced. His fingers moved over the keyboard.

Cee-Cee twisted in her chair to face Manny on her left. "That should give you time to tell us what you know."

"I already told LaShaun—"

Cee-Cee cut him off. "How long have staff in Dallas been feeding you information?"

Manny met her intense scrutiny without batting an eye. "Probably about a month or so after we met. You mean Kirsten."

"And a couple of others. Are you Legion moles?" Cee-Cee believed in getting right to the point. Her question made Jonah's head jerk up. He blinked at her and then looked at Manny.

"Straight answer," LaShaun added. She leaned forward, one arm on the table.

"Hold on a minute. They're just grumblers who think the spirituals are superstitious dummies. There ain't no satanic conspiracy goin' on." Manny rocked his chair back as if escaping even the suggestion of collusion.

"We'll verify your denial shortly. They're being rounded up and questioned as we speak," Cee-Cee said to Jonah and LaShaun.

"But I could have gotten more information," Manny replied with a frown.

"Orders from the top," Cee-Cee replied, her attention back on the cell phone screen.

"You shouldn't have tipped them off. Together, we could handle Legion. Hell, we already did. You said yourself a New Orleans team will clean them out in a few hours," Manny protested.

Cee-Cee put her cell phone on the polished tabletop. "They don't think we can take the chance now. Especially once they found out Legion approached LaShaun."

"Which has nothing to do with *me*." Manny slapped a palm against his chest.

"Like I said—"

Manny cut her off. "Yeah. You'll check whether I'm lyin' real soon."

"Hello, Jonah and everyone." Dr. Bakir's voice came through the laptop speakers. "Sorry to keep you waiting. Am I coming through clearly?"

Jonah stopped tapping the keyboard and turned it so the rest could see her. "We're good."

"Excellent," Dr. Bakir started to continue, but paused. She pushed her face closer to her camera. "Is that...?"

"Emmanuel Young, yeah, doc," Jonah said.

"Oh my." Dr. Bakir moved back again.

"Damn, everybody knows my face," Manny muttered.

"Hello, doctor. So, what you got for us?" Cee-Cee said.

"The symbols are Old Aramaic. From the Neo-Assyrian Empire. It was the lingua franca of the time, beginning around the eighth century BCE. Though a few of them are actually Paleo-Hebrew alphabet letters, which are a variant of the Phoenician alphabet. Eventually, Aramaic was accepted by rulers, what some coined as Imperial Aramaic. Fascinating. So, by the time of Jesus—"

"We can put the linguistic history lesson on hold for now," Cee-Cee broke in. "We need to know if there's a message that might be material to our investigation."

A patient smile spread across Dr. Bakir's olive complexion. "Cee-Cee, still a bottom-line woman of action. But in this case history is relevant. With the rise of Christianity, many groups or cults rose in opposition. Some reportedly with the backing of the fallen angel. Several of them started while Jesus was still alive. They created a few symbols of their own to communicate. This was common, especially after the Christian church became so powerful in later centuries."

"Which forced them underground. They backed the losing side since the efforts to stamp out the spread of Christianity failed," LaShaun said.

"Yes, yes. They became the hunted. A real reversal from the days when Christians were slaughtered in the hundreds, thousands even. But back to the present and our message, before Cee-Cee grows too impatient," Dr. Bakir said with a laugh.

"I kinda see where this is going, doc. Legion sent some of its people here. We have a murder victim who may have gotten in their way somehow," Cee-Cee said.

Dr. Bakir gasped. "That's right. I became so engrossed in research and translation, I forgot for the moment. The message is a warning to those who oppose 'The True Path.' That's a phrase used by one offshoot of a cult that eventually became Legion. Before the term Christianity came into use, the followers of Jesus the Christ referred to their doctrines as The Way."

"The True Path isn't just opposing Jesus, but every religion that worships the one God," Jonah put in.

He grinned when the others looked at him in surprise. "My TEA history classes come in handy."

"Correct. The message warns that those who wage battle against The True Path will suffer. Not an exact translation since some Old Aramaic phrases don't exactly match modern English." Dr. Bakir started to go on, but paused with a smile. "But I won't test your patience by expounding further."

"Thanks, Dr. Bakir. Every bit of info counts." Cee-Cee wore a distracted frown.

"I'm glad I could add something valuable." Dr. Bakir's affable expression was replaced by a solemn one. "The appearance of Legion is worrisome. I've heard the rumors going around the TEA community."

"Yeah," Cee-Cee murmured.

"Well, I have another class to teach. Let me know if I can help again." Dr. Bakir waved into the camera at them all.

"Thanks, doc." Jonah closed the video app on his laptop. He turned it around so only he could see the screen again. "Well, another clue."

"I don't understand what Mr. Baptiste could have done to be a threat to Legion. At least nothing enough to provoke such a deadly response." LaShaun looked at Cee-Cee.

Jonah answered first. "Right. He's been breeding and providing dogs to TEA members forever. No secret to Legion."

Cee-Cee turned to LaShaun. "Did Chase mention anything else about his murder, something odd?"

"Two puppies were missing. His wife told Miss Rose when she visited. A Pharaoh Hound and a Tibetan Mastiff. They're very valuable," LaShaun replied.

"They're not just worth a lot of money. They bond with those with psi powers especially. They're among the most ancient dog breeds in existence."

"Makes sense. Legion would want puppies to train instead of mature dogs. So, robbery could be the motive," Jonah said.

"And the message only means he fought back to stop the dogs being taken," LaShaun added. Then she frowned. "But why would Legion give away their presence here over two puppies?"

"Which happens in the same area where monazite deposits are found. A substance that also has supernatural value. I don't trust coincidences," Cee-Cee said.

"What's puppies got to do with the TEA deaths and some rocks from the swamp?" Manny spoke up.

Cee-Cee blinked at him as if just remembering he was in the room. "Thanks for the information about Devil's Swamp. We'll handle things from here."

"Hey, wait a minute. I—"

"Message from headquarters, in Canada," Jonah announced. His jaw dropped. "They want an urgent video chat."

"The wireless connection here probably isn't secure enough. See if they'll wait until we're back at the hotel. I have our TEA wireless hub." Cee-Cee glanced at Manny and back to Jonah.

"Things are bad if you don't trust your own local club members," Manny said in a dry tone.

"TEA isn't a club," Cee-Cee clipped

"No worries. I'm using our VPN, we're good." Jonah's fingers moved fast and he turned the laptop.

"Wait—" Cee-Cee jerked a thumb at Manny.

"An emergency sub-council transmission has been authorized to the Constantiam Team Field Unit Three," a male voice intoned from the laptop.

The TEA logo appeared. Seconds later, the logo vanished. Three people, including Frank Miles and Secretary General Desmond popped on the screen, each in a separate mini-display. A larger image of a group of three more also appeared as they logged on.

"What the..." Manny gawked at the laptop screen. His mouth hung open.

"Shush, and stay out of the way," LaShaun muttered to him. "Keep up the noise, and Cee-Cee will make you leave for sure."

"Hello, Chief Officer Cuevas," Desmond said. "I understand the circumstances, but we thought it necessary to communicate vital information quickly." Then he was distracted when someone spoke to him.

"He means I'm here," Manny whispered. "They oughta make me a soldier since I gave up the best tips so far. I—"

"Shut it," LaShaun said through clenched teeth.

"We're called operatives, and not even on a cold day in hell," Cee-Cee answered in her own harsh whisper.

"Mr. Young, I think you know who I am," Desmond clipped. He continued before Manny could respond. "So, you're well aware that we're watching you. We know about the house one of your aunts kept up for you. The renovations are lovely, by the way."

"Shit." Manny jammed both hands in his jean pockets. He moved farther away even though he wasn't in front of the laptop's camera.

"We can impact your parole status. Do we understand each other?"

"Yeah," Manny shot back. He stomped to a chair and dropped on it hard.

"I'm not going to go along with framing him just because TEA wants Manny out of the way," LaShaun said as she leaned forward.

"TEA doesn't use nefarious means to achieve ends, Mrs. Broussard." Desmond scowled at LaShaun like a school principal chastising a student. "We won't need to manufacture evidence that he's violated several of his conditions. Mr. Young knows what I'm talking about."

LaShaun gave Manny a sharp look. "Meaning?"

Desmond's frown deepened. "Back to more pressing matters. We've identified the second murder victim. Devin Cross is a TEA operative who was sent to Louisiana. He was working to uncover a drug operation used to fund a New Orleans Legion cell. We estimate they were moving up to two million dollars in meth, ecstasy, and heroin every six months."

"Someone found out and killed him, huh?" Jonah looked at Cee-Cee.

"Could explain why he dropped off our radar for almost a month," Desmond replied.

Cee-Cee spoke up. "And drove over a hundred miles to dump his body in Vermilion Parish? I—"

"Yeah, yeah. You don't believe in coincidences," Jonah said. "Could be they wanted to make sure he wasn't found."

Manny got up and walked around the table to join the others. He looked at Desmond on the laptop screen. "Except he was."

"That area is regularly patrolled by security officers that work for the dock owners," LaShaun replied. "But someone from out of town wouldn't necessarily know that. To New Orleans crooks, Vermilion Parish is probably just one big backwoods."

"They could have taken him to a swamp near New Orleans or to Lake Pontchartrain. Hell, I can think of a dozen places closer to dump a body," Manny put in. He wore a pensive expression as he stared at a wall.

"I'll bet you can." Cee-Cee stared at him, her dark eyes narrowed to slits. "Tell us more."

Manny snapped back from his musing. "Hey, I'm just talking like anyone who knows the state. I've been hunting all around south Louisiana."

"We know about your 'hunting' trips," Cee-Cee replied tersely.

"I meant... Oh, never mind." Manny slumped into a chair. He brooded as he muttered low to no one in particular.

"We'll address Mr. Young's culpability for past crimes later," Desmond broke in before the exchange could continue. "We need to find out if Officer Kelly followed a lead to Vermilion Parish or was indeed merely dumped there after he was killed. Mr. Young is quite correct. There were any number of places the killer or killers passed up."

"Which is a good reason to think Cross came here for a reason," Cee-Cee said. "We'll connect with Team Three."

"As the leader of Team One, take charge," Desmond said to Cee-Cee. "I'm texting you their details and more instructions on our secure message app."

"Yes, sir." Cee-Cee picked up her smartphone. She made sure Manny couldn't see the screen.

While Cee-Cee shared information with Jonah, who nodded. The other TEA officials on the video chat murmured to each other. LaShaun studied Manny for a few minutes. He sat gazing down, his brow creased as in deep thought.

Her tingle returned. Manny looked at her after a few seconds.

"I didn't do nothin'," Manny whispered, forcing the words out hard. "None of this stuff got anything to do with me."

"I wasn't thinking it did," LaShaun said quietly.

Jonah left his chair next and sat by Manny. Cee-Cee put in earbuds so only she could hear the orders from her superiors. Jonah nodded in Cee-Cee's direction.

"She might not join your fan club anytime soon, but Cee-Cee has figured out that much, too."

"Yeah, this is all TEA-related, though how... Cee-Cee is right. Too much coincidence. Mathieu Baptiste was in touch with one of the dead top TEA officials," LaShaun said.

"Who might not have died of natural causes," Jonah added.

"Right. Then a John Doe murder victim found here turns out to be with TEA. Legion shows up, and TEA factions are fighting over Devil's Swamp." LaShaun tapped out each point as if drawing a map on the table. But it led to nowhere. She sighed and shook her head, baffled by a string of facts that didn't seem to connect.

"Got it, sir." Cee-Cee unplugged the earbuds and motioned for Jonah and LaShaun to join her again.

"Mrs. Broussard, please accompany Chief Officer Cuevas to inform the local authorities about Mr. Kelly's identity. Tell them about the investigation of illegal drugs in New Orleans. Regular law enforcement can deal with the local dealers. We'll follow-up on Legion. Expect instructions from the Criminal Division, Mr. Parker."

"Sir, how much should we tell Lieutenant Broussard?" Jonah said.

"Consult with Commander Wagner. As of now, you'll concentrate on what happened to Kelly. Chief Officer Cuevas will concentrate on the mining operation. Of course, you'll coordinate your efforts. Since this case has become complicated, splitting your duties is more efficient. Mrs. Broussard should assist CO Cuevas. Everyone clear?"

"Excuse me, secretary-general. Question," a male voice said.

"Yes, Mr. Esnard," Desmond replied.

"I believe at least one member of PPA should be sent. Just to avoid questions and conflict. Even skilled operatives can be misled the longer they're in the field," another official said.

"I appreciate your input, but the council has decided. Ms. Cuevas and her team are veteran field investigators," Desmond replied in a clipped tone. Other voices chimed in.

Cee-Cee grabbed her earbuds. "Mute the audio, Jonah. Now."

Joshua complied as Cee-Cee plugged into the discussion. "Awkward."

"Who's that dude, and what's he talking about?" Manny asked. He blinked rapidly as he stared at the screen.

"Predictive and Prognostication Analytics. That's a relatively new division, well if you consider sixty years new. TEA has been informally in existence almost seven hundred years, and formally organized about one hundred fifty years ago. So, sixty years is like yesterday. Anyway, the council has been using that division as a way to ease tensions between spirituals and scientists."

"And it hasn't worked, I guess?" LaShaun switched her gaze between the screen and Jonah.

"Not so far. That's Garland Esnard, legendary self-made man. He made a fortune in the mining industry in western Canada. Some say he dealt in Congolese blood diamonds while supporting dictatorships in the nineties. An old-school tough guy."

"Quiet," Cee-Cee hissed at Jonah with a squint. Then she went back to listening.

Jonah leaned toward LaShaun and Manny, voice low. "Esnard is firmly in the all-science camp."

"Mining, you said." LaShaun turned her full attention back to the laptop video chat.

"Yeah, he... Hey, I'm not sure why he's on the call. We're talking about the local murders." Jonah glanced at the screen.

"Is he involved in the local company?" LaShaun's psychic version of a Geiger counter, the itching tingle, went off.

"Not that I know of. He sold his last company for millions. Now he works in the archaeology section Helping us find artifacts related to our work." Jonah frowned at the screen as if working through facts in his mind as he talked.

"Four murders over swamp mud. And y'all think I'm crazy," Manny retorted. He started to go on, but stopped as he looked at the laptop.

Garland Esnard's face now dominated the screen. He seemed to be addressing the entire group with Desmond moved to the background. Desmond's tight expression said he wasn't pleased with the development. After a few moments Desmond gained control again to lead the discussion. LaShaun ignored the TEA drama. She studied Manny. His demeanor seemed to hover between puzzled and anxious.

"What's going on with you?" LaShaun said as she moved closer to him.

"Nothing. Just, um, thinking about mining in a swamp. That's mostly dredging. They work on barges. You gotta know how to handle boats and work equipment. But engineering, that's like going to college." Manny looked at LaShaun. "Right?"

"Yeah." LaShaun was more interested in observing Manny than the subject.

"Well, that's it." Cee-Cee put away her wired earbuds in a case.

"Fill me in on the gory details. Did Desmond slap Esnard back in his place? Did people take sides and a fight break out?" Jonah rubbed his hands together as he waited for Cee-Cee to respond.

"They talked about the role PP&A might play here in the field. I pointed out that we needed to stay flexible and mobile. Those folks mainly show up with a trunk full of gadgets. Then they want to debate every grain of sand found. I was more diplomatic, of course," Cee-Cee said with a slight smile. "Bottom line, Desmond decided against it. Most of the commanders agreed. Esnard conceded after a while."

"G is smooth, that's what folks call him. Anyway, he's known for using the soft approach to get his way in the end. A sledgehammer in a glove, they say," Jonah said.

"Uses his words like silk or a blunt object, depending on the situation." Manny rubbed his forehead hard. A grimace twisted his face.

"You recognize the technique, I see," Jonah quipped.

"Mr. Young perfected the method to lure in his victims," Cee-Cee replied in a cold voice.

"I'm not guilty," Manny snapped with heat. Then he blinked hard. "At least I'm pretty sure of it."

"Well, that's definitive. Thanks for clearing it up for us," Cee-Cee said. She muttered to herself in Spanish.

Manny stood to face her. "Look, I helped you people a lot. The least you could do is give me some benefit of the damn doubt. Why would I try to help LaShaun if I was a monster?"

"Because you want to suck her into raising more questions about your conviction for a heinous crime. Maybe reduce your restrictive parole conditions. Use your slick lawyer to even get your conviction overturned," Cee-Cee said, ticking off the points on one hand. "I can go on, but we don't have time. Your help is appreciated, but we won't need you from here on."

"Gee, your gratitude warms my heart."

"You expected us to share a group hug and welcome you into our confidence? Please." Cee-Cee looked at Jonah. "We'll regroup, connect with Del and the others. Get on it tomorrow."

"Check." Jonah nodded as he packed up his laptop and other items.

Cee-Cee gave LaShaun a pointed look before she strode out. Manny observed the two women, probably taking in what wasn't being said. LaShaun knew Cee-Cee didn't want to say anything else in front of Manny. Seconds later they heard her voice talking to others in another part of the theater.

"Well, that's the thanks I get. Now I don't have any friends at TEA, damn it." Manny shoved both hands in his jean pockets. The effect made him look taller with both arms against his body. Anyone looking at him would think he was a mild-mannered thirty-something who might be fun at a bar crawl.

"You can make new friends, stop hanging with the wrong crowd," LaShaun drawled.

"Folks say he's the wrong crowd." Jonah shrugged when Manny gave him a sharp glance. "See you later, LaShaun. And you, Manny, try to stay out of trouble."

"Hey, there are more lovely ladies to meet at TEA. Some of them are open-minded."

LaShaun winced at his observations. "That's not reassuring, Manny."

"I gotta like you, dude, but don't let anyone else hear you say that. Especially Cee-Cee. Bye." Jonah left, still laughing at Manny's cheekiness.

"Everything I say comes out creepy, you mean. Like I'm planning to seduce my way into another round of slaughter," Manny said with a smile.

"You gotta admit, you've got a lot to live down." LaShaun slung her crossbody over her head.

Manny threw up both hands. "I can't win. You see why I need you to find out the truth about those murders? That's the only way I'll have anything close to a normal future life."

"We've got four recent deaths, an internal war between people with massive psychic powers, and Satan's minions prowling the bayous. I think you'll agree we have to address your issues later." LaShaun looked at him. "What got you rattled a few minutes ago? Something happened during the video conference that—"

"Like you just said, a lot of serious shit is going down. Guess it just hit me all of a sudden," Manny broke in. "School bus should be dropping your kid off soon."

LaShaun gasped and pulled out her cell phone. "Damn, I lost track of time. Don't think you're getting around telling me the truth. We'll talk later."

"Sure thing. Hey, I'm gonna help y'all out with this TEA crap. Chief Officer Cuevas doesn't have to know. I figure the sooner I clean up y'all's mess, the sooner we can get back to proving I'm not the Blood River Ripper." Manny followed LaShaun out.

"Manny—"

"You know I'm right. Without me, y'all wouldn't have found out about the local mining connection," Manny said.

"Yes, we would have. Don't underestimate Cee-Cee and Jonah," LaShaun said over her shoulder.

"Not for a while, and every minute counts." Manny trailed LaShaun to her SUV. He opened the door when she used her remote to unlock it.

"Go home, concentrate on not violating your parole, and don't do anything unless you talk to *me*." LaShaun threw her bag into the SUV and stabbed a forefinger toward his face. "Swear."

Manny held up a palm as if taking an oath. "I promise to be a good boy on the grave of my low-down, murdering father."

"Lord, give me strength not to shoot this fool." LaShaun slammed the door and started the engine. She groaned when Manny gave her a jaunty good-bye wave as she drove off.

Chapter 11

LaShaun muttered a few cuss words when she passed Ellie's school bus on Highway 14. The driver waved with a smile, which meant she didn't know Ellie was home alone. Maybe a miracle happened and Chase was home early. Though with two unsolved murders, LaShaun doubted it. Even more worrying was the news report on the radio about a home invasion in the small community of Gueydan. She didn't have to call Chase to know he had his hands full. Plus, no need to get him freaked. Telling him she'd missed getting Ellie off the bus would not go well.

"For once let Mrs. Busybody Marchand be at my house," LaShaun said as she pulled onto Rougon Road. She glanced at the digital clock on her dashboard. Fifteen minutes late.

When she finally reached their driveway, LaShaun's heart thumped faster. No sign of Ellie. She wasn't on the porch of their Creole cottage style house. The SUV tires spit out gravel as she braked hard. LaShaun put the car in park, engine still running, and jumped out.

"Ellie! Mama's home. Sorry I'm late, baby. Where—"

LaShaun stopped at the sound of Beau's barking. Tingling along her arms and up her back announced serious trouble. LaShaun tried to slow her breathing. Her hand went to her jacket pocket. She suppressed a cry of dismay. On her way home, she'd locked her pistol securely in the console to keep it safe from curious little hands.

"Damn it, please. Open. Open."

LaShaun whispered a prayer as she fumbled with the keys, first pulling them from the ignition. Then she had to find the small one to the console. Moments later, the derringer in one hand, she jumped off the rocky driveway onto the grass to avoid crunching footsteps. Beau barked, then growled, then barked furiously. The sound moved in a circle. When LaShaun reached the back of their home, she froze in terror. Ellie stood looking up at a tall figure shrouded in black. A blue, hazy mist ringed their property, obscuring the view across a pasture. Their nearest neighbor, the Marchand family, would not see anything happening. When the figure reached out an arm, LaShaun raised the gun.

"Ellie, step away," she yelled.

"She just wants to play," Ellie replied in a small voice, her gaze still on the figure.

A woman? LaShaun became even more horrified. "We talked about strangers trying to be friends, remember? Now trust Mama and back up."

"Look at the smoke she made. People can't see through it. I could win at hide and seek all the time." Ellie's delighted giggle floated out, making the scene even more bizarre. She didn't seem to realize the danger.

"What are you?" LaShaun addressed the figure.

"Your child is extraordinary. Those bunglers at TEA have no idea how to maximize her potential. Soon she'll realize her superiority to them all." The figure turned from LaShaun to look at Ellie. "Then, my dear, you can make your own choices. I've shown her what the future could be like."

"Mama doesn't approve." Ellie looked from the figure to her mother and back again. "I think you should leave now."

"We have more to discuss," the female voice deepened, making the mist appear to vibrate.

Ellie blinked and then frowned at her. "Mama..."

"Listen to me," LaShaun broke in. "This... thing is evil."

"Ellie will learn soon enough that evil is relative. The lies she's been told are chains that bind her true power. You're too far gone, Mrs. Broussard. But Ellie is still open to the possibilities." The woman's voice implied a smile beneath the hood that hid her face.

"You decide to come for a little girl? That's low even for Legion." LaShaun strode forward, gun still pointed at the woman's head.

The woman ignored LaShaun. Beau launched himself at the figure when she moved toward Ellie. She didn't seem threatened at first. Then a screech came as the dog crashed into her. More shocked screams filled the air as Beau's large paws raked the hood. Somehow the cloak didn't come off.

"Run, baby. Run!"

LaShaun stood helpless. She couldn't shoot for fear of hitting Beau. Ellie watched the battle between human and dog with fascination. Then she dashed to the back patio. Ellie ripped open a bundle and tossed a powder at the fighting duo. The woman let out one more agonizing scream. She managed to break free from Beau's jaws and dash for the woods. LaShaun watched as Beau chased the figure until both disappeared into thick brush. The mist began to clear when the woman vanished from view. Echoes of her scream flowed back to them. He returned moments later and shook himself, then trotted over to stand next to Ellie.

"We got here fast as we could," Xavier Marchand Sr. panted as he broke through the thin remains of mist. His knee-high rubber boots had mud splotches all over them. He spun around with a huge wrench in one hand.

"Mama is calling Mr. Broussard," Xavier Jr. said. He ran past his father to the edge of LaShaun's lawn, shotgun in hand.

"No, Jax. He might not be alone in them woods," his father shouted after him.

"Maybe I should fire off a shot just to let 'em know they better get gone and not come back." The younger Marchand hefted the shotgun in preparation.

His words shook LaShaun out of her stunned state. "No, don't! They're gone. I'm sure of it."

"Been crazy around here lately, what with folks turnin' up dead." Xavier Sr. looked around as if checking for more threats. Then he raced over to Ellie. "You okay, sweetie?"

"Yes, Papa Zay," Ellie said, calling him the nickname his grandchildren used. Her small face turned up to him with a guileless expression. "I'm okay. Was that a burglar?"

"Probably some kid prowling around to steal livestock. Never thought I'd see the day when we had this kinda goings-on." Xavier Sr. scowled at the woods where the woman disappeared. Then he put on a smile as he looked at Ellie again. He placed a large hand on her slight shoulder. "Don't you worry. They won't be back."

"I think me and James should go check just in case," Xavier Jr. replied, referring to their part-time hired hand. "We'll take the ATVs to cover more ground."

Betty Marchand huffed as she ran across the prairie between their properties. "A deputy is on the way. I called our other neighbor, Mason, and his nephew. They gonna check the woods from their direction."

"Good idea, Mama." Xavier Jr. nodded to her and left before his parents could say anything. His long legs and youthful vigor took him yards away in seconds.

"Go after him, Xavier. You know that boy's been spoiling for some action since he got back," Betty

Marchand said to her husband. Then she turned to LaShaun.

Xavier Sr. took a last look around before he followed the younger Marchand. "Wait for me, son."

"He's like that every time he gets back from Louisiana National Guard training. I just hope these politicians don't decide to send more of our kids off to some crazy foreign war. Jax got a baby on the way."

LaShaun shook her head to clear it. Betty Marchand had managed to respond to a crisis and share family gossip in one swoop. Xavier Jackson Marchand Jr., called Jax to distinguish him from his father, was the youngest of their three sons.

"Hmm." LaShaun looked at Ellie. Her daughter stood next to Beau, a hand on his back. She was talking to him, but LaShaun couldn't hear what she said. "Uh, you called Chase at the station?"

Betty nodded. "Yeah, but they said he was out. Let's make sure our little miss is fine." Mrs. Marchand moved to Ellie. "Did that bad man try to hurt you, honey? What did he say? Tell Mama Betty."

"It was a tall lady, but she didn't scare me," Ellie replied in a small voice.

"A woman? Well I never. She must have had somebody with her. But folks know y'all don't keep cows, goats, or chickens."

Ellie's eyes sparkled. "Oh, she didn't—"

"Ellie, take Beau in to get some water. All that running around must have him thirsty," LaShaun said.

"Beau is made to chase shadows. He's the perfect guard dog for us." Ellie hugged Beau's neck with one arm, the bag still in her other hand.

"What's that you got?" Betty reached to take it.

"Dog snacks," LaShaun said, grabbing it before the nosy woman could. "Or toys. She loves action figures. Go on inside while I talk to Mrs. Marchand."

"Don't worry, Miss Betty. Me and Beau will keep the shadows away." Ellie marched off with Beau at her side.

"Shadows and keep us safe? What an odd thing for a child to say..." Betty's voice trailed off when she spotted the derringer in LaShaun's hand.

"I keep it for protection. Chase works such long hours. You know." LaShaun had forgotten she still had it out. She slipped it into her jacket pocket.

A siren announced someone from the sheriff's department had arrived. Ellie came out of the house again and raced toward the sound. "The cops have arrived," she squealed with glee.

Mrs. Marchand started to ask more questions, but LaShaun ran after Ellie. She followed, no doubt eager to get more news she could spread. They all arrived just as M.J. climbed out of her unmarked cruiser.

Ellie skidded to a stop. "Where's Daddy?"

"He's at the state police troop in Acadia Parish, baby girl. What's goin' on?" M.J. noticed Mrs. Marchand.

"Our neighbor," LaShaun explain with a pointed look.

"Ok." M.J. smiled at Mrs. Marchand. "Afternoon, ma'am."

Betty, sharp-eyed as ever, didn't miss the silent exchange. "We scared off a prowler. Ellie says it was a woman, which is pretty peculiar, don't you think?"

"We?" M.J. repeated. She looked at the house. When she walked to a nearby window, the others followed.

"My husband and son, Jax. We heard the shouting and hustled over here. Then the woman took off. Guess we scared her off. Our neighbors are looking to see if she brought anybody with her. I guess your backup officers are out searching, too."

"Just me. Any sign she tried to break in the house?" M.J. strode on, doing her job. She peered at windows, walked on and looked at the front door, and kept going. The others trailed after, watching her.

"Didn't have a chance to check," LaShaun said.

"No," Ellie piped up in a cheerful tone. "I got off the bus. Mama wasn't home yet, so I let myself in the back using our code. Then I heard somebody call my name, so I went outside."

"Which you're not supposed to do," LaShaun said in her best firm voice. "We'll talk about that later."

"Oh my, you must have been so scared, baby," Betty jumped in. Her eyes lit up, as if the nuggets of information were gold.

"I had Beau and my mojo." Ellie looked around at the ground and then at LaShaun.

"You mean the bag?" Betty's eyes got wider with each passing second.

"Mojo is her stuffed rabbit. Let's get you a snack while Auntie M.J. checks around. Be sure and tell Jax and Mr. Marchand thanks for me. You've all been such a help." LaShaun nodded to M.J., took Ellie by one hand, and started for the kitchen door again.

"I could fix Ellie's snack so you can stay with Chief Deputy Arceneaux. I have those lemon squares you love back at the house, Ellie," Betty said.

"Ellie only has fruit or yogurt before dinner, but thanks for the offer. You've done more than enough. I don't want to take up any more of your time. I know how busy you are running the family business and everything." LaShaun kept talking to keep Ellie from speaking up again.

"Well if you think I can help..."

"I got it from here. Take care now." LaShaun pushed Ellie ahead of her through the door. She sighed with relief when it bumped shut behind them.

"Guess I should have left out the part about mo-jo, huh?" Ellie said with a shrug. She marched over to the bowl of fruit on the kitchen island and selected a banana. "I didn't know we had yogurt. And sometimes I have a cookie before dinner."

"Mostly not," LaShaun huffed, annoyed Ellie had picked up on her fib. She glanced out the window. Betty Marchand stood on their back lawn, gazing around with interest. When she realized LaShaun was watching her, she gave a sheepish smile and headed home. LaShaun faced Ellie again, arms crossed. "Please explain to me how you know about mojos and who gave you one."

"Monmon Odette," Ellie said around a mouthful of banana.

"Holy ancestors." M.J., mouth hanging open, stood in the open kitchen door. Then she pulled it shut behind her.

"And I made it myself. I found the recipe in a family book." Ellie slipped off the bar stool and was gone before LaShaun could answer.

"No signs anyone tried to break in. So I'm guessing they either came from the road out front or through the woods in back. The deputy patrolling this section will check it out. Maybe someone saw a car or truck parked." M.J. perched on a stool at the kitchen island. She took out a notepad. "Tell me what happened."

Ellie skipped back in holding a book and held it up for them to see. It was bound in dark blue leather with silver lettering. "You said history is important to learn, especially about our family because people have so much to say about the Rousselle family."

"You in trouble when the kid quotes you," M.J. murmured. She shifted to lean back as if waiting for the show to begin.

"That didn't include creating your own gris-gris and reciting spells," LaShaun said in a firm tone.

"But it worked. The lady in black had..." Ellie frowned, which looked incongruous on her smooth baby face. "Evil intent. That's what grandfather Robert LeGrange called it."

"He's was your twice great-grandfather. Monmon Odette's great-grandfather. And she was your great-grandmother." LaShaun recited part of the Rousselle lineage without thinking. She took the book from Ellie.

👁

"Okay." Ellie took a seat again and ate more banana.

"Well that's a relief. For a minute there I thought she was gonna say..." M.J.'s voice trailed off.

LaShaun shook out of her reverie. With a side-eye at M.J., she spoke to Ellie. "Forget the family history lesson, young lady. You are never, I repeat, never to follow any kind of instructions on spells and the like. The only family recipes you should concern yourself with are for cookies, cakes, gumbo, and such. Are we clear?"

"But Mama—" Ellie went still when her mother continued to give her the look. Her small mouth turned down in a sulk. "Yes, ma'am."

"Lord save us all from babies who can conjure," M.J. muttered low.

"I'm not a baby. I'm a big girl, and Monmon Odette says she learned the old ways when she was my age," Ellie said with confidence. "I read it, the parts I could understand."

LaShaun heaved a sigh. "When you get older and can understand more, I'll help you learn. Right now you could easily make a mistake and do more harm than good."

"Like when me and Hayley tried to fix the walkie-talkie." Ellie tilted her head to one side as she looked up at LaShaun.

"Exactly. You took it apart, but you didn't know enough to put it back together. So, it quit working." LaShaun chucked her daughter's pretty little chin. "No more experimenting."

Ellie frowned for a few seconds as if thinking hard. "But I knew it would work. Monmon Odette told me so. Experiment means you're not sure what will happen. I looked it up once for school."

"Ellie." LaShaun fixed her with the mama look again.

"Okay, I'll check with you first. I have one assignment. But it won't take long though. Bye Auntie M.J." Ellie hopped from her seat and headed off. "C'mon, Beau. We've got work to do."

"Later, baby," M.J. called after her.

Beau gave a bark, but didn't move. He seemed quite comfortable in his bed in a corner of the family room. LaShaun could have sworn his response indicated it wasn't his homework. When Ellie called again, an insistent note in her girlish voice, he hauled himself up. He took his time going toward her room.

LaShaun slapped the book on the counter. "I think we could both use a cup of strong coffee."

M.J. was about to reply when her two-way radio went off. A male voice crackled from where it was clipped to her waistband. "Yes, McGruder."

The male deputy reported two people had seen a dark-colored SUV parked along the highway. He and M.J. exchanged information for a few minutes before ending the call.

"Not likely you'll find anything. Legion is good at covering their tracks," LaShaun said. She filled up the clear glass coffeepot with water, poured it in, and sat again. The soft hum of the machine promised to reward them soon.

"You mean those cult nut-boxes are back? Now there's good news," M.J. said with a snort. "Well, at least we have a file on the members who were local. I'll brief my guys who to look out for. Not that they can't blend with all the Mardi Gras tourists."

"I doubt they'd risk sending the same people," LaShaun said.

"And as I recall, you took out a few of them. Two are still serving time," M.J. replied.

LaShaun had previous run-ins with cults. She waded into the fight with no hesitation. Then she was single with no children. Now. The image of Ellie's tiny figure staring up at the hooded woman sent a chill through her. LaShaun placed a hand over her belly. As if on cue, Chase strode into the kitchen. When he spotted LaShaun seated at the kitchen island, he blew out a breath.

"How's Ellie? Is she still upset?" Chase took off his dark-brown Stetson, tossed it onto the breakfast table, and crossed to LaShaun. He wrapped both arms around her. He spoke to M.J. while hugging LaShaun. "Bill's chasing down the leads on that SUV."

"We're fine. Ellie's fine." LaShaun smiled at him. She brushed her fingers on one of his cheeks.

"She didn't look upset at all. Took battling evil right in stride." M.J. chuckled, got up, retrieved three mugs, and poured them all coffee.

"What?" Chase yelled. His eyes widened when LaShaun described Ellie's adventure. "My God."

"She's okay..." LaShaun's voice died away because Chase rushed down the hall to see Ellie was safe for himself.

"You left out the part about your grandmother instructing her on banishing bad spirits." M.J. put the mugs down with a thump.

"That can come later. First, he needs to see Ellie's not hurt for himself. Then he can digest more."

"You mean the fact that his first grader can handle demons on her own. I'd share that bit of news a little at a time, too." M.J. wore a crooked smile for a second and then her expression grew serious. "But this is no joke. They came to your house."

"Yeah." LaShaun considered the implications.

Chase strode back in. He still seemed on edge. Instead of sitting or reaching for a mug, he crossed his arms. His lawman mode was still in full effect. "From the top, exactly what happened."

"Long story short. I got home a bit late, so Ellie had already gotten off the bus. She was playing in the backyard with Beau, apparently, when this person showed up." LaShaun flinched when Chase glowered at her. "I was at a really important meeting. You're going to want to hear what—"

"More important than our daughter?" Chase snapped.

"Don't you even try it, Chase. Remember all the overtime hours you put in? I see the days and nights you're not home have slipped your mind," LaShaun shot back with enough heat to melt ice.

"So, now it's about *me*. All because you put Third Eye business ahead of our home life. You're carrying my baby for God's sake," Chase shot back.

"Excuse me?" LaShaun sputtered.

Chase held up a palm. "Okay, *our* baby. You have to be careful. Spooky crap happens when your sorcery pals are in town."

"TEA doesn't cause 'spooky crap'—they show up to restore order," LaShaun countered.

"Last time I checked, restoring order was our job." Chase pointed to himself and M.J. "Just stay out of it. Isn't being my wife and Ellie's mama enough for you?"

"Oh, now your mother is coming out. The guilt trip of not staying in a 'woman's place.' Unbelievable." LaShaun clenched her fist and looked around. Not having another outlet, she kicked the leg of one bar stool.

"See what I mean, M.J.? TEA shows, and she's all worked up, ready for a fight. You're not some iron woman, LaShaun. And you're pregnant," Chase shouted.

"Don't be ridiculous; I can take care of myself. I didn't even have to land a punch this morning when—" LaShaun stopped.

Chase seemed to tower over her even taller than his six feet two inches. His dark eyes flashed. "When what, LaShaun? Tell us the real reason you were late."

LaShaun clicked her tongue and let a few moments of silence stretch. "Members of Legion blocked the road when I was on my way to meet Cee-Cee, Jonah, and... Manny. But they didn't attack, they were trying to recruit me."

Chase didn't answer right away. He pulled a hand over his face and turned in a circle before he faced LaShaun again. "Manny Young, and now a cult. Anyone else you've decided to have lunch dates with we should know about? Like maybe Dracula?"

"Don't be a drama king. I told you, they only wanted to talk. And Manny provided TEA with valuable information."

"Listen to yourself, LaShaun. I have to face ugly crimes every day. I don't want you and Ellie added to the list." Chase pointed at LaShaun's increasing girth. "Especially now."

LaShaun started to toss back an angry reply. The genuine anxiety in his voice checked her. She softened her tone. "Honey, I can handle anything that comes at us. And Ellie seems to as well."

"She's just a baby. My little girl," Chase blurted out.

"Your baby girl kicked butt today. Well, sort of. Whoever or whatever made the mistake of coming here got a nasty surprise." LaShaun grinned at the image of Ellie casting a repel incantation on the woman. Her grin faded at the look Chase gave her.

"We decided Ellie would have a normal childhood, LaShaun," Chase snapped. "Or have your supernatural pals talked you into throwing that out?"

LaShaun inhaled and exhaled a few times. She reminded herself that her husband's apprehension was understandable. "Stop making TEA the bad guy, Chase."

M.J. had followed the exchange as if observing a tennis match; looking at them in turn, sipping from her mug. She rapped her knuckles on the countertop to get their attention.

"Chase has a point. Even more caution is warranted on the home front," M.J. said in a mild tone. She stood and smoothed down the front of her shirt.

"*Thank you*." Chase looked from M.J. to LaShaun.

"Which I'm sure LaShaun will do, if she hasn't begun to already," M.J. added.

"Of course I will. At least somebody has trust in my ability to protect *our* child." LaShaun raised an eyebrow at Chase. "Thanks for reminding him, Chief Deputy."

"I trust you, it's just..." Chase raked his dark-brown hair with the fingers of one hand. "Tell me exactly what Ellie did today."

"She's been reading Rousselle family journals, and I didn't know," LaShaun added to preempt an accusation. "She learned a spell to fight off an opponent. Some kind of powder—a mojo or gris-gris."

"Sounds like both. Mojo is a spell, at least in the old ways. Gris-gris is the actual talisman or object used in the spell. A lot of folks use them interchangeably," M.J. said. When they looked at her in surprise, she shrugged. "Not saying I believe it."

"Right." LaShaun said with the ghost of a smile.

"What I am saying is Ellie probably caught the woman off guard, and when your neighbors showed, she ran off. Fast thinking for a first grader. You've taught her well." M.J. nodded to them both. "But we've got to get back to work. Deputy McGruder will stay in the area tonight. I think we can spare one more deputy to cruise this way. Chase, we've got another lead on one of our cases. LaShaun's friends have identified our first murder victim."

"What?" Chase gaped at M.J. and then stared at LaShaun.

LaShaun nodded and heaved a sigh. "He was a TEA operative."

"They'd better tell us everything about him. No holding back or claiming it's some kind of confidential magical information," Chase said with force.

"They call it classified need-to-know information," LaShaun murmured.

Chase groaned in exasperation. "Somebody needs to explain to these folks they're not the damn CIA or FBI."

"They're fully cooperating as far as I can tell," M.J. put in before he could continue his rant.

"That's what I learned at the meeting this morning, so TEA officials contacted your office immediately. See? They're not screwballs running around doing crazy stuff." LaShaun looked at both M.J. and Chase.

"They claim he was working security for the mining operation on Devil's Swamp. Seems the company is now owned by them. He stumbled on a drug deal going on out in the swamps," M.J. fixed LaShaun with a steady gaze for a few seconds.

"Sounds plausible," LaShaun replied. When both Chase and M.J. frowned at her, she tried to assume a blank expression. "Why are y'all looking at me like that?"

"Like we really buy that explanation from the shadowy global organization of wizards," Chase said. He made a loud, snorting sound to punctuate his skepticism.

M.J. shook her head at him. "What my less-diplomatic colleague is trying to say is, nothing TEA does is so simple."

"TEA has a non-profit foundation and business interests, a for-profit subsidiary. The for-profit side owns businesses. It funds a lot of the research and tech development. The mining company is one. And every company has security. Not simple, but nothing strange." LaShaun looked at them in turn.

"Tell us again, exactly, what are they mining," Chase said.

"A rare mineral called monazite. It's used in a lot of high-tech equipment. They also dredge for gravel and sand used in construction. Not that I know a lot about that stuff," LaShaun added quickly when Chase's eyebrows went up.

"You're quite the little fountain of info right now," Chase said.

M.J. looked at her phone when it buzzed. "Text from the boss. He wants to meet with us. He's talked to the head of security at the mining company." She looked at LaShaun. "Are we gonna get the truth from these folks?"

"Sure," LaShaun replied.

"Humph." M.J. glanced sideways at Chase. She headed for the door. "I'm on my way."

Chase nodded, his gaze still on LaShaun. "Right behind you."

Minutes later, they heard the hum of M.J.'s vehicle engine, followed by the crunch of tires as she drove away. Seconds ticked by. Ellie's voice talking to Beau added background noise to the silence. Chase stood, fists resting on his narrow waist. LaShaun could well understand why that stone face could wear down a suspect.

"What? What?" LaShaun repeated when he didn't answer.

"Your answer about TEA sounded like a practiced dodge. A way to keep from telling the whole truth and nothing but the truth," Chase said.

"Based on my experience, they do cooperate with regular law enforcement." LaShaun stepped close to him, brushed his lips with hers, and patted his handsome cheek. "The important thing is, Ellie is fine."

"You'll talk to her about, you know." Chase mimicked the stereotypical hand movements of a wizard casting a spell. When LaShaun giggled, his eyes narrowed.

LaShaun put a hand over her mouth and cleared her throat. "I'm going to give her a good talking to, soon."

"Call if anything else happens. Anything odd, which sets the bar low in this family," Chase mumbled as he walked off.

"Let's just hope she doesn't try that stuff at school," LaShaun whispered.

"Wait, what?"

"I said we'll talk as soon as she finishes her school work," LaShaun called after him.

Chase started to speak, but his cell phone rang. He looked at the screen, frowned, and answered. Minutes later, still talking, he waved good-bye as he went through the door. LaShaun stood in the frame watching him back down their driveway. She put on a bright smile for him; a happy work-at-home mother sending hubby off to a day at the office. A tug drew her attention down. Ellie stood next to her, waving as well. Then she grinned up at LaShaun.

"Mama, we had fun today. Didn't we? That lady tried talking me into doing what she wanted."

LaShaun grabbed one of her small, soft little hands. She marched Ellie into the kitchen and kicked the door shut. "What happened out there was not a game. You need to understand—"

"I can be like Jonah one day. And you, too, Mama. You're strong and pretty, and—" Ellie broke off her flattery when the landline phone rang. "You have to answer. It's important."

"Finish your homework," LaShaun called over her shoulder as she stomped to the phone. "Unavailable" displayed on the caller ID screen.

"Your visitor this afternoon—she's not Legion," Manny announced.

Chapter 12

The next morning, LaShaun sat in Cherry's Coffee and Confections questioning her sanity. Manny stood across the shop at a long white counter with a glass case. Pastries, cookies and more were on display. Tables with chairs cover in red fake leather were arranged around it. He was on his best behavior, charming the waitress. They'd met in Milton, a small unincorporated community a few miles from Lafayette. He strolled over with a paper plate loaded with an apple pastry and two glazed donuts.

"Angel says it's King Cake Day." Manny sat at their table.

"That's not king cake," LaShaun said, pointing out the obvious.

"Yeah, well, I've had two helpings already. Decided to try something different." Manny lifted his refilled red mug, sipped, and let out a sigh. "You know the best thing about being in the free world again?"

"There's isn't a big scary felon taking your food." LaShaun glanced around. The crowded shop buzzed with conversation and activity.

"No one is staring at us," Manny assured her. He licked icing from his right thumb. "Decent coffee."

"Hmm." LaShaun bounced one knee beneath the table, still observing their surroundings.

"Relax. Folks around here haven't been paying attention to the news. Lafayette has its share of crime thanks to the illegal drug trade. Human trafficking is a problem, too. Can you imagine? So sad." Manny shook his head.

"Dude, really?" LaShaun looked at him.

"Okay, okay. Just making conversation." Manny gazed back at her, sighed, and wiped his mouth with a napkin. "I'd give anything to just be... normal. Talk boring shit every day. A faceless hick in a little bitty old place. When I finish parole, I could move to a big city. A friend says you can get lost, start over easier. Just let yourself get swallowed up. Or maybe even leave the country."

"Manny..."

"Anything is possible when you're really free. Right now, I got this invisible chain on my leg. They ready to snatch me back for any reason, even if it's on a lie." Manny's good humor had soured in seconds. He looked at his plate as if in distaste.

"Y'all need anything else? I got more coffee," the waitress said. A gold name plate pinned to her white blouse had "Angel" in black letters. She held up a glass pot.

"Believe I will, thanks so much." LaShaun smiled at her as Angel poured.

"Why don't you let me box up a slice of praline and cream cheese king cake for you, ma'am. Baked this morning. Dayshawn is the best baker for miles around." Angel nodded toward the open window behind the counter. A beefy black man in white worked to fill orders. He cooked up scrambled eggs, sausages, and more.

"You've talked me into it," LaShaun said. "He must be good with all these people filling the place."

"Even tourists down here for Mardi Gras heard of us. They drive from Lafayette just to get breakfast. Be right back." Angel flashed a smile at Manny.

Manny winked back and watched her go. "Nice lady, and no, I'm not trying to get in her pants."

"I didn't say anything." LaShaun held up both palms.

"Dayshawn was inside, but he done turned his life around." Manny's dour mood seemed to have lifted. He sipped more coffee. "Ah, that's good stuff."

"You mentioned—" LaShaun broke off when Angel approached with a small white takeout paper box. "Thank you."

"All on my tab." Manny smiled at Angel.

"Sure thing. You and your sister have a great day, you hear?" Angel beamed at him and hustled off.

Manny wore a sheepish expression when LaShaun glared at him across the table. "I didn't want Angel to think we were, you know, a couple."

"But you're not trying to sleep with her," LaShaun drawled.

"Angel is different from, I mean my father had me thinking of women in a certain way. I've never been on a dinner and a movie type date. Females were to be used for... you know. In therapy they call it gaining insight." Manny looked off into the distance.

"Uh-huh." LaShaun stared at him through the steam from her coffee as she drank.

"I like Angel. I'm normal in that way. Like any other guy," Manny blurted out.

"Why am I here?" LaShaun's question was as much to herself as to him.

"I want to give you some leads on my case." Manny dug into the pocket of his jean jacket.

"Your case?"

"Yeah. I understand you've been busy with that TEA stuff. But I figure Cee-Cee and Jonah got a solid handle on things. You can back out, what with the baby coming and Ellie needing attention. Hey, I heard about what happened at your place. Look, if you need me to keep an eye out—"

"Whoa, slow down. First, I never said I'd take 'your case.' Second, I'm not a licensed private investigator. Finally, and more to the point, there's no evidence pointing to anyone else. Except maybe Orin. Which is the reason you got parole, remember? That and your... mental state." LaShaun had lowered her voice as she spoke. She glanced around to make sure no one took a special interest in them.

"Yeah, well, I read the evidence from the state police too. At least two male DNA samples were found that haven't been identified. People arrested or convicted of certain felonies after 1999 had DNA samples taken. Now if the cops around the state have been doing their jobs, they should have looked for a match. I'm thinking they didn't even try. Just assumed it was me."

"Manny—"

He waved a hand to stop her. "Just listen before you blow me off. Nobody listens to me. All my damn life. Maybe if... well, no use in beating my brain against the *maybes* that never happened." He stared into the depths of the dark-roast Louisiana brew. Angel appeared.

"That must be cold by now. Here's a fresh cup." She gave him a brief smile before bustling off again. Manny barely had time to thank her.

LaShaun watched the young woman for a few seconds. Then she looked at Manny. His morose expression, and Angel's soft treatment of him, moved her. Maybe past common sense, she mused.

"Okay, tell me," LaShaun said.

"Two of the victims had unidentified male DNA on them. The girl found out in Cameron Parish, you know in the Sabine Wildlife Refuge, and the girl found almost in Orange, Texas. That's two of the six they say I did. Some female DNA, too." Manny nodded.

"A female serial killer." LaShaun frowned.

"Humph, I hadn't even thought of that. But it's possible." Manny had regained his animation. "Yeah, I know it's uncommon, but what if—"

"Let's not get ahead of ourselves. Both victims had a history of prostitution, at least when they needed money. So, finding multiple DNA isn't unusual under the circumstances."

"In a murder investigation, every avenue should be pursued. That's what my attorney argued, and that wasn't even about this extra DNA. At the time he was talking about my dear old *dad*, may his soul twist in agony forever," Manny said in a tight voice.

"The court ruled that given your father's history, and that you partied together, he *might* have been a suspect. The investigators and DA didn't hide evidence, just maybe moved quickly since you were connected to both. And the other four." LaShaun raised an eyebrow at him.

"I had an active social life. Sue me," Manny quipped.

"Oh, you went to court all right. Instead of a lawsuit, you ended up in prison," LaShaun shot back.

"We proved all those girls either lived around here or traveled here. Part of the same drug and party crowd. More reasonable doubt."

LaShaun studied him for a few moments. His dark gaze searched her face for clues. She made sure he wouldn't push into her mind. Not again. She'd shared one too many disturbing visions with Manny in the past.

"Excellent reasons why you don't need *me*. Look, you're already walking around enjoying donuts, taking rides in the country."

"I'm not free, damn it," Manny snapped. When several heads turned their way, he sucked in air and let it out. "Being on parole means I'm still a prisoner. The Louisiana Department of Corrections owns me, LaShaun."

"And there's not a thing I can do to change that. What am I gonna do, have DNA examined and—" LaShaun blinked hard as the slow smile that spread across his face. "Oh, hell no."

"TEA has the best forensic labs in the country, hell maybe the world. And they have a criminal division. You're close to Cee-Cee and Jonah. Throw in psychic resources, and I could be cleared." Manny sat back. "Just saying the words..."

"You seriously think TEA will just roll out the welcome mat and let me use their facilities? I don't have any pull to do something like that, Manny. You're out of your mind." LaShaun gave a grunt, sipped lukewarm coffee, and grimaced. "Angel doesn't care if you sister doesn't have a fresh cup of brew."

Manny laughed and waved until he got the waitress's attention. "Refill. And a raspberry donut for me. Suddenly, I'm hungry again. Must be getting close to lunchtime."

Angel arrived seconds later holding his order. "Oh Manny, you're so funny. It's barely nine o'clock. You two enjoy."

"She knows it's my favorite. Thanks so much." Manny beamed at her.

"You have the metabolism of a hummingbird to eat so much and stay slim," LaShaun muttered.

"You have to watch the sugar and calories. She's got a baby bakin' in there," Manny said to Angel with a nod at LaShaun.

"Congratulations," Angel said to LaShaun. "And if you want another donut, just say the word." Then she looked at Manny. "You're going to be a great uncle, I just know it."

"Yeah, pretty exciting," Manny replied with a cheeky grin at LaShaun.

LaShaun forced a smile for Angel's sake. "I'll skip the donut, but thanks."

"When Angel left, Manny leaned forward with an eager expression. "Now about that DNA."

LaShaun opened her mouth to say "no" with as much force as possible. Then his words about Legion hit her even stronger. "You said the woman who was at my house wasn't a Legion member. Then who is she?"

"I have a feeling those TEA deaths go deeper than your pals think." Manny glanced around. Then lowered his voice. "My friend says the spiritual faction of TEA has a fanatical side. They're willing to do whatever it takes to win. And they figure if they get you and Ellie to their side, they've got a huge advantage."

"Wait, what?" LaShaun looked at him.

"The local mining operation is right in your backyard. TEA bought the company last week. Pretty smart folks, gotta hand it to 'em. Now the spiritual crazies think you can help them take control. That mineral is supposed to amp up supernatural skills, right? Ellie is a little celebrity with her mind-bending power. Oh yeah, they know all about her." Manny nodded slowly.

LaShaun tried to wrap her head around the plot twists. "So, the three clowns that stopped me the other day..."

"They're Legion all right. Legion and the TEA spiritual crazies decided they need to recruit Ellie. Nobody forcing your baby girl, not without serious blowback." Manny chuckled. "They've found that out more than once. Matter of fact, the woman was sent to confirm it."

"Which means they want her even more." LaShaun flinched. Her supernatural senses sent what felt like static shock over her body.

"I hear she's got a rebellious streak. From her mama, no doubt."

"She's got a daddy, too, you know." LaShaun huffed in annoyance. "So, you're telling me folks are scared of my first grader."

"Hell yeah, and they're right. They all heard about what happened when them fools kidnapped her." Manny lifted his mug and drank deeply.

LaShaun sat in thought for a time as Manny polished off his last donut. "Eventually, they're going to look for someone even stronger than Ellie."

"They who?" he said, wiping icing from his fingers with a napkin.

"Both, Legion and the radical side of TEA," LaShaun said, a deep dread taking root in her gut.

"If I had to guess, I'd say Legion will try first. TEA figures she's closer to being on their side. People she loves and trust are TEA."

LaShaun stared at him in surprise, speechless at his astute assessment and insight. "You have so much potential if..."

"If I'm not a psycho serial killer with one step in the Satan-worshiping collective," Manny finished for her.

"I wasn't going to put it like that exactly," LaShaun said. "Back to my child. No matter what she can do, or they think she can do, Ellie is still a baby. She needs protecting."

"Legion hasn't gotten around to the more powerful psychic option. Plus, they got a global search on their hands when they do. So, we got time." Manny said.

"But how much?" LaShaun felt like taking off to Ellie's school to make sure she was safe.

"I'd say it's gonna take them at least a month. Then they'll figure out their best option is right here in Louisiana." Manny tilted his head to one side and gazed at LaShaun.

LaShaun frowned at him. "Another kid is as strong? Then we better find her, or him, first. I...." She blinked hard as the realization hit.

"Yeah, me." Manny laughed and clapped his hands.

"Oh. Shit. Bricks." LaShaun shoved her chair back to put more distance than the table between them.

Manny's laughter died away as he wiped his eyes. His mirth vanished, and he grew serious. "I have a lot of faults, but hurting kids ain't one of 'em. And I hate people who do. You might have heard about what happened when they sent me to prison the first time."

"You ended up back at the forensic hospital because you had a breakdown," LaShaun murmured.

"That was the official story. Cover-up so the guards and warden didn't catch more heat. They already had investigators on their asses about conditions at The Farm," Manny said with a grimace. He used the old-school nickname for the infamous Louisiana State Penitentiary at Angola.

"I thought they sent you to Dixon first," LaShaun replied.

"Very effective cover-up, huh? Once the psychiatrist said I was stable, they transferred me to Angola. Met a guy who had molested and tortured little girls. I choked him out. Guards got to us before he died. Dude has brain damage though."

LaShaun shuddered at Manny's smile of grim satisfaction. "That's awful."

"Piece of garbage got hard talking about what he'd done to a four-year-old, baby girl of a woman he shacked up with. Still feeling sorry for him?" Manny drained the last of his cup.

"You have a propensity for extreme violence." LaShaun quoted part of a report in Manny's voluminous criminal records.

Manny clicked his tongue. "You know, I never understood that. I mean, what the hell else kind of violence is there?"

"Manny..." LaShaun shook her head as she studied him.

He leaned forward. "I knew exactly what I was doing and why. I met women who liked it rough, and it was fun. But unless something happened to me I don't remember, I've never felt an urge to kill my sex partners. Or anyone." Manny shrugged. "Well, I don't count Orin."

"Right." LaShaun winced at her own acceptance of his logic.

"Which is why I think all these murders were a setup. My family… well, you know the story." Manny looked away with a frown as if mentioning them caused pain.

LaShaun nodded. The Young family history had opened up to reveal a toxic soup of incest, domestic violence, drug addiction, and alcoholism. She knew Chase would disagree. He'd argue that many people had it worse and didn't slaughter other human beings. Still, LaShaun couldn't help but feel sorry for the little boy born into such a hell. Manny's pale-white complexion contrasted by his dark Cajun hair and eyes made him look haunted. After a few seconds he transformed. The charming, boyishly handsome façade returned.

"But back to our girl." Manny nodded.

"Our girl?" LaShaun started at the lightning change in him and the subject.

"Nothing is going to happen to my godchild. So, you can stop worrying about those Legion jokers. The religion fanatics from TEA are content to let her 'mature' as they call it." Manny nodded.

LaShaun knew others would think she was crazy, but she felt relief. She believed Manny would protect Ellie. Then she gasped at the psychic tingle up her spine. He already had, which meant he was strong indeed. Her whole body relaxed and the urge to check on Ellie subsided.

"You have about as much chance of christening Ellie as I have of becoming queen of the universe. And what do you mean mature?"

"You know, let her get older. Enter those tween or teen years and get even more defiant. They're counting on nature taking its course. And those LaShaun genes kicking in. Girl, you didn't tell me what a rebellion hellion you were back in the day. I've heard stories. Whew." Manny let out a low whistle.

LaShaun pushed aside her irritation. "You've still got sources in TEA. Get them to arrange for a DNA analysis."

"They don't have the clout. I'm talking a file clerk, a receptionist. Though I did make friends with a guy who's in IT, not high up though." Manny shrugged.

"Damn, you made a lot of friends in a short period of time," LaShaun retorted. Then an image came to her. "The meeting the other day, at the theater in New Iberia."

"Hmm." Manny glanced around and waved at Angel. The waitress nodded with a pleased smile. "No hurry. Just ready for the check," he called to her.

"Was one of those new friends on the video conference?" LaShaun stared at him hard.

Manny made a big show of pulling out money to pay for their meal. Seconds later Angel hovered near. "Like I said, all my new friends are bit players. Those guys on the video conference. They're the top of the food chain. Am I right?"

"Pretty much." LaShaun continued to watch him.

Manny favored Angel with a winning smile as he handed her money. The waitress gushed a bit and left. Then he turned back to LaShaun. "So, I got a plan."

"A plan," LaShaun echoed, her energy still focused on sifting through her gut instinct reaction. Something was off.

"Yeah. If TEA wants to study me like I'm a bug or something, fine. I want something in return. I've helped in two TEA investigations. I even helped you catch Orin." Manny wagged a forefinger at her.

"I'll see what Cee-Cee says. She's got some clout," LaShaun replied. She looped her purse strap over one shoulder.

Manny sat straight with a surprised look on his face. "Really? No argument? No telling me it would take a cold day in hell?"

"It's pretty obvious even by TEA standards you're unique. They might consider examining your guilt or innocence part of their research. I'll talk to Cee-Cee. I gotta go. Errands to run, and I don't want to miss Ellie's drop-off again. Chase would go ballistic."

"You agreed pretty fast, too fast." Manny squinted at her.

"Look, you got parole because there was evidence you might not be guilty. Since TEA is treating you like a lab animal anyway, might as well give them incentive." LaShaun stood.

"Yeah, okay," Manny said after a while.

"Hey, show more gratitude. Or maybe you put that infamous Manny Young charisma on the research team leader."

"Doesn't work on her," Manny said promptly. Then a sly smile curved his mouth up. "She's on guard about me."

"Gee, I wonder why?" LaShaun quipped. "One condition of me continuing to help you."

"I knew it was too easy. What?"

"Don't lie to me, or hide anything. The minute I find out you've tried to play me our deal is dead."

"Would I... okay, okay. I won't even say it. I have bared my soul to you so far." Manny placed one hand over his heart.

"Manny." LaShaun let her eyes send the warning, but she must have sent more. He flinched as if she'd touched him.

"No need to poke me with a supernatural branding iron." Manny rubbed the backs of both hands. When LaShaun's expression remained merciless, he sighed. "Okay, sit down. This will only take a minute or two."

LaShaun took out her cell phone, checked the time and for messages. "You got ten minutes."

Twenty minutes later LaShaun was almost home. Manny had told her about more of his unsavory activities. These were crimes he'd never been arrested for, let alone convicted. Most of it involved theft in one form or another. He'd taken part in more of his father's sadistic orgies than he'd let on. He'd avoided looking her in the eye the longer he talked. Could the Blood River Ripper feel shame?

Once home, LaShaun got Beau to jump into her Forrester for a trip to the groomer. And he wasn't happy about it. He did his version of grumbling, low woofs of dismay, as he seemed to realize the route they were taking.

"Look, those nails of yours need clipping. I'd prefer to have a professional do it rather than risk hurting you. So, quit your whining, dude. I'm paying for the works. A massage, ear cleaning, even a new bandana. How about that?" LaShaun laughed at Beau's loud double bark. "I'll take that as a 'yes'."

By one o'clock that afternoon, they were on the way home from Doggie Boutique and Spa. Beau sported a yellow and navy-blue bandana that complemented his now glossy coat. Within one mile of home on Rougon Road Beau poked his head between the seats. He barked softly, as if sounding an alert. LaShaun followed his gaze. A solitary figure stood on the shoulder. LaShaun didn't see a disabled vehicle. There were no houses along that stretch, so it seemed odd. Then her SUV's engine sputtered and died. The Forrester rolled to a stop slowly as the figure stepped on the center yellow line of the road. Beau raised on all fours and growled. Clouds moved in to blot out the sunshine. Within seconds the area looked dark, as if a curtain had dropped. LaShaun's whole body lit up with the characteristic tingle. No weather system had rolled in. The figure had caused this change, and it only affected the space around them.

"Get out of the SUV. Staying inside won't help you anyway," a voice reverberated in the vehicle. The figure's lips hadn't moved.

LaShaun jumped when Beau thumped against the door in the backseat. His barking became insistent, his efforts to get out more frantic. "Beau, don't. You're going to hurt yourself."

"Get out here. We need to talk," the voice repeated. The androgynous sound gave no clue as to its gender.

"Fine. You wanna play this game."

Beau had hopped across the seat to crouch next to her up front. Sliding back the lid of the console, LaShaun put the derringer in a pocket and opened the door. Beau leapt out, his large paws hitting the pavement seconds before LaShaun exited the SUV. He assumed the stance of a hunting dog ready to pounce. The figure seemed to shimmer in and out of focus the more LaShaun stared.

"Restrain that animal or else."

LaShaun pushed through the psychic camouflage. The effort gave her a slight headache. She felt like electrified ants were crawling all over her body. "You came to my home. Threatened my daughter."

"I didn't threaten the child. I offered her a better life." The figure lifted its arms in a motion as if sweeping back a hood. Her pale skin stood out against deep reddish-auburn hair pulled into a tight bun.

"This stunt won't scare me into giving you what you want. So, your other option is to harm me. You'd still have to go through her father. Even without supernatural abilities, Chase is no easy target." LaShaun took a step forward. So did Beau. She grinned when the woman moved back as if surprised.

The woman stiffened as if remembering her resolve. She glared at them. She was dressed in a black catsuit. She might have been cosplaying a comic book villain.

"You and your husband would be gone if I wanted. Just like that." The woman snapped her fingers. Thunder seemed to roll out from her hand to surround them. The air crackled. "But I'm hoping you'll see the huge advantages I offer Joelle."

"Ellie is smart. She'd figure out who hurt us and make you pay." LaShaun sneered at the woman. "So, pack up the rest of your clown outfits and go to hell."

The woman stomped a foot. Pieces of the paved road flew up, leaving a crack. "I'll do what's necessary."

"So will *we*." LaShaun frowned. The woman's face contorted into a mask of pain.

Beau started forward, but LaShaun grabbed the collar beneath his new bandana. He strained forward. A low growl built in his throat unit a bark that sounded more like a roar came out. The woman flung both arms out. Streams of steam seemed to come from her fingertips. She screeched once, then again.

"I'm in control," she shouted. Her voice seemed muffled by the atmosphere around her. "You'll do what we want or else."

Beau shot forward and yanked LaShaun a few inches with him. The force of his momentum broke her grip. LaShaun pulled out her gun. But the woman seemed to be fighting herself more than trying to attack.

"Your lame-ass skills won't help you, not against me." The woman scowled.

As she raised an arm as if to point at LaShaun, Beau reached her. LaShaun blinked in shock as his jaws opened wider than she thought possible. Beau clamped down hard enough that the woman howled. Then he whipped his head from side to side. She beat on him with her free hand. Stumbling around, she tried to land a kick. The two engaged in a wrestling match as LaShaun watched, feeling helpless. She ran back to the SUV, grabbed her phone and fumbled until she tapped in 911. Somehow the dispatcher understood the rapid-fire call for help. Then she managed to unlock her phone and call Cee-Cee.

"Come, quick. Lock on my location," LaShaun gasped. She trembled as she watched the bizarre, deadly dance. Dog and woman. A wave of hot air crashed into her. Like someone had flipped a switch, the sound vanished and the scene went dark.

Chapter 13

LaShaun woke up to a confusion of sensations. A firm, smooth surface lay beneath her. Voices, some shouting. Others speaking in level but urgent tones. Movement all around. She fought to focus her fogged vision, blinking hard. When she tried to lift an arm a sharp ache and stiffness stopped her. Fright slapped into her. A hand rested on her shoulder with a light touch. Then a male voice she didn't recognize spoke up.

"Take it easy. You're okay. Vital signs are pretty good. Though I'm not sure what the heck hit her." Then he moved away to tap on something, an instrument.

"We got here fast as we could. Beat Chase and his people, so we lucked out."

"Humpt," was all LaShaun managed to get out. Her throat felt raw, dry. The second voice's familiar sound helped quell her rising hysteria. She ignored the pounding pain in her head and turned toward it.

Jonah's smooth face appeared as if from behind a gauzy veil. He seemed to hover in the sky over her. No, she was lying down. "Where... what..."

Chase pushed Jonah aside. "Baby, you're fine. The EMTs say no broken bones or blunt force trauma. Don't worry about giving a statement. Just relax."

"Ellie," LaShaun croaked and tried to sit up.

"M.J.'s grandmother met her at the bus. She's fine. No one went to our house. I've got a deputy there," Chase said rapid-fire, knowing which questions to answer before she asked them. "Same woman?"

LaShaun nodded yes, then winced at the fresh pain the motion brought.

"She's in rough shape. When you're able we need to figure out what the hell happened here. No way did Beau cause those weird injuries," Chase started to say more, but someone called his name. "M.J. just got here. Gotta go, but don't worry. I'm close by."

"I'll take care of her, dude," Jonah piped up over Chase's shoulder.

Chase scowled at him. "You folks dragged her into this black magic mess. If I find out—"

"Boss, you wanna see this," a female deputy said.

"I'll talk you two later." Chase pointed a finger at Jonah's nose and then strode away.

LaShaun tried to rise, but two sets of gentle hands pushed her back. They didn't need to exert much effort since she felt weakness along with the pain. Jonah's face popped back into her line of vision. He grinned at her.

"You sure know how to keep life interesting. Oh, and Ellie says hello. She knows you're going to be fine. Heck, she told me before I said anything. She's watching some kiddie show," Jonah said in a chatty tone.

"I'm glad you both are enjoying the afternoon." LaShaun winced at the laborious effort a complete sentence took.

Chase reappeared. "Okay. You're going to the hospital to get checked over."

"See ya later, sis. I'm glad you're okay." Jonah squeezed her hand.

"Thanks for showing up. I..." LaShaun realized her lips weren't moving. No sound had come out.

"We got your back. Always," Jonah said. Then he looked at Chase. "Let us know if she's admitted."

"Wait, admitted? I don't need..." LaShaun didn't have strength to move. Her voice came out as a weak rasp.

"Okay. We're ready," Chase said to someone she couldn't see.

"But—"

"Here we go, babe." Chase pulled a thin blanket up to cover her chest.

The scene faded to black as LaShaun tried once again to make her wishes known. No hospital. Check on Beau. Find out who the woman is and why she acted so weird. Then suddenly none of it matter as she drifted into a land of dreamlike wonder.

****

"Somebody is going to tell me what's going on right now," LaShaun said.

"Shush, or we'll give you another dose of sedative. You're going to disturb the other patients." A middle-aged black woman gave LaShaun's shoulder a pat. "I know you've been through something, but settle down. You're safe."

"Who—"

"You're in Vermillion General Hospital. I'm Mrs. Sheffield, your nurse. Well, one of 'em on this floor anyway. I got the wonderful duty of checking on you this shift. Half the others are scared of you." Mrs. Sheffield chuckled to herself. She tapped the keyboard on what looked like a laptop on a rolling cart.

"Scared?" LaShaun blinked at her in curiosity. The woman reminded her of Miss Rose and M.J.'s grandmother.

"Mavis, I..."

The older woman paused in typing to shake a finger at LaShaun. "Hey, hey. None of that. I'm old enough to be your mother. I'm *Mrs. Sheffield* to you, youngster."

LaShaun smiled at the good-natured admonishment. The woman's smooth, brown skin like milk chocolate made her look younger. "You mean older sister."

"Now don't be thinking you'll get around me and these rules with sugar sweet words." The nurse grinned back and return to her notes.

"Yes, ma'am. Why are they scared of me?" LaShaun looked around the hospital room.

"Some silly nonsense about voodoo or witchery going back over two hundred years in your family. That true?" Mrs. Sheffield cast a glance at LaShaun then back to her screen.

"It is. Now I guess you're gonna run out of here." LaShaun found the button and raised her bed.

"Pooh." The nurse never paused in tapping keys.

"So you're a modern who believes in science." LaShaun reached for a cup nearby and sipped water through a straw.

"Uh-huh. And my Aunt Nola Ray taught me how to protect myself. I stay prayed up. Now, tell me what day and time it is." Mrs. Sheffield took out a pen light. She shined it in LaShaun's eyes and peered into them.

"Wednesday, maybe around four o'clock?" LaShaun blinked when the light clicked off.

"AM or PM?"

"PM. I wanted to make sure to meet my daughter when the bus dropped her off. But I got..." LaShaun's heart started to pound as the events came back.

"She's fine," Mrs. Sheffield said in a gentle tone. She patted LaShaun's shoulder a second time. "Your husband brought her to see you. They're waiting for me to finish."

"I don't want her to get scared or upset." LaShaun blinked as tears formed. Then another terror seized her. "My baby—"

"Is just fine. Active little rascal, too. Whatever happened didn't make you miscarry," Mrs. Sheffield said quickly. Then she grinned. "That dog of yours must have superpowers, too. Heard that crazy woman didn't get a chance to lay one finger on you."

"How's she doing?" Chase said before the nurse could go on.

"Ha, I figured you wouldn't stay out of here for long." Mrs. Sheffield beamed at him. "I'm finishing up. So, I'll leave her in your strong hands. For now."

"Thanks." Chase nodded and watched the nurse leave. Then he kissed LaShaun. "Feeling less dizzy?"

"Much better now that I see you." LaShaun put both arms around his neck. She pressed her cheek against his for a second and let go.

"Ellie almost caused a riot until I agreed to bring her." Chase grinned.

"So, she's had her snack?"

"You mean dinner. And she's thrilled to be up past bedtime. It's almost ten o'clock, hon." Chase brushed a hand through LaShaun's thick hair.

"You're kidding." LaShaun's mouth fell open.

"And you're going to stay. Just for the night," Chase added in a firm tone. "It's for the baby."

His last sentence made the protest dissolve on her tongue. LaShaun rubbed her tummy and relaxed against the pillow. "Yes, sir. You're right. I can't go charging after villains. At least not until a month or so after I give birth."

"What am I gonna do with these hard-headed Broussard women?" Chase blew out air. "Be right back."

Moments later he returned holding Ellie by the hand. She pulled him along, eager to go faster. Chase repeated that she couldn't run in the hospital. When he let go, Ellie raced to the bed. She tried to climb up, but couldn't.

"Hey, be careful. Mama's had a little accident. You don't want to shake her and our baby," Chase said. He gave Ellie a boost onto the bed as LaShaun made room for her.

"My brother is just fine. He told me," Ellie said promptly. "And I know that lady tried to hurt Mama."

"I'm going to choke Jonah for—" Chase broke off. His eyes grew to the size of saucers. "What did you say about your brother?"

Ellie giggled, both small hands over her mouth. "I'm just playing with you, Daddy."

"Don't give your father a heart attack, munchkin." LaShaun struggled not to laugh.

"Cute," Chase drawled. He pulled the large chair closer to the bed.

"Don't be mad at Jonah. I asked him for the whole story. I knew it wasn't an accident anyway. And you were busy making sure Mama was okay and talking to the other policemen." Ellie spoke in such a practical, non-little-girl tone, Chase seemed struck speechless.

"But next time wait for Daddy," LaShaun said while combing her fingers through Ellie's thick, tight curls. She had two buns on either side of her head with rhinestones pinned in. "Azalei did your hair up. I recognize her style."

"Miss Clo took me to Aunt Shirleen's. She had brownies with lots of walnuts, just the way we like." Ellie snuggled into the crook of LaShaun's arm.

"Sounds delish." LaShaun smiled at Chase.

"Uh-huh. Then Cousin Azalei came home from work and we played beauty salon. See? Mardi Gras." Ellie held up her hands to showcase green and gold polka dot nail polish.

Chase held up both palms when LaShaun gasped. "I swear I didn't notice with everything going on."

"They're like stickers or something. Easy as Monmon Odette's pie," Ellie piped.

"Huh?" LaShaun blinked at her and yawned.

"That's what Aunt Shirleen says." Ellie kissed LaShaun's cheek. Then she slid off the bed.

Chase leaned forward to cushion her descent to the floor. "Mama's—"

"Sleepy. She and baby need rest. I'll go talk to Jonah while you talk grown-up stuff." Ellie scooted from the room, managing to swing open the door. She was gone, leaving Chase staring after her in astonishment.

"Soon I'm gonna have two of 'em," he mumbled and shook his head. Then he turned to LaShaun again. "Speaking of the baby and your TEA friends, let me warn you. I let them have it for putting you at risk. No, let me finish."

"Cee-Cee didn't make me do anything. They weren't even with me," LaShaun said, finding energy for the brewing argument. She pushed up to sit straight against the firm pillows.

"LaShaun—"

"No, Chase. Jumping on my friends is unfair. Not to mention you're treating me like a child. As if you have to regulate who I hang out with. Seriously." LaShaun gave him an evil-eye stare.

"I was upset, okay?" Chase leaned toward her and took one hand. "If anything happened to you, to our baby..."

LaShaun's anger melted at the look of anguish on his handsome face. He had a few lines on his forehead that she only just noticed. She smoothed a hand over his forehead. "I'm sorry, darlin'. You didn't sign up for... all this."

"Hell yes, I did." Chase's voice softened. He pressed her hand to his cheek. "Now I'm going to let you two get to sleep. I'll be here first thing to pick you up. The doc says an overnight stay would be best."

"No." LaShaun pressed the button. The hospital bed went down in a smooth motion. She threw the sheets back. "I'm going home."

"The doctors want to observe you overnight to make sure you don't have a concussion, LaShaun. Don't be stubborn." Chase stood as if to block her.

"Get my clothes." LaShaun moved stiffly, but the pain had eased.

"The clothes you had on are gone, but I brought a clean set. Which you can put on *in the morning* when I pick you up." Chase placed both hands on her shoulders. The motion stopped her from slipping out of the hospital gown.

"They've run all kinds of tests, and we're good. I'm just going to sleep all night. I can do that at home. Plus, Ellie will be reassured if I'm there to see her off to school as usual." LaShaun smiled at him. "Now move. And what do you mean my clothes are gone?"

"Guess in the confusion the bag got misplaced."

"Oh my God. My gun. It's been in my family for generations." LaShaun clapped a hand over her mouth.

"I picked it up at the scene, babe. It's in the truck," Chase said

"Whew! Thanks, babe."

"The important thing is for you to follow medical advice." Chase huffed in exasperation as she ducked under his arm to reach the closet.

"I'll call my OB-GYN bright and early tomorrow, get an appointment, and get checked over. See? I'm not being totally unreasonable." LaShaun handed him the gown. "I hope you remembered clean underwear."

"Of course I did. Hey, put that stuff back." Chase tried to stop her progress.

LaShaun gently pushed his strong hands away. She faced him, wearing only panties that stretched over her growing tummy. Chase frowned at a light blue bruise on her shoulder. He kissed it. LaShaun caressed his dark, straight hair. "You're so sweet. Now, find my socks and shoes."

Chase stood back with a sigh. He retrieved the trainers. "I already got you an appointment, by the way. For tomorrow."

LaShaun turned, and Chase hooked her bra. Then she shimmed out of the old panties and put on the ones he'd brought. She dropped them in the bag. "But you were just demanding I stay here until tomorrow."

"Yeah, well. I'm no psychic, but I had a feeling you'd buck doctor's orders," Chase retorted.

"Honey, don't let Ellie's confident act fool you. She's still a little girl who needs to feel safe. That means having Daddy and Mama around when trouble breaks out."

"You're right. I wasn't crazy about leaving you here alone, but I didn't want to leave Ellie with anyone either." Chase leaned down as she steadied herself against him to step into comfortable yoga pants.

LaShaun pulled an olive-green, long-sleeved heavy sweater over her head. Seconds later she was fully dressed. "I hope they find my boots and denim jacket. Those are my favorites."

"I'll make sure the nurses track 'em down." Chase started to say more when the door opened.

Ellie tiptoed in dramatic fashion, a finger to her lips. She pulled Jonah in after her and shut the door. Then whispered, "I sneaked Jonah past the nurses. You're only supposed to have one visitor at a time, and family."

"Joëlle René Broussard, you better behave." Chase shook a finger at her.

"Mrs. Sheffield gave me a wink as we 'snuck' by." Jonah stayed close to the door as if ready for a necessary quick exit.

Ellie crossed to Chase and looked up at him with a sweet smile. "Jonah's here to help, Daddy."

"Yeah, well..." Chase rubbed a hand over his face. "Sorry I yelled at you earlier."

Jonah grinned at him and waved a hand. "Already forgotten. Understandable, with a pregnant wife and kid to worry about. Well, I don't completely since I'm blissfully free. But you know."

"Oh, brother." Chase shook his head, but his mouth twitched as if he was fighting a smile. His cell phone buzzed. "Better take this. I'll be back in a minute."

LaShaun eyed Jonah. "Tell me everything."

"We'll have a full briefing later." Jonah slid a side glance at Ellie and back to LaShaun. "Some details have to be confirmed."

LaShaun nodded. She handed Ellie a nightgown Chase had hung up, her cell phone, and a few other items. "Honey, pack the rest of Mama's things in the bag. For me."

"Okay." Ellie dragged the bag across the floor. With a determined expression, she arranged her mother's belongings in pockets.

"We took your clothes," Jonah said. "TEA forensics wanted to have a go at them." He broke off when Chase returned. Jonah mouthed "Later" when Chase had his back to him.

"My deputies have things under control. Let's break the news to Mrs. Sheffield." Chase tugged one of Ellie's pigtails. "Good job helping, baby girl."

Mrs. Sheffield took the news as expected. She scowled with disapproval through the paperwork. Both LaShaun and Chase had to sign forms confirming they acted against medical advice. But the veteran nurse went further. She practically had them swear before God LaShaun would see her obstetrician.

"And you say you already have an appointment?" Mrs. Sheffield asked a third time. She squinted at Chase in a way that made him squirm.

LaShaun fought a giggle. Her big, strong husband had the look of a high schooler being grilled by the principal. "Eleven AM sharp, and we won't be late. I'll take this hospital discharge summary with me. Scout's honor."

"Bet you were never a Girl Scout. You're allergic to rules and authority," Mrs. Sheffield retorted. "Here's a short list of what you can take for pain. Won't hurt the baby. And stop running around here like some crime-fighting Marie Laveau. Slow it down."

"I'll make sure Mama follows instructions," Ellie piped up.

"Humph, at least somebody is showing some sense. Keep 'em in line, baby." Mrs. Sheffield beamed at her fondly.

"Thanks for everything, Mrs. Sheffield. Okay, let's go, ladies." Chase turned to leave.

"Hold it. Mrs. Broussard is not walking out of here. One rule I will enforce." Mrs. Sheffield nodded at a nursing assistant who appeared with a wheelchair.

"Don't argue," Chase muttered aside to LaShaun.

"Wouldn't dream of it," LaShaun whispered back. She faced the nurse with a smile.

They left under the watchful stare of Mrs. Sheffield. LaShaun gave her a final wave as the automatic glass doors whisked closed. An hour later they arrived home. LaShaun started awake, realizing she and Ellie had fallen asleep during most of the ride. It took another hour for Chase to get Ellie bathed and settled into bed. LaShaun managed a soothing shower after giving her sleepy daughter one last goodnight kiss.

Chase disappeared, no doubt checking in with either M.J. or his deputies. Then he took a shower, dressed in pajama bottoms, and climbed into bed next to her.

Chase brushed her right cheek with the fingers of one hand. "Good night."

LaShaun grabbed his shoulder before he could turn on his side away from her. "No you don't. I want to know what you've found out."

Chase sighed and propped pillows behind him. "You mean besides figuring out Cee-Cee and Jonah took your clothes? I could charge them with removing police evidence."

"Anything could have happened in the chaos, you don't know..." LaShaun clicked her tongue when he cocked his head to one side. "I wasn't physically touched, so technically my clothes have no forensic value to the police."

"The fact that TEA took them means they do. I didn't pin both your pals to the wall because I had my hands full."

"Okay. Get right on it first thing after sunrise. Explain that my sorcery friends think there's some magic pixie dust on my clothes. Get the state police lab right on the job." LaShaun lay a hand on his broad chest and grinned at him.

"Um, yeah. And there was the part about coming up with an explanation." Chase scowled in irritation.

"TEA has one of the best forensic departments in the country, maybe the world. They'll handle my clothes with care, and I'll make sure Cee-Cee returns them. But they won't mean much to your people. The woman never got close, let alone touched me."

"Yeah, we figured as much. You were a good twenty feet apart."

"How's she doing, by the way?"

"You should rest instead of demanding a full briefing." Chase smoothed a tendril of her thick hair.

LaShaun gasped and sat up suddenly. "And where's Beau?"

"Honey, you—"

"He's not in the house, is he? Chase, come clean. Ellie was too exhausted to notice tonight. But in the morning when it's time to feed him, she's going to be upset." LaShaun had an irrational urge to go look for their faithful pet.

"Calm down. Irvin Baptiste will bring him home as soon as possible. No, he wasn't injured." Chase grabbed LaShaun's hand.

"What then?"

"The woman died. If a dog causes injury, and especially ones that are fatal, Animal Control has to quarantine them. It's the law," Chase added quickly when LaShaun shivered.

"They can't put him to sleep, Chase. He's a member of our family." LaShaun blinked away tears. "Ellie will be devastated and..."

"Shush and let me finish. The coroner's initial findings are it's unlikely she died from Beau's bites. Maybe she went into shock. She sure didn't bleed out. Those bites weren't deep enough. He didn't go for her throat either."

"Then why did they lock him up?" LaShaun swiped tears from her face, but still wasn't consoled.

"I said initial findings. Tomorrow she'll do a full postmortem. The woman's family got in touch. They want to bring her home soon. She's Jewish, and their tradition is to have a funeral within twenty-four hours of death. Forty-eight at most. They've made arrangements with Wilbert's Funeral Home to take the body to the airport. Naturally, we want to cooperate. Dr. Amory will complete the exam quick."

"She's from out of state?"

"She lived in New Orleans for the past two years, but her family is in Missouri. She has a history of mental issues. They reported her missing about three weeks ago. Seems she stopped taking her meds." Chase pulled the sheets up around LaShaun and gently rubbed her stomach. "She was diagnosed as bipolar years ago. According to her sister."

"But how did y'all find out who she was so fast?"

"Driver's license in her pocket. Though we haven't found her vehicle yet." Chase yawned. Then he lay flat after pushing the pillows down again. "Nothing supernatural. Your TEA friends will be disappointed."

"They took my clothes. And if I know Cee-Cee, who is super-thorough, they're all over the scene." LaShaun stared ahead, deep in concentration.

"Yeah, well, for once we know more than the wizards. Poor woman probably meant no harm. Bet we'll find out she had health issues."

"Irvin Baptiste, related to Mr. Baptiste," LaShaun murmured. She didn't know him, but her psychic sense had kicked in.

"His second son. He's over Animal Control. Followed his dad's footsteps to work with animals. He also is helping his mama and other brother with their business," Chase mumbled. "Now be a good girl like our daughter and go to sleep."

"Yeah." LaShaun barely registered his last words.

She resisted pointing out having another Baptiste involved was an odd coincidence. Better to let Chase drift off to sleep undisturbed. LaShaun lay still for twenty minutes. Then she eased out of bed. First, she checked on Ellie, who tossed a couple of times. It was if she sensed her mother nearby. Exhaustion won, because Ellie didn't wake. Then LaShaun went to family room. Her laptop sat on a side table. Legs crossed yoga style, she perched on the sofa and logged onto TEA's secure message app. She wasn't surprised that Cee-Cee immediately answered.

Chapter 14

"Hump day," Chase announced to no one in particular. He drank from his glass of orange juice and let out a big sigh. "Not that the weekend means I'll be off fishing."

"Too cold to fish anyway," LaShaun replied. She fidgeted with a napkin. "Let me help. Being treated like an invalid sucks."

Chase put his glass in the dishwasher and closed it. He said nothing while he pushed buttons to start it. Then he wiped the counters. "We dodged a bullet putting Ellie off about Beau this morning. I let her sleep late on purpose. Rushed her through getting ready for school."

"He'll be okay, right? There's no reason for him to stay locked up in doggie jail." LaShaun pushed down irritation with the world. She wanted to be doing something. And she wanted their dog home now.

"Irvin is taking good care of Beau. His father gave him to you, after all. I'm guessing he knows Beau isn't like other dogs."

Chase bustled about the kitchen. He straightened chairs at the breakfast table. Then he wiped the inside of the microwave oven. LaShaun watched him, knowing his mind churned even as he did the mundane. So did hers, except she didn't have the distraction of busywork. He left, and moments later she heard the hum of the washing machine. When he came back, Chase had a basket of clean laundry. She followed him into the family room.

"Tell me what you found out last night." Chase glanced at her sideways for a second and started folding.

"I tried not to wake you." LaShaun sat on the sofa with him and helped.

"You didn't, but I know you. So, what did Cee-Cee or Jonah say is going on?" Chase sat back because LaShaun had taken over the folding duties. He studied her as she stacked Ellie's tiny undershirts into a pile.

"The woman is a TEA member, but she dropped off the radar suddenly a few weeks ago. Her family contacted TEA to help find her. She's an avid supporter of the spiritual faction. She became one of those who joined the radical fringe. TEA is going to do their own autopsy. Her husband gave consent." LaShaun finished with the clothes and towels. Then she crossed her arms. "All so strange."

Chase gave a sharp laugh. "Gee, I hadn't noticed. I guess Irvin Baptiste is a TEA member, huh?"

"Not sure." LaShaun gaze off at nothing as her mind turned over the puzzle of events. "Manny figures in this whole thing somehow. He's still convinced he didn't kill anyone. I think he's desperate to prove he's not like his father or brother."

"I can see how living with Orin Young would screw up anybody's mind. But it's no excuse for murder, especially not the way those poor women died." Chase grimaced. "I can't scrub images of those crime photos out of my brain."

"I agree. It's just..." LaShaun shook her head. "I know there are those who choose evil. I'm not sure Manny is one of them."

"Whether the devil made him do it, he enjoys killing, or he's nuts, doesn't matter," Chase said. "Folks who kill have to be stopped. Not my job to play head doctor or priest. The result is the same, and the world needs to be protected."

"Spoken like a true officer of the law," LaShaun replied. "But understanding why helps you catch criminals."

"I agree. We caught Manny. The system put him away. That's how it's supposed to work." Chase frowned.

"The system did work, honey. What if his father only let Manny believe he killed those women? Orin's DNA was also on at least one victim, possibly two." LaShaun looked at Chase.

Chase sat quiet for a few moments. Then he stood, put the folded laundry into the basket, and headed down the hallway. "C'mon, let's stop talking shop and get ready for the doctor. Maybe if we get there early, they'll take us in."

"Okay." LaShaun followed him.

They got to the doctor's office a good thirty minutes before LaShaun's appointment. News had spread, because the nurse and other patients eyed them with frank curiosity. Three other women, all in various stages of looking very pregnant, sat in the waiting area. They didn't seem to mind that LaShaun was ushered through moments after checking in. Once in the exam room, Chase helped LaShaun undress. Dr. Hollensworth, a blond woman in her mid-thirties, joined them. Her examination complete, she sent LaShaun down the hall to get a sonogram. Chase let out a long, loud sigh when Dr. Hollensworth announced that all looked normal.

"Fetal development is on schedule, and the placenta is intact. You might want to avoid more action-adventures though," Dr. Hollensworth said, both blond eyebrows raised as she gazed at LaShaun.

"I certainly didn't go out looking for this one," LaShaun muttered as she struggled to sit and get off the exam bed.

"Keep up with the prenatal vitamins. No eye of newt or tongue of frog," the doctor quipped. She giggled at her own joke. Her nurse's eyes went wide. "It's a joke, Melissa. Mrs. Broussard is like any normal expectant mother. I had no idea when I moved here from Colorado folks would take this stuff so seriously."

"I'll be back with the paperwork," the nurse replied with a weak smile and left.

A second nurse appeared to lead them back to the exam room. After she got dressed, Chase and LaShaun met with the doctor in her office. Twenty minutes later they were driving home. Chase's cell phone rang. He used the Bluetooth to answer hands free. M.J.'s voice came from the truck's speakers.

"How's my girl doing?" M.J. said.

"I'm good. My baby's a fighter, too," LaShaun replied before Chase could.

"I don't doubt it. Dr. Amory is sure Beau didn't kill this woman. The pathology reports on what did will take time though. She didn't bleed a lot, but there's some abnormalities with her internal organs. No disease or anything, at least the doc doesn't think so." M.J.'s bewilderment came through in her tone. "Maybe it's just a weird coincidence a disturbed woman crossed paths with LaShaun."

"Right." Chase shot a side-eye at LaShaun before looking at the road ahead again.

"Do I want to know? Scratch that, do I *need* to know at this point?" M.J. said.

"See if any of the forensics from Mathieu Baptiste match back to our new dead visitor," Chase said.

"Will do, and the first victim found. I knew this week would go downhill." M.J. ended the call.

"We're thinking the same thing," LaShaun said after a time. I—" Her cell phone played a Solange tune as a ringtone.

"Speaker," Chase said promptly.

LaShaun sighed. "Chase..."

"Fair is fair. You listened to my call with M.J.," he shot back.

◉

"True." LaShaun accepted the call. "Hey, Jonah. What's up?"

"Hello Jonah, and how are you this fine day?" Chase said.

"Now that I know LaShaun and baby Broussard are okay I'm good. I told Cee-Cee," Jonah replied in a cheerful tone.

"How do you—" Chase huffed out. "I don't know why I bother to ask."

LaShaun patted Chase's shoulder. "Nothing magical. I texted him, my aunt, and Azalei while I waited for you to get the truck. They were all so worried."

"Hey listen, things have gone from kinda strange to mind-blowing. Garland Esnard is in Lafayette. He's a member of the Central Canadian Regional Council. He's been shadowing Manny," Jonah said.

"I knew Manny was up to more than he let on." LaShaun tapped a fist on one thigh. The gesture would have to satisfy her need to punch something.

"I wouldn't have recognized him. Don't know the dude. But I remembered him from the video call the other day. Haven't had a chance to tell Cee-Cee." Jonah let out a long, dramatic sigh.

"Okay, Jonah. What have you done this time?" LaShaun detected something in his tone.

"I kinda didn't follow orders."

Chase let out a snort. "Wow, I'm shocked."

"I was supposed to be on a plane back to the regional headquarters in Dallas, but..." Jonah cleared his throat. "I stayed to make sure Ellie was okay and no other Legion members tried getting to her."

"Or nutty TEA folks," Chase mumbled. He shrugged when LaShaun shot a hot side-eye his way. Then, louder, he said, "We got keeping Ellie safe covered. So don't blame us when your butt hits hot water."

"No offense, but the kind of backup I provide is way different. Besides, it's not that I think they could hurt or kidnap Ellie. I just don't want them planting ideas in her tiny, powerful head. Trust me, I know how it works."

"Bull. Our little girl wouldn't choose the dark side," Chase said promptly. "Now confess, you stayed because you met a woman."

"This has nothing to do with Brianna," Jonah said. "Damn it."

"I'm gonna get recruited into Hogwarts at this rate. I've been on target figuring you wizards out," Chase quipped.

"Don't mind him, Jonah. You know the old saying, it's better to ask for forgiveness than permission." LaShaun shifted her attention back to the subject of Manny. "I think your disobedience led to a vital clue."

"Let's hope Cee-Cee and the other bosses think so. Anyway, Esnard seems to have dropped out of sight. No surprise. Almost like the guy can shapeshift."

"Oh please." Chase looked at LaShaun. "I mean, you don't' really think—"

"Or maybe he's able to interfere with people's perception of what they're seeing. Native peoples have a long tradition about those who can change shape."

◉

"I'm going to find out more about this guy. I can't hang around, though. My pal says they're asking when I'm gonna report in. He's been covering for me." Jonah didn't say good-bye or hang up. Silence stretched as LaShaun stared down at her phone.

"LaShaun is going to rest, Jonah. Don't even think about asking her to do legwork for you," Chase said.

"No, but *you* could talk to Manny. I mean, you guys had him in your sights for a minute for these two murders. Right?"

"Let me get this straight. Now you want to recruit me to... Oh, hell no. I've got three dead people, no answers, and a job to do. You think I'm some rent-a-cop? No." Chase wheeled the truck onto their driveway off Rougon Road.

LaShaun looked at him. "Makes a lot of sense, though. I mean, we're still not sure Mr. Baptiste's murder isn't connected to TEA, and the other murder victim."

"Newton Cross, aka Devin Kelly," Jonah added.

Chase's jaw tightened as he parked under the carport. He tapped the steering wheel for a few seconds. "Repeat that."

"I was going to tell you, but with everything going on..." LaShaun's voice died away under his withering gaze.

"I'll let you explain, LaShaun. Bye," Jonah said, his voice muted. A soft beep signaled he'd ended the call.

"Um, bye," LaShaun said to the empty connection.

"Well?" Chase gave her an expectant "can't-wait-to-hear-this-one" look.

"All these pregnancy hormones, taking care of Ellie... We got distracted by a half dozen developments. Devil's Swamp, mining, Manny, and well." LaShaun realized she was babbling and stopped.

"Uh-huh."

"Devin Kelly was tracking a Legion drug ring. You said yourself, there's nothing that connected him to Mathieu Baptiste. Cee-Cee didn't find anything connecting them either. No phone calls, emails, texts. Nothing."

"Uh-huh." Chase continued to study her.

"I know what you're thinking, but we're not dragging our problems onto *your* turf. See, there's this battle for control within TEA about the direction the entire organization should go in." LaShaun pressed her lips together when he raised a palm like a traffic cop.

"Does Cee-Cee, Jonah, or anybody at TEA have information on who might have killed these two men?"

LaShaun swallowed hard. She knew Chase's dead-calm tone was deceptive. She slipped her phone back into her leather bag. "Honey, we'd never conceal the identity of the killer or even a suspect from law enforcement."

"I thought we'd agreed you'd maybe freelance on select cases, but not let them recruit you."

"I meant 'we' as in members of TEA. We all have a moral obligation to help protect the world. And I figured Cee-Cee would tell you about Cross. Sorry." LaShaun rubbed his arm as if to soothe him.

"When she decided it suited her needs, or rather TEA's." Chase heaved a sigh and took the keys from the ignition. "You're going to put your feet up. No, argument. I'm working from home today since it's mostly reports. I'll meet Ellie at the bus and fix her snack. Make sure she does any school assignments. My father is bringing us dinner."

"That's so sweet of Papa Broussard." LaShaun smiled at the image of her father-in-law cooking. No doubt he wore his favorite apron.

Chase came around to the passenger side and helped LaShaun down from the truck. "Take it slow. Yeah, I know what the doctor said."

"Being pampered feels nice." LaShaun patted his cheek. When he lifted an eyebrow at her, she hugged one muscular arm. "Don't be mad at me. Or Jonah."

"Okay. I'll accept TEA wasn't deliberately withholding vital information in my murder investigation. *This time*." Chase held up a forefinger at her.

"Yes, sir." LaShaun gave a crisp salute, which made him roll his eyes.

They went inside and, true to his word, Chase insisted that LaShaun do nothing. He ordered her to take a short nap on the sofa. With a glass of pineapple juice, her phone, and the television remote within LaShaun's reach, Chase was satisfied.

"Just drift off and forget about everything for a while. Ellie's at school. Dinner is taken care of, and I'm close. By the way, Irvin's son will bring Beau home today. M.J. called to let them know he's cleared of that woman's death."

"They don't have to go to any trouble. I could pick Beau up. Dr. Hollensworth didn't say I can't drive. It's not that far." LaShaun lifted her chin.

"Irvin's sixteen-year-old is thrilled for any excuse to drive, just got his license," Chase countered.

"He shouldn't miss school because of us."

"He takes courses half a day and works with his father the other half." Chase's mouth quirked in a sly smile. "You can stop worrying about the young man's education. You're not to leave this house for the rest of the day."

"I wasn't trying to... Fine. You're right anyway. I should give the baby a peaceful afternoon." LaShaun sighed and arranged the throw Chase had placed on her lap. She relaxed against the soft sofa back.

"Uh-huh." Chase gave a grunt of skepticism and walked off. "I'll check on you in a bit."

"Okay." LaShaun craned her neck to follow his progress down the hallway. He was headed for the study. Once there, he'd had to connect with the office and make calls. LaShaun went to the kitchen island and opened her laptop. Cee-Cee answered her message fast, which meant she was waiting to hear from her.

****

The next day dawned cold and windy, yet the sun was out. Ellie went off to school happy because Beau was home. He walked her to the bus stop as Chase watched from their front porch. He returned to the kitchen to find LaShaun had cleared the table and was sweeping up crumbs.

"Don't say it. I'm fully capable and feeling energized," LaShaun said before he could comment.

"Okay." Chase gave Beau's head an affectionate pat, which elicited a soft woof of appreciation.

LaShaun put the broom back in the walk-in pantry. Then she faced him, arms crossed. "Well?"

Chase leaned against the counter and took out his work cell phone. "Well what?"

LaShaun walked past him and poured herself a cup of peppermint herbal tea. Her grandmother's recipe had been handed down from her great-grandmother. "I'm waiting for the lecture to take it easy, forget about TEA, etc. etc."

"Morning sickness today, huh?" was all Chase said. He didn't look up from his phone. "Anything in your family journals about pregnant psychics?"

"How amusing, Mr. Broussard," LaShaun retorted. "There's some kind of funny business going on at Devil's Swamp, Chase."

"Unless you mean criminal activity, I can't do a thing." Chase tapped the phone's screen for a few minutes. Then he sighed and turned his attention back to LaShaun.

She smiled at him. "You want to hear the wizardry details. Admit it."

"Just don't expect me to take action or mention anything to M.J. or, God forbid, Dave," Chase said.

Dave Godchaux, the sheriff, had a firm "Don't ask, don't tell" policy when it came to LaShaun and the supernatural. He most cared about protecting the innocent, solving cases, and getting re-elected. In that order, to his credit. LaShaun knew he was a true friend. But she also knew not to test that friendship when it came to official investigations.

"Rules established, and no. It's not anything you can investigate. I think the real struggle is to control the production of monazite. If either side of the two battling factions can harness its use, they'll get the upper hand."

"The magic dirt that can create psychic superheroes," Chase said.

LaShaun glanced at him sharply, but he wore an impassive expression. "Or villains."

Chase stood straight and grimaced. "Oh. Shit."

"Exactly. The equivalent of giving a weapon of mass destruction to a power-mad dictator. Except multiply it by however many people use monazite to enhance their powers."

LaShaun stopped when a bell trilled on her laptop, the tone that signaled an incoming TEA message. She read it and looked at Beau. The dog's ears went up and he lifted his head.

"Irvin didn't mention anything about Beau acting strange to you, did he?" LaShaun walked over to stroke Beau's back.

"He was restless, on edge. But nothing unusual since he was in a strange place. He tried to get out, probably to get home. Why?"

"Beau bit that woman more than a few times. Jonah says preliminary TEA tests of her tissues and blood show high levels of Cytokines." LaShaun went to her laptop and looked at the message again.

"I see." Chase grunted. "I have no clue what that means."

"Her body developed some kind of immune response, like a germ or virus had invaded her body. Except, not exactly. Anyway, the pathologists are intrigued. And there were other unusual findings."

"She'd been smoking weed, according to the coroner. Could have been mixed with anything. They're still testing." Chase glanced at Beau. "Shouldn't bother our boy though."

"Hmmm." LaShaun tapped the keyboard and sent a reply. Another message popped up seconds later as Cee-Cee joined the conversation.

"I gotta go. The woman's brother and sister are coming. They're going to meet the hearse that'll take the body to the airport." Chase crossed to their mudroom to get his on-duty equipment.

"Okay," LaShaun said, still typing away.

Chase came back dressed in his favorite suede jacket. The Stetson hat he wore and leather boots completed his Cajun cowboy look. The department-issued pistol in the holster on his belt sealed it.

LaShaun looked up at him. "You look good enough to eat, Lieutenant Broussard. Let's get married and have babies."

"That sure as hell wasn't what you said when we first met. I thought you was gonna call me a racist hick cop," Chase joked.

"And you thought I was a crazy voodoo priestess and maybe a murderer. Now look at us." LaShaun crossed to him and kissed the end of his nose.

Chase pulled her into a firm embrace. "Should I even try to talk you into staying home and away from your TEA best pals?"

"I'm open to negotiations if it means you lose all the work tools and those pants." LaShaun winked up at him.

"Girl, stop trying to interfere with an officer doing his duty and answer the question."

"I'm just gonna meet with Cee-Cee and talk, bat around theories, leads for *them* to follow. Then I'll be home in time to meet Ellie at the bus stop. I swear on the graves of my ancestors." LaShaun held up a palm.

"Are any of them still in there though?" Chase laughed as he ducked a swipe aimed at his head.

"I promise, no chasing bad guys. No matter how bad I want to take another look at the mining—"

"LaShaun." Chase tensed and scowled at her.

"No trips to Devil's Swamp," she said, wincing at the severe look he gave her.

****

LaShaun kept her promise. She did meet with Cee-Cee at the local Holiday Inn Express. Cee-Cee sat cross-legged on the king-sized bed with reports spread around her. LaShaun was on the edge of her seat literally, waiting for an update. Her friend studied the papers, moving them around as if shuffling cards in a deck. Cee-Cee frowned and clicked her tongue a few times.

LaShaun rocked forward in the chair. She had waited with something less than patience at the desk across from the bed. "Questions are gonna spill out of my guts all over the floor in a second."

"Oh dios mío, such drama. Must be the hormones," Cee-Cee mumbled and gave LaShaun a look.

"I wish being pregnant gave me the power to pull answers outta you," LaShaun retorted.

"And irritable, too. Definitely the hormones. Both my sisters got like that when they were pregnant. Okay, okay. Don't hit me." Cee-Cee pretended to shield her head with both hands.

"Talk and you'll be safe," LaShaun shot back.

Cee-Cee's smooth, lightly tanned face became serious. "First up, Allison Hargrove. The dead woman," she added before LaShaun could ask.

When Cee-Cee heaved a sigh, LaShaun forced herself to wait a few seconds before she blurted out a prompt. "Allison Hargrove is who?"

"A member of TEA. She was with the commercial enterprises division. Business development, to be exact." Cee-Cee looked at LaShaun. "And she's part of the spiritual faction. There's a fringe element on both sides. People who want to take more radical, aggressive action to push their agenda."

"Huh?" LaShaun blinked at her

"The more conservative folks favor compromise and dialog. Then there are those who want a hostile takeover, so to speak. The side that believes in science has the majority on the council. At least for now."

"The High Protectorate Council, you mean. They meet annually in Helsinki," LaShaun said, eager to keep her talking.

"Yeah, though they alternate every two years to a different city. They'll meet in New York in October." Cee-Cee shook her head as if clearing random thoughts. "Anyway, Allison went off even more than the most fanatical in her circle. Her death exposes just how far they're willing to go. We suspect they've been experimenting with monazite."

"Not through approved TEA lab protocols, you mean." LaShaun gasped. "They want to enhance their paranormal abilities to get an edge. And do what, wage war?"

"You know, a few days ago I would have laughed at such a wild idea. But now..." Cee-Cee held up a page and extended it to LaShaun. "Take a look. I printed this out from the Abbeville Museum."

"The legends of Devil's Swamp. Stories have been told for well over three hundred years, including by the Atakapa tribe. They say those with mystical powers would go to the swamp to connect with the great spirit," LaShaun read out loud and then looked at Cee-Cee. "You think they ingested monazite as part of some ceremony or ritual."

"The librarian said I'm not the first person to take an interest in Devil's Swamp history. The place isn't exactly well known outside this area. She assumed interest is connected to the mining." Cee-Cee stretched her legs and stood to work out the kinks.

"You recognized any names on materials checked out?" LaShaun grabbed more papers and read.

"Most of those books don't circulate, too rare. She did let me make these copies, the same as the other people. So, no names. But." Cee-Cee wore a fierce smile of satisfaction.

LaShaun looked up when she didn't continue. "You're onto something."

"Mr. Bernard, a historical society member who volunteers at the museum, got suspicious of some visitors. He set up a camera for security purposes. He stopped a woman trying to steal an artifact and a document." Cee-Cee grabbed her tablet computer from the bed. After a few swipes and taps, she held up the screen to LaShaun. "And he took a liking to me and showed me this."

"Allison Hargrove." LaShaun jumped to her feet and snatched the tablet from Cee-Cee. "What the hell?"

"I'm probably not supposed to share this with you, but—" Cee-Cee crossed to take the tablet back again. She swiped through to another set of photos. "You recognize this guy?"

"Not really." LaShaun peered closer at the gray-scale images of a man with dark hair, lighter at the temples. His features tickled at something buried inside her head.

"Garland Esnard, all the way from Central Canada. Quebec City to be exact." Cee-Cee tapped one photo of him standing behind Allison Hargrove.

"Yeah, Jonah told me about him." LaShaun stared at him hard. "He was on the video call. He's part of the spiritual fringe?"

"No, that's what's so confusing. Esnard hasn't been a figure on either side, much less the extreme groups. At least we didn't think so until now." Cee-Cee frowned at the photos as she swiped through more screens.

"He's shadowing Manny for some reason. Why?" LaShaun didn't like all the unanswered questions swirling around them.

"I sure as hell intend to find out, big wheel or not. Counselor Esnard has some explaining to do. He's what my old boss back at the Austin office calls a wild card. Threw headquarters for a loop, I can tell you."

"He knows you and Jonah are in the area. A local TEA member wouldn't know who he is, but... I don't get it." LaShaun squinted at the tablet as if the answer would float from it.

"His profile says he's a descendant of Acadians. Maybe he figured to get in and out without detection. But if asked, he could come up with a plausible reason for being here." Cee-Cee grimaced. "Nah, that sounds thin. And from what I know of the guy, he's smart. Like super-smart."

"Not if he's been to Louisiana before. A stretch, but it would do in a pinch." LaShaun shrugged.

"Which means coming was worth the risk," Cee-Cee replied.

"Or monazite is so important, it's worth the risk," LaShaun said. "Which has what to do with Manny?"

"No clue. Esnard isn't part of the TEA commercial enterprises division. Although everyone is interested in the stuff."

"But he was here with Allison."

Cee-Cee shook her head. "The same time as Allison, but they weren't *together*. We can't find any indication they knew each other."

LaShaun watched as Cee-Cee switched from still photos to video footage. They watched the twenty-second clip in silence. Both sat on the edge of the bed thinking for a time once it ended. Then LaShaun stood.

"Manny is the link. He's more likely to talk to me alone."

"Girl, your husband is going to be pissed."

"One last conversation, and I'm going to leave the rest to you and Jonah," LaShaun said with a grin.

"Uh-huh."

LaShaun laughed as she headed for the door. "Why doesn't anyone believe I can stay out of the action?"

Chapter 15

An hour later LaShaun sat in the office of the program responsible for Manny's supervision. The forensic outpatient program was in reality both mental health treatment and monitoring. Khalid Bell, the social worker, also functioned as almost a second parole officer. He could trigger the process to send Manny back to secure custody. Not only did Manny have to comply with conditions of his parole, Department of Corrections rules, but he also had to follow through on treatment. The lanky young man led LaShaun to his office. He was dressed in business casual style. He had the smooth, light-brown skin of a Creole. He smiled, and his hazel eyes lit up. On the surface he appeared to be a fresh-faced recent college grad. Yet beneath the striped cotton shirt and tan slacks, LaShaun noted the rock-solid muscles. He was older and tougher than he looked.

"Thanks for letting me come on short notice," LaShaun said as they shook hands.

"Just so happened my schedule opened at the last minute. I was going to a court hearing, but it was canceled. The guy went back inside. Too risky."

LaShaun froze. "You mean..."

"Oh, no, not Manny. Someone else." Bell gestured an invitation for her to sit. He followed suit and looked at her with curiosity. "But I'd probably have made time for you anyway. Manny is a special case. I've never had a client like him."

LaShaun glanced around the office. Bell's college degrees and other credentials hung in frames on the wall. "I'm surprised you haven't recommended he get sent back, too. I mean, with a nickname like the Blood River Ripper."

"Public scrutiny is still intense even after a year of him being out. And he's odd, to say the least. But so far, he's played by the rules. I don't have any reason to recommend to the court that he be locked up again," Bell said.

LaShaun studied Bell's frown of dissatisfaction. "Why is that a problem? The local citizens should be relieved."

"They haven't forgotten the details of his crimes. The talk about him having supernatural powers don't help. Not to mention the media fascination with his every move. I've had to throw out that 'Ghost Team USA' character three times. He finally stopped showing up."

"Stay awake. Once James Schaffer smells a big ratings story, he's going to low-key stalk you. Ask me how I know," LaShaun said with a scowl.

"Yeah, but I have handcuffs."

LaShaun stared back at him and then burst out laughing. "A clear advantage I don't have."

Bell laughed with her. "Seriously, though, this building is Department of Corrections property. I could report him to the state police for remaining on the premises without authorization."

"Don't count on him going too far. Stories about Manny helped make Schaffer a ghost-hunting reality TV star."

"Yeah, and reporting on you," Bell said.

"Hmmm." LaShaun grimaced.

"You visited Manny multiple times at the Feliciana Forensic Hospital."

"Twice, and we're not best buds."

"He trusts you, though. I can tell he thinks you're the only person on his side. Beside his aunt and sister. They help him but keep their distance." Bell glanced at the digital clock on his desk. "And he's running late."

"Just five minutes," LaShaun replied with a glance at the clock as well.

Bell stood at knocking on the office door. "He'll bend a rule until it looks like a pretzel."

"You don't have to tell me, dude," LaShaun muttered.

Manny wore a wide grin when Bell swung the door open. "Morning, Khalid. Hey, LaShaun. Traffic is a killer, but I'm not too late. Bet she got here early so y'all could talk about me."

"Morning, Manny. Come in and sit. Can I offer y'all something?" Bell started to leave but stopped when Manny shook his head.

"Nah, man. Thanks, but let's get right to business. Why am I here?" Manny looked relaxed despite his point-blank question. He slumped into the second chair facing Bell's desk.

"Mrs. Broussard had quite a drive to visit you, Manny." Bell's measured tone seemed to imply a warning.

Manny held up both palms. "Pardon me for being so direct. Y'all wanna chat about the weather and sip tea first, fine by me."

LaShaun glanced from Bell to Manny and back again. She picked up on the undercurrent of tension. Bell, for all his mild-mannered demeanor, was an instrument of institutional authority. The need to maintain a certain balance was an unspoken rule between convicts and guards.

"Chill, y'all. It's all good," LaShaun said.

Bell's handsome, youthful face eased into a smile. "Mrs. Broussard wanted to ask you some questions and get input from me."

"My life is an open book," Manny said. He swept out both arms in a dramatic gesture.

LaShaun grunted a laugh at the guileless expression he affected. "Sure it is. Has anyone other than Cee-Cee and Jonah been in touch? Ms. Cuevas and her partner, Jonah Parker," she added when Bell looked puzzled.

"Right, the people who work at the clinic in Dallas. Manny's parole officer got clearance for them to visit." Bell nodded and glanced at Manny.

"Yeah, Dallas," LaShaun said with care, avoiding an outright lie. When Manny flashed a smirk, she hoped Bell didn't notice.

"The usual couple of reporters I had to blow off. That TV guy is a pain." Manny made a sour face.

"Schaffer?" LaShaun felt a flash of anger. The man was like a gnat, always buzzing her head.

"Yeah, him. Like I need more publicity to put an even bigger target on my back," Manny retorted.

"What about any other representatives from... Dallas." LaShaun stammered with a side look at the social worker.

"Nope." Manny gave a shrug but didn't meet LaShaun's gaze. He stood. "If that's all then I'll go back to enjoying my day off. Gotta work the zoo this weekend. I'm damn lucky they didn't fire me. No thanks to your husband dragging me in for questioning."

Bell looked at LaShaun. "Well?"

"That's it then. Thanks. I won't take up any more of your time, Mr. Bell." LaShaun stood. "Say, Manny, let's get some coffee and those donuts you love so much. My treat. We can talk about your case."

"My case?" Manny glanced at his social worker and then at LaShaun.

"Sorry, I..." LaShaun cleared her throat.

"Manny told me he asked you to investigate and possibly clear his name," Bell spoke up.

"Yeah, well I'm over it. I figure after all these years there's nothing to find." Manny waved a hand.

He nodded to the social worker and walked out of the office. "See ya later, K."

"Good-bye, Mr. Bell. Manny, wait up." LaShaun strode fast to catch up to him. He had reached the lobby and had pushed open the glass door by the time she did. "Slow the hell down."

"Wow, what a beautiful day. Can you believe Mardi Gras is next week? February twenty-fifth. Came early this year, huh?"

"Manny," LaShaun snapped.

"I'll miss the crowds. Easy to get lost in 'em, not feel like I'm being watched all the time." Manny walked to his truck.

LaShaun reached him and grabbed his arm. When she tugged on it, he faced her. "You came to me all fired up to prove your innocence. Now all of a sudden, you've lost interest like it's no biggie. What the hell is going on with you?"

"Look, anything you find out won't matter. I'll always be a psycho serial killer to the world. I'm the boogey man, the bad guy they need me to be." Manny scowled as he put on aviator sunglasses.

"The truth always matters. I thought it mattered very much to *you*," LaShaun said. "At least about whether or not you're a vicious killer who has no control."

"But I do have control. Over my life, at least some even on parole. A lot more than when I was locked up. You think the powers that be want me digging up skeletons?" Manny shook his head.

"Did the district attorney or someone in law enforcement warn you off?" LaShaun glanced around, suddenly conscious they were quite exposed. All she needed was a photo of her talking to Manny on a news website.

"Ain't no reporters around. I checked. Your TEA pals might be, though. They block me from picking up on their vibes." Manny took his keys out and jangled them. "I gotta go. You take care of yourself. Make sure that new baby gets here healthy."

LaShaun forgot about who might be watching. She walked up close to Manny and peered at his face. At five feet eleven inches, he wasn't that much above her five feet seven inches. She still had to tilt her head up to look at him. Her intense expression was reflected back in the mirror-like lens of his sunglasses.

"If someone has threatened you let us help," LaShaun said low. She took a quick look around as she talked.

"LaShaun, leave it alone," Manny said. He unlocked the truck door.

"So, going into the history books as the Blood River Ripper is okay with you?" LaShaun crossed her arms.

"I'm gonna piece together what I can of my life. Plenty more sensational murders will happen. Eventually, folks will lose interest in me. I'll finish my time and maybe relocate." Manny put on a crooked smile. "You know, while I still got youthful good looks and charm going for me."

"I don't buy the act, Manny. You're making me want to investigate even if you fire me," LaShaun said. She gave him an equally phony smile.

Manny's amused façade slipped a notch as his lips pulled down. "Forget everything I said about investigating those murders. Better for us both if you do."

"But Manny I—"

"Thanks for the offer of coffee, but I got a hot date. That cute waitress is meeting me for lunch at the Crawfish Café. See what I mean? Normal life for me."

"Does she know who you are though?" LaShaun said in a gentle tone.

Manny paused in the act of climbing into the truck. "Your concern for my feelings is touching. Yeah, I told her right off, and that evidence threw doubt on my conviction. She's willing to believe in me."

"She's a special woman then," LaShaun said.

"When I'm with her, I don't feel like trash." Manny got into the truck and shut the door. "But I thank you for all you done so far."

"I haven't done much. But listen—"

"You did a lot more for me than anyone has in a long, long time."

LaShaun shaded her eyes from the sun. "Manny, at least let's talk a minute. You've got time before your lunch date. It's only ten thirty."

"Don't you worry, the check's in the mail as they say."

Manny flashed a smile as he turned the ignition. The engine rumbled loudly. He waved good-bye, waited for LaShaun to step away, and then backed out of the parking space. She watched in frustration as his taillights disappeared. A voice over her shoulder made LaShaun jump.

"Everything okay, really?" Khalid Bell gazed at Manny's truck as it turned onto the street. Then he looked at LaShaun.

"Yeah, sure," LaShaun said with a nod.

"Seems odd Manny not wanting you to investigate. His father was a nasty piece of work. Sounds like looking into what that guy did would be promising." Bell raised a dark eyebrow at LaShaun. "I'm also a trained investigator, do a bit of private detective work as a sideline. Mostly employment background checks. Nothing that conflicts with my work."

"He's worried I'll turn over more bad family history. He could be right." LaShaun shrugged and put on her own sunglasses. "Can't say I blame him."

"Hmm, I gotcha. Saying the Young family was dysfunctional is an understatement." Bell looked down the street Manny had driven, even though the truck was gone.

"Yeah," was LaShaun's only reply. The social worker didn't know the half of Manny's strange story.

****

"Thanks for meeting me at home. I'm trying to remember I'm pregnant and to be home in time to get Ellie off the bus." LaShaun spoke over her shoulder. She moved around the kitchen doing routine chores.

Jonah grunted. "How can you forget you're incubating a whole new human being in there?"

"I don't feel too tired yet, and the morning sickness is almost gone. But you're right. I have to wear my big clothes left over from when I was pregnant with Ellie." LaShaun tugged out the sides of her shirt. She wore the oversized top over black leggings.

"You're hardly showing. My pal Shelly back at the Austin TEA office got huge. Amazing that a tiny baby came out. I thought she was having the Incredible Hulk." Jonah stuffed a few red grapes in his mouth.

"I hope you didn't make that crack to her. We're emotional, you know. A pregnant lady will cut you," LaShaun quipped and waved the knife she was using to slice vegetables.

"Don't I know it. Shelly's partner said she cussed him out when those labor pains kicked in. Even slapped him." Jonah laughed again. "After-school snacks. Brings back fond memories of our housekeeper Maria. I saw more of her than my parents, and got more affection. But you didn't call me over here for a play date with my baby sis."

"No, this is business. Hold on while I get this in the oven."

LaShaun put sliced onions, celery, and green bell peppers in a shallow baking dish. Then she rubbed olive oil on the chicken parts. Finally, she sprinkled the meat with a blend of salt, black pepper, and cayenne pepper. Once she loaded the dish in the oven, she cleaned her hands and joined him at the kitchen island. The smell of fresh snap beans cooking in a pot filled the air. LaShaun also planned to cook rice later.

Jonah inhaled and let out a sigh. "I got time since Cee-Cee is at the New Orleans office."

"Of course you can stay for dinner," LaShaun said, taking the less-than-subtle hint.

He grinned. "Cool. So, what's up?"

LaShaun grew serious. "Manny says Esnard hasn't contacted him."

Jonah matched her change of mood, a solemn expression on his youthful face. "And you don't believe him?"

"No. Well, yes." LaShaun shook her head to clear it.

"Hmm, okay." Jonah went to the sink and rinsed his hands. He came back drying them using a paper towel. "Let's tune in."

"He's got power psi powers to block us," LaShaun replied.

"He can't stop energy from all other sources at once."

Jonah took both LaShaun's hands into his. She stood and faced him. Ten minutes went by. LaShaun focused on the sounds of bubbling from the pot. She listened to the soft tick-tick from a decorative antique clock on the wall. Images floated through her mind, but a gentle pressure from outside nudged her. Jonah urged her not to strain, just to let her sixth sense flow. His ability paired with hers in compatibility, clearing away psychic tension. She let out a long exhale and opened her eyes. Jonah, eyes already wide, gazed back at her.

"That's a high-risk move," he said.

"You've guessed what I plan to do," LaShaun replied. She didn't need to make it a question.

"Felt it, like a splash of warm water. Not telepathy." Jonah tilted his head to one side. "Cee-Cee has to know. She's the lead on this field op."

"She won't object." LaShaun pulled free of his grasp.

"You'd do it anyway. I should go with you." Jonah wore a frown of concern. When Beau trotted up and nuzzled LaShaun's hip, Jonah nodded. "Beau senses trouble, too."

LaShaun ran a hand down Beau's back and patted his flank. "You already know I have to go alone."

"Not tonight though, LaShaun. Tomorrow morning."

"Sure. Chase will feel better about it, but it won't make a difference." LaShaun shrugged when Jonah flinched. They both understood the stories about magic and midnight were myths. Those with especially strong psi abilities weren't limited by time of day.

Jonah glanced at his smartwatch. "Then we'll take precautions. Let's get started. We've got just over an hour before Ellie's home."

They worked in tandem to set up natural and supernatural backup should LaShaun need it. Jonah never left home without an array of gadgets. LaShaun had her own ideas about Plan B, including her derringer. Jonah pressed her to take a second smartwatch. Pressing a button deployed small darts that delivered an electric shock. The charge would disrupt the electromagnetic field generated by the neural activity of a powerful psychic.

"And this, in case you need extra power." Jonah pressed a TEA-modified stun gun into her hands.

"Fine." LaShaun relented and took the tools to her bedroom. She put them in the safe concealed in their walk-in closet. She returned to the kitchen to find Jonah sliding the dish back into the oven.

"Timer went off, so it was time to baste." He put the large spoon back into its cradle. "Ready to make the cornbread?"

"In a bit. When the chicken is about done, I'll do the rice." LaShaun chuckled when he went to the pantry. Jonah came back with canisters of flower and cornmeal. "You're going to make some girl a wonderful husband."

"Please, no horror stories until Halloween." Jonah gave a melodramatic shudder. "I get dizzy just thinking about being tied down."

They joked with ease for another thirty minutes. Jonah beamed when LaShaun let him greet Ellie's bus. He was already outside when the horn blew. Moments later they burst into the kitchen, both laughing with delight at being together. They went to the backyard as though the house couldn't contain their energy. When Chase pulled up an hour later, he joined their kickball game. LaShaun waved to them from the bay window. Later, the back door opened and Chase came in.

"Well, the kids are having a good time," he quipped, nodding to Jonah.

"Yes, they sure are." LaShaun paused in the action of stirring the cornbread batter. She stared out at a smiling, relaxed Jonah. "His parents are multimillionaires, you know."

Chase let out a low whistle. He hopped on a barstool at the kitchen island. "Seriously? Lucky kid."

"When they weren't ignoring him, they mistreated him. He's never told me the details of how bad. Jonah likes to think he's a committed loner, but he'll have a family." LaShaun smiled as she went back to stirring.

"Is that an official vision of his future?" Chase quipped.

"Maybe, but just look at him." LaShaun nodded toward the window.

"He's more complicated than you might think. And don't forget free will." Chase pointed up to the ceiling.

"Le bon Dieu, eh? We'll see." LaShaun smiled.

"I'm a mere mortal so no spoiler alerts. Guess we should call in our three kids," Chase said with a laugh.

They spent an almost normal family evening with dinner, small talk, and lots of joking. The fun moved to the family room once the dishwasher was loaded. Then the world of murder cases and TEA intrigue intruded. It started with a Carlos Santana guitar riff and Everlast singing "Put Your Lights On."

"That's a dark tune," Chase said and spooned more banana pudding into his mouth.

Jonah took out his cell phone and glanced at the screen. His relaxed expression faded by degrees as he read. He looked at LaShaun. "For dark times."

****

The next morning Ellie was about the only one in a good mood. She'd convinced Jonah to spend the night. LaShaun was happy she didn't pick up on the grim thoughts of the adults. Ellie's little girl chatter help lift the clouds until she disappeared onto the school bus. Jonah was first to heave a deep sigh. He faced LaShaun and Chase with a grim, tired expression.

"Did you sleep at all?" LaShaun rubbed his shoulder as they all walked back to the house.

"A couple of hours maybe. Ellie needed me to be here this morning. Otherwise I would have slipped away after she fell asleep." Jonah rubbed his face. He slumped onto a barstool at the kitchen island when they were inside.

"Or you needed to see her," LaShaun said. "When was the last time you spoke to your parents, or any family member?"

"You know we don't have that kind of relationship. They're fine without me. Always have been." Jonah yawned. "I talk to my aunt and uncle-in-law maybe once a month. They're about the only ones who don't think I'm a freak. I'm good."

"Uh-huh." LaShaun put a cup of hot chocolate in front of him. Then she added a dollop of whipped cream on top.

Chase chuckled as he studied them. "You two."

"What?" LaShaun and Jonah said at the same time.

"Nothing. So, another update from Cee-Cee?"

"Forensics has been running tests on tissue and body fluid samples from the dead woman. It's a challenge. They had to pretty much invent protocols on the fly. LaShaun gave us the key though." Jonah nodded to her.

"I thought you got up during the night," Chase said.

"For a little while. My mind was working overtime, too. I figured the woman might have ingested monazite. The side effects haven't been studied in humans."

"You were right. Took them all night, even with TEA's advanced forensic toxicology equipment. A bit of magic helps," Jonah said with a weary grin.

"And?" Chase took out his own buzzing work cell phone.

"I was up all night working with Del and Cee-Cee to track her movements. Bottom line, we think the radical group of spiritualists are doing their own testing. But here's where it gets weird."

"I shouldn't have to say this, but it's already weird," Chase muttered.

"Alison Hargrove stole a vial of monazite. She sent them a message that she took it for the cause. Here's a video of her. She performed some kind of ritual before she swallowed a solution." Jonah showed them on his phone.

"Damn," Chase said, drawing the word out as he watched.

"I'm no psychiatrist, but she sure looks manic to me," LaShaun said.

"She started having vivid visions, talking about the apocalypse, and then she vanished." Jonah sighed. "It gets worse. She wasn't the only one who ingested the solution."

"But she had mental health issues. Like any drug, it just made her even more crazy," Chase said.

"The forensic team is meeting as we speak. Their working theory is monazite has some bad side effects. They're flying in specialists from two countries. They treating it the same way the CDC would treat an outbreak." Jonah gulped his hot chocolate. He licked a bit of whipped cream from his top lip.

"Great. A crowd of crazed wizards roaming around. Please tell me they're not all in Vermilion Parish," Chase said. "How the hell do I explain that to my boss?"

"Don't say anything. It's not like you guys can handle this situation anyway." Jonah grabbed his backpack where it hung on another barstool. "I gotta move. Listen, don't go see Esnard since I can't be backup."

"I agree. M.J. is in court on an old investigation she did a couple of years back. I have to be at the station to interview a person of interest related to the TEA murder victim. Let it go, LaShaun," Chase said in a firm tone.

"Aren't you curious how he knew to follow Alison Hargrove? Esnard came all the way down here from Canada. He's got some kind of involvement."

"Shit, there's so much intrigue going on within TEA these days. I'll bet we got secret investigations going on all over the damn place." Jonah put on his backpack.

"Let Cee-Cee and Jonah sort it out. Then they'll tell you what's going on." Chase kissed the top of LaShaun's head. "Stay home. Bake those chocolate chip and walnut oatmeal cookies we love so much."

Jonah pecked a kiss on LaShaun's cheek. "And save me some. We'll connect the dots on Esnard. Promise. Bye."

LaShaun accepted their coddling without argument. "Sure. Love you both."

Jonah left first. Chase rubbed LaShaun's tummy with a soft smile. He said good-bye to the baby with comical goo-goo noises. Then he was gone, but not before emphasizing that LaShaun wasn't being left out.

"Bye sweetie," LaShaun called as Chase walked down the back steps.

She waved as he turned around his Ram truck and drove away. The picture of the dutiful wife and mother. Then she turned on her heels and went back inside to get dressed. LaShaun had every intention of getting answers from Garland Esnard.

Chapter 16

Garland Esnard looked up from his complimentary hotel breakfast. “Good morning, Mrs. Broussard. I wondered how long it would take.”

LaShaun glanced around the dining room. Most of the other guests had cleared out, probably gone to parades and other tourist attractions. A sparse scattering of people lingered. An elderly couple at the next table gathered up their belongings and left. The hotel employee glanced at Esnard and made a wide circle around him. LaShaun noticed the other tables around him were empty.

“I cleared the area for you.” Esnard leaned forward and lowered his voice to a whisper. “My skill is energy manipulation. Basically, I can repel people. Sometimes objects. Not well understood, but then so much of what we can do is a mystery. I’ll get you a coffee.”

"No thanks," LaShaun said as he started to rise. She sat across from him when he eased back into his chair.

He nodded. As he calmly went on to finish his scrambled eggs, LaShaun studied him. Esnard's brunette hair was mixed with gray. He wore a striped short-sleeved shirt tucked into dark blue jeans. He had a slight paunch, but LaShaun guessed he was lean as a younger man. She also estimated that he was somewhere south of fifty years old. Lines in his face indicated he'd lived hard. He would have been handsome, or close to it. Yet there was something in his gray-green eyes, a hint that he could turn cruel in seconds. His genial façade covered it for most people. LaShaun wasn't most people.

An expensive leather jacket was draped on the back of the chair next to him. With a satisfied sigh, he finished eating the last of his food. Then he sipped coffee while gazing at LaShaun over the rim of the cup. Only the hotel housekeeper remained, picking up cups and trash left behind. Soon she disappeared.

"You have questions." Esnard nodded as if to prompt her.

LaShaun didn't bite. She gazed back at him for a few seconds before she spoke. "You followed Alison Hargrove to Louisiana."

"The unfortunate troubled woman who died recently. Tragic for her family. I get reports like many high-up TEA officials." Esnard nodded again.

"You're not that high up. You're a third-in-command communications officer based in Quebec, but originally from New Jersey. Well, you lived there for almost twenty years," LaShaun said.

"Sixteen. You lived in Los Angeles for almost ten years. Left Beau Chene under a cloud, as they say. You were lucky to dodge a murder charge. Naughty." Esnard tsk-tsked and waved a finger at her, then went on. "Your grandmother had a not-altogether-good reputation. Your mother died when you were young. I could go on."

"Let's not get into a pissing contest on who has the most dirt," LaShaun snapped.

"This is no game, Mrs. Broussard. If it was, you wouldn't win. I can assure you I know more about you than you do about me." Esnard's good-humored mask slipped. A glint of enmity flashed brightly, then vanished. He got up and strolled over to the serving buffet. He took his time getting a glass of apple juice from a dispenser.

LaShaun's supernatural sixth sense set off alarms. He was right. There was some critical missing piece she didn't know. Her mind ticked through possibilities. She touched his leather jacket and got an unpleasant shock. The images weren't clear, like an out-of-focus, grainy video. Secrets, deadly and foul. LaShaun wanted to search the pockets to get a better read on the man. When Esnard returned she drew her hand back.

"So, you knew Alison Hargrove even though her close associates had no idea where she'd gone. Which suggests you were part of her experiment."

"I have ancestral connections to Louisiana. With the mining operation yielding interesting results, I took the opportunity to visit. See the dredging process up close and research the family tree." Esnard relaxed against the faux wood chairback.

Lying. He knew that she knew and couldn't do a damn thing about it. Not yet, LaShaun thought with fierce determination. She shivered when his smile widened. LaShaun hoped her growing, inexplicable fear of him didn't show.

"Which side are you on?" LaShaun said.

Esnard flipped a hand as if swatting a fly away. "Both have degenerated into idiocy. I'm a centrist, open to all possibilities. Extremism opens one up to serious error."

"In other words, you'll play both sides against the middle until a clear winner emerges. Then you'll use every chance to benefit yourself," LaShaun said without thinking. He blinked in surprise but recovered fast. Still, she'd caught the reaction. Her smile of satisfaction seemed to annoy him.

"You're not as clever as you think," Esnard said in a clipped tone.

"I will figure out what you're up to, Monsieur."

"You're already two steps behind. I'm not your biggest worry. Better get that call." Esnard's smug grin returned.

LaShaun started at the abrupt subject change. Before she could demand more answers, her cell phone played a zydeco tune. She didn't have to look at the call ID to know it was the school. She walked away to answer.

"Maybe I'll extend my stay after all. Things are about to get interesting." Esnard crossed his legs and laughed.

LaShaun spoke to the school principal for a few seconds and then hung up. She headed for the exit but spoke to Esnard as she strode past him. "We aren't done."

"Tell Manny I said hello," he called back.

LaShaun spun to confront him again. "What did you just say?"

"You seem tied to that disturbing man. Maybe your fates are linked. Not a pleasant thought given his history. You have a daughter and a child on the way. Be careful of the company you keep."

LaShaun's cell phone buzzed again. She already knew it was Chase. The urgency to leave propelled her to jog from the dining room and across the lobby. A hotel desk clerk gasped at LaShaun's speed. Then he sighed in relief when the automatic entry doors slid open seconds before she got to them. She slowed once she reached her SUV.

"Honey, I'm on my way," LaShaun breathed when she answered Chase's call with one tap.

Luckily no local cops caught LaShaun. She violated speed limits to reach Ellie's school ten agonizing minutes later. The school resource officer didn't stop her as she raced to the office. Chase was there with Ellie cradled in his arms. Only then did LaShaun allow herself the luxury of losing control. She cried out and wrapped both arms around them both.

"She's okay. The nurse says we should get her checked out just in case," Chase said.

"Mama." Ellie sniffed as she hooked an arm around LaShaun's neck.

LaShaun knew that Ellie was scared only because of the reactions of the adults. She willed herself to exude calm and hugged Ellie back. "It's okay, sweet girl."

"What the hell happened?" Chase said, a dangerous edge to his voice. He let LaShaun take Ellie.

"There was a mix-up. The food service staff thought a parent had sent cupcakes for the kids as a treat. When the cafeteria manager came, she realized it was a mistake. Any such additions to the menu have to come through her and this office. I'm sure there's no reason to be concerned." Mrs. Rouzan, the principal, replied in an even voice. "No need for panic."

"I'm going to have those things tested." Chase had already started texting as he spoke.

"The local bakery is one we've had deliver cakes and cookies here before," the school secretary put in.

"They either came to the wrong school or a parent got the wrong date," Mrs. Rouzan added.

"Parents often send treats on their child's birthday or to contribute to a special class day," the secretary piped up again.

"So, you've confirmed all that with the bakery?" LaShaun put in, hoping to head off a full explosion from Chase.

"Well..." Mrs. Rouzan glanced at her assistant, who shrugged.

"I'm sure it's fine," LaShaun said quickly before Chase could notice. He had switched to talking on his phone.

Chase ignored everyone and walked close to LaShaun. "I've got people on the way. You both okay?"

"We're fine, babe. You go ahead."

"I like strawberry frosting," Ellie whispered to no one in particular. She sniffed before burying her face into LaShaun's shoulder again.

"Won't be long," Chase replied and strode off, phone to his ear.

LaShaun turned to Mrs. Rouzan. "Walk me through what happened."

"One of my teachers called Mrs. Peterson, the parent we thought sent the cupcakes, to ask a question. When Mrs. Peterson explained she didn't know anything about cupcakes, well..." Mrs. Rouzan glanced at her staff.

"I told the teachers not to give out the cupcakes until we investigated, but a few had been eaten," the cafeteria manager, head of food service at the school, put in.

"We had no reason to think—" Mrs. Rouzan floundered for a few seconds. "I mean, we'd never immediately assume some kind of deliberate attempt to hurt the children."

"Just a mix up, maybe even the wrong school. That has to be it," Valerie Simpson, Ellie's teacher, said. She looked at her colleagues, all of whom nodded assent.

"Still, it's our policy to keep parents fully informed in case of reactions due to food allergies. Is there something we need to know? Lieutenant Broussard seems to suspect some kind of threat or crime.

We should know if there is any situation connected to his work or your... what you do," Mrs. Rouzan stumbled over trying to categorize LaShaun's psychic investigations.

"We would have, of course. This took us by surprise." LaShaun felt tugging and realized Ellie was pulling away. She let her climb down.

Ellie tugged at her school uniform jumper to straighten it. "I'm fine. I only had one cupcake anyway. I was about to eat another one when Miss Tina stopped me."

"And good thing, too, dear," the cafeteria manager said. "We don't know where they came from."

"But they were for me special. My name was on the bottom of them." Ellie smiled brightly. "A treat. Maybe Papa Bruce sent them."

LaShaun gasped and looked at the principal. "You didn't tell us that part."

"All of the cupcakes were labeled," Mrs. Rouzan replied. "We just thought the parent knew each child's preferences or food sensitivities."

"We provide that information if they offer for their child's birthday, Valentine's Day, and other events," Mrs. Simpson added.

"I want to go back to class. We had a science experiment that's going to be fun." Ellie's small voice held a note of complaint.

"We'll see," Mrs. Simpson said with a patient smile.

"But I want to make fog in a jar. We're studying weather and stuff," Ellie explained, looking at LaShaun.

"The children aren't harmed, so I don't see why not," Mrs. Rouzan said. She turned to the cafeteria manager. "Store the cupcakes."

"Already done. I'll put one or two aside for the police." The older woman nodded and march off.

"Mrs. Simpson, you can take Ellie and resume you class activities. I don't see why we should disrupt the school day," Mrs. Rouzan said.

"Great idea." Mrs. Simpson grabbed Ellie's right hand and started to leave.

"Wait just a minute." LaShaun grabbed Ellie's left hand. They stood with Ellie between them.

"Mama, take a chill pill," Ellie said, her girlish voice firm and serious.

LaShaun recognized a favorite phrase of her Aunt Shirleen, whom Ellie had taken to quoting. Though she started to protest, a sense of calm settled over her. LaShaun let go of Ellie's hand and stepped back.

"I understand. The children should finish their fun school project." LaShaun heard the words coming from her mouth as if from a distance. She felt relief at complying.

"Yay!" Ellie looked especially pleased with herself. Her pretty brown eyes sparkled.

Chase returned looking more at ease. "On second thought, no need to panic. The kids seem okay."

The cafeteria manager returned with a white bakery box. "Here ya go. I put all of cupcakes left in there, including the one with little Joëlle's name on it. Oh, and the wrapper left from the first one she ate. Found it in the trash."

"I doubt we'll need those," Chase said.

"Well, everything is settled and back to normal. Very good." Mrs. Rouzan smiled.

The cafeteria manager put the box on a desk. She seemed more relaxed as she sauntered back to her duties. Mrs. Simpson nodded with a vacant expression. Chase had gone from sixty to zero. He beamed at Ellie as if he had no thought of being upset. LaShaun gazed around at them all and then at Ellie again. Ellie's superior grin began to fade in degrees the longer she stared at her mother. LaShaun got a jolt, not just a tingle. Her body felt a searing heat for a few seconds. She glanced down at her arms expecting to see burnt skin.

"I don't like needles," Ellie said.

LaShaun felt pressure in her head. Then she pushed back hard. "You're going to get tested, young lady."

"No." Ellie shook her head.

"You're going to do as you're told." Jonah seemed to have appeared out of nowhere.

"How did you know?" LaShaun gaped at him in shock.

"Chase. He figured me and Cee-Cee needed to know." Jonah turned to Ellie. "Cut it out, baby sis."

"You know what's she doing?" LaShaun said.

"Hey, Chase. I'll take these for testing." Jonah grabbed the box of cupcakes.

Chase shrugged. "Up to you."

"Everything is okay now. Really," Ellie said. She looked from LaShaun to Jonah. Then she stomped a foot in frustration.

"Not going to work, kiddo," Jonah said. "I'll make sure another box is put aside for Chase. His head is gonna clear up soon. Then he'll get back to being in charge and wanting normal forensics done."

"I didn't do anything." Ellie pouted when both adult psychics looked at her.

"Yes, you did. But part of it isn't her fault," Jonah said to LaShaun.

"Oh Lord. Alison Hargrove went insane on the stuff." LaShaun pulled Ellie against her. She knelt to stare into her child's eyes.

"We think she and the other kids will be fine." Jonah lifted the box lid as he spoke.

"*Think* isn't good enough," LaShaun replied.

Ellie shook free of LaShaun's attempts to examine her. "I'm not a baby. I have everything under control."

"Yeah, that's the problem." Jonah put the box down again.

LaShaun glanced at the other adults. "It's like they're in a bubble. Or in a parallel universe and can't hear us."

"Uh-huh. Interesting." Jonah stepped back with his smartphone pointed at the group.

"What in the world are you doing?" LaShaun frowned at him.

"Video for later analysis. Easier than explaining this phenomenon to the team." Jonah recorded a few more minutes.

LaShaun, holding Ellie by the hand in a firm grip, spoke to Chase. He blinked at her and returned to normal. In minutes he'd taken a second box from the principal. Chase checked to make sure Ellie and LaShaun were indeed fine one last time. Then he went back to the sheriff's office. After a quick side conversation, LaShaun and Jonah agreed on a plan. Over the next few hours LaShaun took Ellie to the local pediatrician. Saliva, blood, and urine samples were taken, over Ellie's tearful objections. Like any parent, LaShaun soothed her during the needle prick. Later, she bought Ellie a frozen yogurt waffle cone.

"For being a brave girl," LaShaun said. They sat in a sweet shop in New Iberia.

Jonah talked on his cell phone several yards away. LaShaun texted updates to Chase. She assured them Ellie seemed fine. Still, LaShaun studied her every move. She whispered another prayer of protection as she watched Ellie relish each lick of her treat. Jonah came back.

"That looks yum." Jonah smacked his lips.

"Mama can buy you one, too," Ellie piped up.

"Jonah's got a good job. He can buy his own," LaShaun teased. She caressed Ellie's hair with one hand and devoured the last of her own waffle cone. Jonah made a face when LaShaun burped loudly.

"Excuse me." LaShaun put a hand over her mouth. She laughed at Ellie's uncontrolled giggles.

"I'ma let it slide since that's baby gas." Jonah grimaced at LaShaun. "Just don't let loose from the other end."

"No promises." LaShaun rubbed her growing belly.

Ellie squealed. "Mama!"

"You think that's bad? Wait until you have to put up with baby poop and farts." Jonah tickled Ellie.

"Ewww!" Ellie screwed up her face and then giggled harder.

"All day, all night. And guess who'll have to help clean it up? Big sister, that's who!" Jonah delighted in her reaction.

"No, no. Not me. Ugh!" Ellie tried to tickle him back.

"Hey, cut it out you two, before they throw us out of here," LaShaun said, amused at their horseplay.

Her admonishment was half-hearted at best. Seeing Ellie behave normally relieved the nagging worry of what monazite might have done to her. Then she flinched as electric tingles made raised goose bumps on her arms. Movement at the corner of her field of vision made LaShaun look up. Manny stood outside on the sidewalk. She blinked and he was gone. Ellie waved to another child who'd apparently been to the doctor as well. They compared colorful adhesive bandages with cartoon characters.

"I'll stay with Ellie. Go," Jonah murmured while Ellie was distracted.

LaShaun was up and out of the door in seconds. Manny stood a few feet away waiting. He nodded and walked off. She followed him. Historic buildings housed antique shops and boutiques along the quaint downtown street. Not that LaShaun noticed. They ended up at a small park along Bayou Teche. Tourists milled around enjoying the bright cool day.

"You and Garland Esnard have history, Manny. I can't quite see it, but—"

"He's a dangerous man. Let it go, LaShaun. Y'all have no idea..."

Manny rubbed his face hard. He turned in a circle as if unsure where to go or what to do. His hands shook when he took a partially smoked cigarette and lighter from a frayed jacket pocket. Wind prevented him from getting a light. After two tries he threw both on the pavement with a curse. LaShaun picked them up.

"Someone sent tainted cupcakes to Ellie's school," LaShaun said in a savage, low voice. "So, if I have to beat it out of you—"

"I can't." Manny swallowed hard and wouldn't meet her intense gaze.

LaShaun gripped his right forearm tight enough that he winced. "You better because we're talking about my baby, my firstborn. You damn well best believe I'll be even more dangerous if you don't."

Manny shook his head. "You don't enjoy torture. You can't kill without blinking or losing sleep; walk around with blood on your hands and body, enjoying the feel of it. The taste of it. Rape men and women with so much force they lose their minds."

"If that's true, then you have to help us stop this monster. We have four dead people. Is Esnard involved, and how do you know him?" LaShaun pressed on. "Look, maybe I don't have sense enough to be scared. But my child, other children, are involved. Mathieu Baptiste was a good man. He didn't deserve a violent death. Neither did those other people."

Manny barked out a sound that crossed between a groan and a laugh. "You wish the body count was that low."

Manny muttered. LaShaun studied him with growing alarm. He seemed on the verge of a relapse into psychosis. He gibbered with an unseen third entity. Spittle formed at one corner of his mouth. He roughly swiped it away with the back of one hand. His eyes darted back and forth.

"Don't go back to the dark place."

LaShaun shook him hard. When he became less coherent, she concentrated. Her hold on his arm tightened. Heat from her skin grew. The baby inside her pushed against her belly and she gasped. Afraid of the effects she might cause, LaShaun trembled with panic. Yet she couldn't let go. Manny knew of a huge danger. She had to get him to talk. As if watching from outside herself, LaShaun raised her right hand. She slapped him hard enough that his head snapped to the side. Then she slapped him again, and a third time. Manny's eyelids fluttered as he staggered away from her. Then he cupped his face and huffed out a noisy breath.

"We better leave," Manny said, his voice hoarse but lucid. He glanced around.

"Leave?" LaShaun echoed in confusion. She blinked out of her daze and back to their surroundings. A group of people stared, frowns of shock and curiosity on their faces.

"Before they decide to take cell phone pictures and post them on the internet." Manny pulled LaShaun along with him, their positions reversed.

Then he spoke to the crowd in a loud voice. "Pregnant lady, hormones going wild. I shouldn't have gotten on her nerves. Woo-wee, lesson learned!"

"You can't get close to Ellie," LaShaun gasped. Manny was pushing her in the direction of the sweet shop.

Manny turned a corner and pointed to a small café. They pushed inside to escape scrutiny. "Let's hope nobody cared enough to call the cops."

"May I help—"

"Coffee, black, and herbal tea for my sister. Lemon and honey flavor on the tea if you got it," Manny said fast before the waiter could finish.

The young man looked at Manny, swallowed hard and nodded. "We do, um. Right." He scurried off but kept looking back over his shoulder.

LaShaun glared at him. "Stop telling folks I'm your sister."

"Just go with it," Manny mumbled.

"You keep giving me orders like I'm supposed to trust you. My daughter—"

"Yeah, yeah. We went over all that. Poisoned cupcakes, the school." Manny waved a hand as if batting away her words. "You notice Ellie being able to do things, like extra special stuff?"

"At the school… She controlled the situation. No, that's not quite it. She managed events. I mean people." LaShaun stopped when the waiter returned and put the cups down. He placed a decorative ceramic box on the table that held sugar and artificial sweeteners. Then a tiny pitcher of cream.

"I said black, and she's pregnant. She can't be putting that unnatural mess in her body," Manny snapped. He exhaled when the young man jumped at his anger. "Sorry, man. Rough day."

"No problem." The young man backed off, both palms raised.

"Esnard, Manny."

"Mama, we found you!" Ellie stood in the door with Jonah. "Jonah showed me the bayou."

"Hey, sweet pea." Manny waved at them.

Ellie gazed at him with interest. "What's your name?"

"I'll be with y'all in a little bit," LaShaun said before Manny could reply. She looked at Jonah.

Jonah whispered something to Ellie, and she grinned with delight. "Jonah's going to show me a toy store. What's it called?"

"Antiques, like your grandmother used to play with." Jonah nodded and they left.

"Be right back," Ellie called as the glass door closed.

LaShaun faced Manny. "Talk. Or this very pregnant woman will slap you into next week."

Manny wrapped his hands around the cup of hot coffee. "You don't know what you're asking. Maybe if you leave things alone it could turn out okay. I mean, still gonna be trouble, but keep it from you. Your buddies at TEA should be able to deal with it."

"Stop talking in circles," LaShaun hissed, but kept her voice down.

Manny sat staring into the cup as if looking for answers. Then he shoved his chair back and stood.

"Good-bye, LaShaun. You've been a good friend, even if you didn't mean to be. I'm glad you can have a life, a family to love."

"Wait." LaShaun gawked at him.

"I don't want to stir up that cesspool. Even more nasty creatures will crawl out."

LaShaun stood to gaze at him eye-to-eye. "What do you mean?"

"I'm exactly what everybody says, a crazy killer. I did it, okay? Sharing DNA with my piece of shit daddy was a stroke of luck. Providing reasonable doubt is the only thing he ever did for me."

"You're lying."

LaShaun blinked as snatches of images flashed through her head. She tried to focus on Manny and the visions. The effort made her queasy. She placed one hand on her stomach and felt the baby kick. She stumbled back and sat down. The coffee shop appeared to fill with mist. LaShaun rubbed her eyes. When she looked around again the room was clear and Manny was gone.

The waiter hovered over her with a look of alarm. "You okay? Your friend paid for everything, plus extra in case you want more tea. Something to settle your stomach, he said. We have peppermint..."

"No, thanks," LaShaun finally managed to get out. "Did the place fill up with fog or smoke?"

"Umm, no. Maybe I should call someone." The young man glanced around, looking for help.

Jonah pushed through the entrance with Ellie by one hand. "Manny whipped past the toy store like something was chasing him."

The waiter huffed out a relieved breath. "Thank goodness. I don't think the lady is feeling well," he said before LaShaun could reply.

"I'm okay." LaShaun remembered the cup of tea. She sipped a bit of the lukewarm liquid.

Ellie marched over to her mother to gaze at her. She put a hand on LaShaun's forehead, then squinted. "You've got a funny tummy again. Time to go home and rest."

"Good idea. I'll fix you a tea to go." The waiter left as if eager to send them on their way.

"Uh, thanks," Jonah called after him. "You gonna tell me what the... what happened?"

LaShaun felt another kick. She put on a smile. "We finished talking, and now it's time to go."

"You found out something and you don't want to talk in front of me." Ellie studied her mother, head to one side. Then she shrugged. "Grownup stuff. Auntie Shirleen says a child should stay in a child's place."

"Does she?" LaShaun pushed to her feet. The waiter came back and handed her a to-go paper cup.

"Yep, but then Cousin Azalei says I'm not a normal child. She was being mean, Mama. Facts is facts," Ellie added when LaShaun scowled.

"I'll still be having a talk with Azalei. You didn't do anything to show them your abilities? We talked about that, Ellie." LaShaun went into mother mode.

"I didn't understand cause I was a baby. Cousin Azalei explained that I had to be considerate and careful." Ellie took one of LaShaun's hands, one of Jonah's and stood between them.

"Your cousin sounds like the perfect babysitter for a psi kid. Doesn't treat Ellie like a freak," Jonah said.

LaShaun's growing anger with her offbeat cousin cooled somewhat. "Yeah, well, don't nominate her for sainthood just yet. Azalei hasn't always been so sweet."

Jonah laughed as they left the shop for the sidewalk outside. "You mean she's got a shady past. Like us."

"That man is really scared, but he doesn't want to hurt anybody. Sometimes he can't help himself." Ellie spoke in a matter-of-fact tone.

LaShaun and Jonah both stopped walking at the same time. Jonah crouched down to Ellie's level.

"Run that by us again," Jonah said.

Ellie pulled a small lollipop from one pocket. "Mama's friend. He left so fast because he's scared."

"Of what?" LaShaun regretted asking the moment the words had come out.

"I don't know." Ellie took the clear wrapping off the candy and licked. "He's got a wrapper on his mind, sorta like this sucker. That's what Papa Broussard calls them. Uncle Bruce says lollipop is nicer to say."

"Ellie, what do you mean his mind has a wrapper?" LaShaun said.

"People like us, they're not easy for me to hear or move like muggles," Ellie said and licked the candy again.

"Hey, you're reading Harry Potter? I loved those books and... Right, sorry." Jonah cleared his throat at one more glare from LaShaun.

"I saw part of the movie, but then Uncle Bruce told us we're too young and turned it off. Too much violence. And he didn't want to give me any ideas." Ellie giggled at the memory. Chase's older brother was another favorite relative of hers.

"So, other psychics can tell if you're trying to use your ability to 'read' them?" LaShaun asked.

Ellie's lips were tinged red from the lollipop. She paused in the intense act of savoring it. "Some. Him especially. Are you going to help him, Mama?"

"I don't know, or even if I should." LaShaun thought about Manny's declaration before he'd left. "Or how."

"LaShaun?" Jonah said, breaking into her thoughts.

"We'll talk later," LaShaun replied.

Jonah's eyes narrowed to slits. "You've got a plan I may not like."

"Now you sound like Chase. C'mon." LaShaun led them back to where they'd parked.

Chapter 17

That evening Chase threw a huge curve in LaShaun's plan. M.J. had come over for dinner. But it wasn't for social reasons. LaShaun didn't want to drop Ellie off with a babysitter. She worried that Ellie might use her newly enhanced abilities. Plus, LaShaun wanted to seem like a responsible normal mother. Fixing dinner, playing hostess might offset Chase's reaction to her plan. His news didn't help.

Chase strode into the family room. He sank onto the sofa next to LaShaun. "Ellie's safely in bed. I made sure she was sleeping. Only took me twenty minutes. Gotta be a record."

"How'd you pull it off finally?"

"We're taking her to the Children's Museum in Lafayette. They're having a paint party Saturday. You need to call Taylor's mama and Mrs. Marchand, see if her nephew can go. I promised," Chase said defensively when LaShaun's eyes narrowed to slits.

"Bribery, seriously?"

"I know, but we need to talk. Big developments in both murder investigations."

LaShaun felt a tingle down her spine. "Implications for TEA?"

"Damn, how do you... Okay, you tell me." Chase crossed one long leg over another and twisted to face her.

"I don't 'see' everything, just flashes," LaShaun replied.

"Right." Chase nodded. He seemed to lapse into thought.

"Well? Don't keep me hanging." LaShaun poked his side with one elbow.

Chase heaved a sigh and looked at her for a beat. "Mathieu Baptiste killed Newton Cross, your TEA operative. We're fairly certain."

LaShaun's mouth hung open as she went speechless for a few seconds. Then she shook her head. "Mr. Baptiste was one of the most gentle and kindhearted men I've ever known. And what in the world would be his motive?"

"I thought about it for a while. They were both TEA connected. So, I had forensics check. They had skin and tissue from each other under their fingernails. Mr. Baptiste died from a hematoma. The doc says it's possible he lived long enough to dump Crosse's body. He returned home not knowing how seriously he was injured."

"But the tattoos. How—"

"Maybe some of Cross's pals got here to help him too late. Found Baptiste already dead, or they finished him off and left a message. A 'don't mess with us' warning."

LaShaun reached out for some kind of image. She focused on memories of Mathieu Baptiste and pictured his friendly smile. Then she called up the sound of his deep, soft voice, the earthy smell from his favorite checked shirts. Chase shook her, causing LaShaun to blink fast to clear her vision.

"What are you thinking?" he asked.

"What a mess," LaShaun said.

"Yeah, well, Dave's happy. I wrapped up two murder investigations at once. And with Alison Hargrove dying of natural causes, he's over the moon. Case clearance rates are his passion." Chase gazed at LaShaun with speculation. "I know you didn't want to hear your friend was a killer."

"If Mr. Baptiste killed Cross, he had a good reason," LaShaun said.

"Oh, right. By a mess you mean for TEA. Members killing each other off and two top officials are dead."

"Don't forget Alison Hargrove ingesting monazite and becoming psychotic. I still gotta find out why Garland Esnard came to Louisiana," LaShaun murmured, thinking aloud more than talking to Chase.

"Maybe he was concerned about her after she disappeared. Anyway, I'm going in early tomorrow. Loads of nice paperwork. The downside to wrapping up cases."

"I'm going to talk to him. Esnard, I mean." LaShaun looked at Chase.

"Long as it's not Manny Young. You don't have a reason to see that wacko again." Chase stood and yawned.

"Hmm?" LaShaun realized he held out his hand waiting for her. "Oh, yeah."

"And don't pretend be asleep and get up during the night to call Cee-Cee or Jonah. I'm going to make sure you sleep sound, too, young lady."

One thing about Chase Broussard, he was a man of his word. With great tenderness, he made love to LaShaun as they spooned. She forgot about everything and everyone else. Until he lay snoring next to her two hours later. Then her thoughts cycled through the labyrinth of clues. LaShaun knew she had to be prepared for Esnard. She just didn't how, or even more important, why.

****

The next morning, she got Ellie off to school and saw Chase off to the sheriff's office. LaShaun promptly texted both Cee-Cee and Jonah. Minutes later they talked via Skype.

"Oh hell," Cee-Cee hissed after LaShaun finished briefing them on what Chase said.

Jonah gave a low whistle. "Our bosses are not going to be happy. We found out more bad news. You wanna tell her?"

"The TEA forensics team did its own double and triple dive into the postmortems on our two dead TEA top folks. Don't ask me how they can tell, but they're thinking those deaths weren't natural. Traces of psychic damage to their tissues."

"Kind of a reverse psychic healing," Jonah said.

"Actually, the correct name is psychic surgery," Cee-Cee put in. "Rare, but we have documented cases of people who can remove disease or a disorder from tissues with energetic incisions that heal quickly."

"So it stands to reason that same ability could be used to harm someone." LaShaun shivered at the prospect of such a diabolical use.

"You got it." Cee-Cee wore a grim expression. Her smooth face had uncharacteristic lines of worry.

"At least this gives my criminal team a line to follow. Kirk died from a hemorrhagic stroke, and Ricci from a STEMI heart attack, which is caused by a blocked artery. Both had the required health exams for those in top positions not long before they died. They came through with flying colors," Jonah added.

"But they could have still had health concerns that were missed."

"At their level of responsibility, the annual physical includes mandatory cardiology exams and MRIs. Not just a stress test but an echocardiogram stress test," Cee-Cee replied.

"Medical procedures that would detect heart or artery disease. Someone with medical knowledge and psychic surgery skills is our double murderer," Jonah said.

"Sounds like a coordinated effort and planning, not just one person." LaShaun looked from Jonah to Cee-Cee.

"Yeah, with a smart leader pulling it all together. One thing we've learned about the battling factions—they're wild. I don't see them being this calculated." Cee-Cee started to say more when her cell phone played "Despacito," a popular Mexican tune. "Be back, guys." Cee-Cee muted them so she could talk.

"I'm guessing we're gonna get called back to the southwest regional office. I already reported to my commander back at Criminal," Jonah said. "You still plan to talk to Esnard?"

"He's connected to Manny in some way. My brain's been going in circles with theories. Then at about three this morning I thought, this is stupid. Go to the horse's mouth, as Monmon Odette used to say. Then she'd add, 'Or the horse's ass, as the case may be.' "

Jonah laughed. "Wish I could have met her. I'm sure we would have gotten along."

"Yeah, both stubborn and enjoy antagonizing authority," LaShaun retorted.

Cee-Cee popped back on. "We're to report back to Dallas. Top brass is meeting about the mining of monazite, Hargrove's autopsy, and the internal fighting. We got folks flying in from all over. And they're interested in why Esnard is in Louisiana."

LaShaun sat forward. "You found out anything about him?"

"Turns out he's not a natural Canadian citizen. He moved there back in the early nineties from Michigan. Before that he lived in New York City. He's moved around quite a bit. But at some point, his identity just stops," Cee-Cee said.

"He somehow re-invented himself?" LaShaun asked.

Jonah broke in before Cee-Cee could reply. "Witness protection. Since the 9-11 attack, changing your identity has been tough, though it's still doable. But the kind of complete scrub I think Cee-Cee is talking about needs serious help."

"Yeah, as in the Federal Witness Security Program," Cee-Cee said with a scowl. "Mostly for criminals or their close associates."

"Manny is terrified of him," LaShaun put in.

Jonah picked up his cell phone. "We've got at least one member at the Justice Department. I think she's a federal marshal, even."

"Only one?" LaShaun said with a sideways grin. "TEA is slipping when it comes to having eyes everywhere."

"Kinda like a lightning strike having someone with psi skills who is also in a federal law enforcement agency. And getting in those ain't easy. Those background checks are brutal." Jonah kept texting as he talked in true millennial fashion.

"Most of us have been naughty boys and girls at some point," Cee-Cee put in with a chuckle.

"Commander Wagner will handle checking out Esnard. That's need-to-know only, top secret. He's pretty influential in Canadian TEA command. She says he was being considered for the international council," Jonah said, referring to his boss in the TEA Criminal Intelligence Unit.

Cee-Cee nodded. "If it gets out the Americans are digging dirt on him, we'll have even more chaos."

"When do we leave?" Jonah directed the question at Cee-Cee.

"I can make a case for you staying behind. I'll tell them you're leaving Friday morning instead of today," Cee-Cee said.

"Wait a minute." LaShaun tried to jump in.

"Two more days in Louisiana. The bosses won't object. They've got my reports," Jonah agreed. "I'll email the office now."

"Right," Cee-Cee replied, already tapping the screen of her cell phone.

"I can handle Esnard," LaShaun protested.

"Manny hasn't told you everything and *he's scared of the guy*." Jonah looked at LaShaun.

LaShaun started to argue and stopped. "I've never seen Manny terrified of anyone except his father. Hey Cee-Cee, did you find Esnard had any connection to Manny?"

Cee-Cee shook her head. "Hit a wall in 1997. He was living in New Jersey. Moved there from New York City. Odd gaps."

"So, he could have been in Louisiana at some point," Jonah said with a shrug. "Did Manny ever move out of state?"

"Just visits to east Texas, which is why he was a suspect in at least one murder there." LaShaun's third eye was trying to show her something. But she couldn't put it together.

"I was never a Boy Scout, but I agree with their motto. Be prepared." Jonah hefted his automatic pistol and nodded. Then he showed LaShaun a couple of his favorite gadgets. "I'm gonna be your backup."

"My husband is a cop, and he had military hand-to-hand combat training. I'm not exactly a damsel in distress myself." LaShaun gave them both a frown of annoyance.

"You got a whole human being inside you," Cee-Cee shot back. "And Chase only has latent psi tendencies. Not to mention he wouldn't know how to use them anyway."

"Like ninety percent of normal folks," Jonah added with a side-glance at LaShaun. "So, let's not waste time arguing and come up with our plan."

"Okay, fine. But you stay out of sight." LaShaun pointed at Jonah. She sighed at the mischievous grin she got in response.

****

Though she'd tried not to meet Esnard in the evening, he'd insisted his morning was full. LaShaun conceded to avoid making him suspicious. She didn't like leaving Ellie, but at least Chase was home from work. Sheriff Godchaux and Chief Deputy Arceneaux were handling media inquiries. For once in weeks, Chase didn't need to work late. His deputy could handle the routine wrapup of both murder investigations. After all, there was no arrest to be made. Alison Hargrove's body had been sent off as well.

Esnard had insisted he treat LaShaun to dinner at Ruth's Chris Steakhouse. The Lafayette restaurant had a subdued, elegant atmosphere. LaShaun dressed for the occasion, but was ready for action. She'd topped her black jeans with a black sweater. To stay warm against the chilly evening, she wore her tan leather jacket.

"I confess you intrigued me, Mrs. Broussard," Esnard said. He sat down after her at their table. He poured himself a glass of wine. He glanced at LaShaun from head to toe. "Obviously, you can't partake. I took the liberty of ordering a wonderful hibiscus and honey iced tea for you. Deliciously hydrating and no caffeine."

"Considerate of you, but you didn't have to buy me a meal. Hopefully, I won't take up much of your time." LaShaun sat back as the waitress placed a glass in front of her.

"By the way, thank your husband for me." Esnard lifted his glass as if toasting Chase.

LaShaun was thrown off by his remark. "Why?"

"For approving of this meeting. He doesn't see me as a threat." Esnard savored a sip of wine for a few seconds.

"Are you?" LaShaun took his cue and sipped the tea. Good for a restaurant blend.

"You tell me," Esnard replied in a mild tone as he brushed a bread crumb from the cream-colored tablecloth.

"I will in a minute," LaShaun retorted with a straight face.

His mouth twitched as if he was trying not to smirk. The effort succeeded in making him look sinister. He meant to rattle her. She knew it, but still shivered. Manny had spoken of him obliquely, as if talking about Esnard outright would increase the danger. She watched him banter with the waitress about his food order. His charm and wit could almost convince her Manny was paranoid. Almost. She focused on his voice, let the sound take her. Then she followed the feeling until... nothing. LaShaun blinked as her clair-audience feelers slammed against a psychic brick wall.

"Lovely Claire is waiting for your order," Esnard said. He'd change the pitch of his voice.

LaShaun recovered enough to smile up at the waitress. "Nothing for me, thanks."

"You have to keep your strength up. Or did you think I'd slip something in your food?" Esnard said once the waitress left. He took care to spread a pat of butter on a piece of roll.

Rage flared at his glib allusion to her pregnancy and the doctored cupcakes. LaShaun's throat went dry at the flicker of enmity in his eyes. She wrestled against the urge to strike out. Instead, she sipped more tea. "You seem to know about pregnant women and what they need. How many children do you and your wife have?"

"I have neither," he clipped. Then he drank wine.

"Sorry. Didn't mean to hit a nerve. But you're still young enough to—"

"I've never been interested in that kind of obligation. More like burden. I'm a career man." Esnard glanced around the restaurant as he spoke.

"I see." LaShaun signaled to the waitress and ordered a second glass of tea.

When the woman withdrew, Esnard studied her for a few seconds. "Most people follow up by asking about my career."

"I'm not most people," LaShaun replied.

"Clearly not."

LaShaun caught the slip into a different, more natural accent beneath the crisp pronunciation. The soft rolling of syllables gave her a glimpse beneath his surface. She decided to push harder.

"Why did you come here? And what did you do to scare Manny Young?"

"Unless you're working as a TEA enforcer, I don't have to explain anything to you." Esnard's right hand curled into a fist on the table surface.

"I'm not. Though TEA is very interested in why a top Canadian official shows up in Louisiana," LaShaun rejoined in a flat tone. She shrugged. "Can't say I blame them."

Esnard's façade clicked back in place. He flashed an amiable smile at her. "Canadians have ties to Louisiana. You've heard of the Acadian Exile, I'm sure. I decided to so some genealogy work. Curious with all the talk about this particular TEA hotspot."

"So, the fight over mining a substance that could potentially double psi abilities didn't factor into your travel. Or the fact that a major possible source happens to be right here," LaShaun said.

"My main interest is history," Esnard replied.

"And it just happened that you were in a museum the same time as Alison Hargrove. I saw the security video footage," LaShaun added with a smile when he looked at her sharply.

"As if they have anything worth stealing. No self-respecting relic thief would set foot in the place," he snapped.

LaShaun tilted her head to one side and studied him. "You were following her. Who are you, I mean really?"

Esnard stared back in silence for a few moments. Then he leaned forward with a predatory smile. "Do I remind you of someone?"

Malevolence curled out from him like a choking, poisonous mist. Her instinct to flee hit so strongly that she half rose from her seat. Determination to get answers pushed her down again. Esnard smiled with satisfaction at the impact his aura had.

"Why I'm here and what I do is none of your business. Listen to your friend's advice. Stay out of my way. I'll stay out of yours."

Energy that felt powerful, yet familiar, filled LaShaun's mind. No, not quite. She didn't get a conscious thought. Light, laughter, and a girlish giggle. The taste of a strawberry lollipop. LaShaun gasped, then placed a hand on her stomach.

"Ellie." She breathed out the name.

"Excuse me?" Esnard's expression tightened the longer he gazed at LaShaun. "Stop, or you'll regret interfering with..."

"You're a master manipulator, Esnard. If that's your real name." LaShaun worked to clear away layers of deception he'd built for years.

Esnard's jaw muscles quivered as he clenched both hands on the tablecloth. He lowered his head to glower at her. "Careful."

"Moving around, ending up in Canada. The FBI, no that's wrong. The NSA decided to let you out of witness protection. The only history you're interested in is what you find out to further your agenda."

"Don't mess with me, girl. Be content to pump out crumb snatchers with your imbecile husband," Esnard snarled.

"You want to get your hands on monazite," LaShaun went on in a relentless voice.

She ignored the curious, and not a few nervous, stares directed at them. Neither of them had raised their voices. Yet the other diners seemed to sense the friction between them. The waitress, intent on her duties, smiled as she approached. She placed a large plate on the table in front of Esnard.

"Here you are, sir. Oysters Bienville, our specialty, with roasted potatoes and braised fresh vegetables. Enjoy." The waitress turned to LaShaun. "Are you sure I can't get you something, ma'am?"

"I'm fine," LaShaun said, her gaze still on Esnard.

"I think we're done," Esnard snapped.

"Oh, right." The waitress blinked out of her peppy mood as she glanced from LaShaun to Esnard. She left them but looked over her shoulder twice.

"I'm going to finish this excellent dinner. Good food, interesting culture. Less interesting people, I'm afraid. It's time to leave." Esnard picked up his fork. Instead of eating, he paused to look at LaShaun. "Is that all?"

"You didn't answer my question about your relationship with Manny Young," LaShaun said.

"We don't have one. I'm mystified why you'd think I do. The man's nothing but an uneducated coonass murderer."

"You've insulted people with the same heritage. Not nice." LaShaun shook a finger at him.

Esnard plucked a plump oyster from the shell. His tongue flickered out to catch buttery sauce that dripped from it. Then he swallowed the oyster and hummed with delight. The entire time his gaze stayed on LaShaun. Her skin crawled as he gave her a lustful head-to-toe glance.

"Tasty. Sorry we couldn't spend more quality time together. Good-bye." Esnard turned his full attention to his dinner.

LaShaun finished the last few ounces of tea in her glass and stood. "We're not done. Not even close."

"On your head be it. Be certain you're willing to pay the costs, though. Mathieu Baptiste learned the hard way."

"Crosse worked for *you*. Mr. Baptiste somehow learned what you were up to, became a threat. Maybe he knew your secrets. You've been in Louisiana before, haven't you?"

"Now you're just throwing anything against the wall hoping it will stick." Esnard took a delicate sip from the goblet of wine and sighed. "I miss the cuisine."

LaShaun resisted the urge to smack the smug look from his face. "Choke on it then."

Esnard flinched in surprise at the harsh retort. LaShaun took advantage of the moment. Without warning, she reached out and grasped his left wrist. Her thumb covered his radial artery the way a nurse would. Warmth spread from his flesh into her fingers, her hand, and finally up her arm. A bitter taste flooded her mouth, like vinegar and bile. Acid burned in her throat. She let go at the same time Esnard dropped his fork.

"Get away from me." Esnard's voice shook. He pressed the wrist LaShaun had touched to his chest. "I said get out."

The restaurant manager strode over. "Is there problem?"

"Not yet," LaShaun replied in a cool tone.

The manager's nervous gaze darted around at the affluent customers. "I think it's best—"

"Enjoy the rest of your evening," LaShaun said to Esnard before he could finish.

As she walked away, LaShaun felt Esnard's fury snake out to touch her. She used her own psychic force to slap it away. Then LaShaun turned to give Esnard a savage smile. His expression for her brought to mind the phrase "if looks could kill."

Jonah seemed to peel away from the shadows in the parking lot. He was stylish, dressed in a black sweater and jeans. He looked like a typical handsome millennial out for the evening. No one would guess he was well armed, ready for battle.

"Did he give anything away?" Jonah glanced at the restaurant entrance as if he expected Esnard to emerge.

"Not willingly, but I got enough," LaShaun said.

Chapter 18

"This is such a bad idea. M.J. is pissed I sucked her into it. Dave would be in cardiac arrest if he knew." Chase shook his head as if wondering at his own foolish choices.

"We can't both go," LaShaun said with as much force as she could.

"I'll be damned if I let you face these crazies without me," Chase replied. He checked his Glock 22 handgun. Then he slid it into the leather holster clipped to his belt. He put a small Ruger in a shoulder holster he wore and put his camouflage sheriff's department jacket over it. Jonah handed them TEA-issue wireless earbuds. That way they could communicate verbally when needed.

LaShaun huffed in frustration at his stubbornness. Jonah stayed out of their argument. He shot glances at them from time to time as he readied his own arsenal. They were in LaShaun and Chase's spacious den, which had in effect become a war room. Del, the TEA operative who'd worked with them before, had agreed to drive in from New Orleans. Her job was to stay with Ellie and protect her if needed. She glanced at the decorative clock on the wall.

"Almost eleven. You sure he's going to make a move tonight?" Del looked from LaShaun to Jonah.

"I shook him up, but he's arrogant. Thinks he's always the smartest guy in the room," LaShaun said. She kissed the rosary handed down in her family for three generations. Then she pocketed it.

"But are you positive?" Del pressed. She studied LaShaun with intensity.

LaShaun heard the real question. Del was asking if LaShaun's psi reading of Esnard had been strong. "I'm as certain as I can be. As any of us when we use our abilities."

"He'll go for a stash of monazite for his own use," Jonah said, repeating the hurried conversation they'd had leaving the restaurant.

"A Legion member who's infiltrated the highest levels of TEA. That will set off a bomb at headquarters," Del muttered. "The bosses were sure we'd rooted out the infiltrators."

"He's not Legion," LaShaun said.

"But you said he's evil." Del frowned at LaShaun.

"Mama, I'm thirsty." Ellie stood in the door. Her pajamas had pink baby animals all over them. She stared wide-eyed at Jonah's gadgets.

"You've had a glass of water, a snack, and been to the bathroom twice. Go to bed, missy." LaShaun stood in front of her to block the scene.

"I can help. Let me come along and—"

"No way," Chase clipped. "Now listen to your mother and go to bed. It's a school night."

"Yeah, that's a reason. Not that she's barely out of diapers," Del whispered aside to Jonah.

"You haven't seen baby girl in action," Jonah whispered back.

"My daughter is going to have a normal childhood," Chase insisted. "As much as I can make it anyway."

"Uh-huh, sure. Same thing my parents said," Del retorted, unfazed by Chase's solid size or dark look. Then she stood. "I'll tuck her in, for the third time."

Chase strode over to Ellie and picked her up. He planted a firm kiss on her smooth cheek. "We'll be home and eating breakfast before you know it."

Ellie gazed at him. They were almost nose-to-nose. Something in his expression must have impressed her not to argue further. "Okay, Daddy."

"Good girl," Chase replied. He walked off down the hall with Del trailing behind them.

"Promise to tell me what happens," Ellie said. Her small voice faded as she negotiated with him.

"That kid is something else." Jonah laughed as he checked settings on two of his gadgets.

LaShaun watched him go through his paces. "Not sure you'll need those. I don't think Esnard will use psi energy or dark arts."

"You put a rosary in your pocket," Jonah retorted with a quick glance at her.

"Take nothing for granted." LaShaun grinned back at him.

Jonah's cell phone trilled a tune and he picked up. He stood the phone up on a small kickstand. Cee-Cee's face filled the screen. "Hey there. We'll be heading out soon."

"I figured. Wanted you to know what I've found out. We can't find any reason to link Esnard to Legion. Or one of the factions," Cee-Cee said. They heard the rustle of paper as she looked down to read.

"What about where he's from?" LaShaun sat down on the sofa so she could see Cee-Cee.

"Not enough information. He claims to have originally been from Canada. That's tough to fake. So, we uncovered that quick. I don't think he's from Michigan or New York though. My colleague at DOJ couldn't dig too much without setting off alarms. Which convinces us that he was in the witness protection program." Cee-Cee looked up again. "Sorry I can't tell you much. We'll need more time."

"You've told me enough. He's got a Louisiana connection, just not the one he claims," LaShaun said.

"You're sure?" Jonah looked at her.

LaShaun nodded. "You know what scares me most? That he's not working for Legion or either of the TEA cliques. Garland Esnard's got his own agenda."

"And he's willing to kill for it," Jonah added. He stood and slung his backpack on.

Chase walked in at that moment. He glanced at his wristwatch. "We'll make it to Devil's Swamp right before midnight if we leave now."

"Call me later," Cee-Cee said from Jonah's phone.

"Will do." Jonah ended the call. He looked from Chase to LaShaun. "We're ready."

Chase led the way to the kitchen door. Beau loped down the hall to walk beside him. "Whoa buddy. Where do you think you're going?" Beau woofed deep in his throat a few times.

Ellie appeared as if by magic. "Beau has to go with you."

Before any of the adults could reply she turned and scurried off. They looked at each other. Finally, Chase shrugged and patted Beau's large head. They headed out.

Jonah followed them in his rented all-wheel-drive Range Rover. Chase drove his truck, which would handle the muddy terrain better than LaShaun's SUV. They didn't speak much. Beau sat calmly on the back seat of the truck's extended cab. LaShaun tapped her fingertips nervously on the armrest, realized the sound she was making, and stopped. Chase placed a reassuring hand on her left thigh. The drive to Devil's Swamp lasted just over twenty-five minutes. They arrived at an unnamed dirt path southeast of the mining operation. Jonah had already parked behind a clump of wild shrubs. LaShaun and Chase got out. They closed the truck doors with care to minimize noise. Jonah trotted over to them.

"I saw headlights flash some kind of signal. Three sets," Jonah said quietly. He scanned the landscape as he spoke.

Chase eased his Glock out of the holster. "Maybe they know we're here."

"I don't think so. But to be safe, let's stay put for about fifteen minutes. If we don't move, they'll come looking for us," Jonah said. He spoke with the confidence of a seasoned TEA field op. "Can you shield us? I'll enhance the force."

"Huh?" Chase looked at LaShaun with a puzzled expression.

"Most of us can use psi powers to block other gifted. One of Jonah's abilities is to enhance the energy of other psychics," LaShaun whispered. Then she looked at Jonah. "Go."

Chase used tactical hand signals to communicate with them. They would move forward a few feet in a line, spaced out and wait. Jonah melted into the shadows in seconds. The time passed with no movement, so they regrouped. The sound of machinery started up.

"He's gotta know somebody would come for him," Jonah murmured. "If he's this confident..."

"Wait. Where the hell is Beau?" Chase turned in a circle. "He got out right behind me."

"Relax. Beau can take care of himself," LaShaun said, one hand on his shoulder.

"They better not hurt our dog." Chase nodded, and followed Jonah through the woods.

LaShaun went to their left, staying at least ten yards away from them. Despite her what she'd said, LaShaun worried what Beau might face. Jonah had made an excellent point. Esnard must have anticipated opposition of some kind. She sent out feelers for any kind of defensive measures he might have set up. The first sign came quickly. On the edge of the woods before reaching water, LaShaun felt pressure. The closer she moved toward the sound of excavation, the stronger came the urge to leave. She reached out to Chase first. Realizing he'd come to a standstill, LaShaun moved toward him. He had knelt behind a large palmetto bush.

"You okay?" LaShaun whispered close to his ear.

Chase shook his head. He breathed hard as if trying to push back against a wall. His jaw clenched with the effort. LaShaun felt it, too, though her powers helped. She swallowed hard, anxious about the physical effects Esnard's negative force might have on Chase. Then the pressure eased a bit. Seconds later it snapped, like a wall of plastic wrap had been ripped from them. Chase blew out air and stood. Before they could speak a shout rang out. They recognized Beau's barking in the same moment.

"I'm steady now. We better move," Chase said low.

LaShaun answered by squeezing his muscular left arm. She stepped back in the line. Seconds later Jonah's voice came through so clear she jumped. Once again, she marveled at TEA tech.

"Sounds like Beau engaged with two guard dogs," Jonah said. "Proceed with caution."

"Check," Chase said, his voice a quiet rumble in her ear.

LaShaun headed for the sound of ferocious snarling. The hairs on her arms stood up. Beau faced off two huge dogs. A Tibetan Mastiff, head to the ground between his enormous front paws, was ready to spring. A Pharaoh Hound, long and lean, stood at attention. It stared ahead as though looking for the best place to attack. LaShaun shuddered at the size of the first dog. She guessed the mastiff stood as high as her elbow. Both dogs had been stolen from Mathieu Baptiste's kennel.

"Okay, guys. I'm praying what Mathieu taught me about Beau works with y'all," LaShaun whispered.

"Wait, what are you doing?" Chase's voice came from her earphone. The urgency in his tone came through.

"Sticking with the plan. These dogs are their first line of defense," LaShaun murmured.

"LaShaun, you... hold on. Jonah is signaling to me," Chase replied.

"Okay."

LaShaun said a prayer of thanks for the distraction. She tapped the button on her earbuds to cut the audio transmission, afraid Chase would rush to her rescue. She edged a couple of feet forward, body at an angle. Mr. Baptiste had trained her not only in dog handling, but how to deal with these special dogs. Beau had a supernatural sense of smell. He could smell paranormal beings or phenomena over large distances. No doubt these dogs shared that ability. Both focused on the threat before them. Beau stood his ground, a low, dangerous growl thundering in his throat.

Please let me be right that you understand Louisiana Creole.

She began a set of commands to heel, mixed with orders to obey. Then she moved sideways to approach all three dogs. She avoided staring at them directly. To face them or look straight would be seen as an invitation to fight. The mastiff responded first by standing to its full height. The sight of the massive hound sent a shock through her. LaShaun threw in a protective prayer Monmon Odette had taught her. Then she realized the Pharaoh Hound had circled to her side. She felt a waved of warmth wash over her. Ellie?

"Mama..." came a whisper like rustling leaves through the woods.

LaShaun shook her head, sure her mind had played a trick on her. A cool breeze picked up, sending chill bumps across her body. The Pharaoh Hound trotted over to LaShaun. It sniffed, then gave a friendly bark. She moved her hand closer to the gun in her jacket. She didn't want to shoot either of the dogs, but would if they attacked. Meanwhile, Beau and the mastiff sniffed each other. LaShaun relaxed when the Pharaoh Hound came to her. It rubbed against her thigh once before racing off into night. The mastiff darted off as well in a different direction. LaShaun went to Beau and rubbed his sides with affection.

"I wish you could tell me what just happened and where they're going," LaShaun said.

She switched her headphones back on. She peered ahead in the darkness. Sounds from the mining machines stopped. Silence dropped down like an ominous blanket. The darkness pressed in like a living, creeping thing.

"What's happening?" she whispered. No answer.

A male voice pierced the night. "Hey!"

Three quick pops pushed her into a dead run. More shouts and grunts rang out. LaShaun's heart pounded as she reached the edge of the bayou. Dark figures struggled to her left and right.

"The barge," Jonah rasped, his voice in her ear sounded desperate.

LaShaun forced herself not to run to him instead. She spun in a circle, then saw the flash of a giant floodlight come on. Light spread in a circle. Esnard stood on the drilling platform. Overhead a helicopter appeared. A huge hook at the end of a cable hung from it.

"Go. Go!" Jonah shouted. He waved his arms frantically.

"I'm good." Chase's deep voice bounced in her ear.

She smiled even as her legs pumped. Chase intuitively knew she needed that last push to attack. She ran to a ramp the mining workers had installed. It stretched from the shore to the platform. Her steps thudded on the heavy metal. Once she reached a control cabin, LaShaun flattened her body against the side of it. She eased her pistol from the built-in holster of her jacket.

"You've already lost. No need to tiptoe now," Esnard called out over the noise of the helicopter.

LaShaun stepped out from her hiding place. He stood on the raised edge of the platform. He pointed up with glee. Esnard clapped his hands hard, applauding as a large tarp slung over his head. He'd managed to hook the tarp so that the helicopter could fly off with it.

"You know TEA will come after you," LaShaun yelled back.

"But they won't find me. Do you think I care about their ridiculous rules and regulations? Power can't be harnessed. Those with it will always rule. I won't live as a sheep being herded by other sheep." Esnard laughed and continued to clap as the helicopter's motor faded. "You lose. They lose."

"So what's next?" LaShaun circled him but didn't go closer.

"I don't want to spoil the surprise." Esnard stepped as if he was going to jump into the water. He grinned at LaShaun and gave a jaunty wave. "My men will keep your husband and friends busy. If one or all die, I'll send you flowers to express my condolences."

"Your dogs deserted you," LaShaun said.

Esnard frowned in confusion. Growling at his back made him jumped. "Where—"

"I like surprises, too," LaShaun said and fired.

Her shot struck his left shoulder like a hard punch. Esnard stumbled back with a look of disbelief. Then he charged LaShaun with a snarl of fury that surged before him. The negative force, his psi ability, almost knocked her off her feet. LaShaun threw her own energy out to repel him, but he managed to reach her. His solid body slammed her to the floor of the platform. He pinned her arms and her gun flew out of her hand.

"I'm killing two birds with one stone," Esnard snarled. He rolled his hips against LaShaun. "Too bad I can't take full advantage of this moment. But I have to go."

He let go of her arms only to close two large hands around her throat. Esnard felt sexual arousal at killing two living people at once. LaShaun's fingers raked the floor to find her gun but couldn't. Esnard moaned with pleasure as she gasped. Her vision clouded over as he squeezed harder. She looked into his eyes. Manny's words came back to her, how she had no clue the level of evil that could be concentrated in one human being. Love for her baby expanded in her chest. First warmth. Then heat, scalding heat. The kind of hatred she had for those cruel enough to enjoy inflicting pain. Soulless creatures who killed, even satisfied their lust doing so. LaShaun pushed a vision of her wrath flowing like white-hot lava.

Esnard gritted his teeth as he fought the pain. A howl tore from his lips and his grip loosened. LaShaun's teeth clenched. Strength built up inside her like steam in a pressure cooker. When Esnard let go, skin hung from both his palms. He stared in horror. Before he could react, LaShaun bucked until he fell from her. She placed a protective hand over her stomach. The pulse of life caused relief to flood through her. Then she directed all of her rage at Esnard. She planted one boot on Esnard's chest and shoved him away. Manny materialized out of a shadowy void. The floodlights overhead burst, plunging the platform into black. He stood over Esnard with a large hunting knife clutched in one hand.

"He's mine," Manny said quietly.

Esnard used his elbows and buttocks to scuttled away from Manny. "You don't have the balls. You never did!"

"Big talk from a man who can't use either of his hands." Manny looked down with a wistful smile. "I've dreamed of this day. I didn't get to give Orin what he deserved. But this... this is gonna make up for it a little."

Chase ran up. "LaShaun, honey."

LaShaun raised a hand, and Chase skidded to a halt before reaching her. "Manny, don't. You'll end up back in Angola."

"Some things are worth the price you pay." Manny advanced on Esnard. "You don't know who he is, what he's done."

LaShaun pushed to her feet, hand still on her tummy. Chase moved forward to support her. He placed an arm around her waist. "He's Ethan Young."

"But he's dead." Chase's mouth dropped open, and he looked at Esnard.

"I need medical attention." Esnard's hoarse voice communicated the agony he felt.

"You'll be out of your misery real soon, *brother*," Manny retorted. He lifted both arms, the knife pointed at Esnard's torso.

"Manny, please. You don't want to be a killer." LaShaun made a circle to face him.

"But I am. I'm the killer my father and my *dear brother* made me. No amount of plastic surgery could hide you from me, Ethan. You'll always have the sick, sour stench of evil no matter how many times you shed your skin."

"I'll make him answer for whatever he's done," Chase called out.

Manny shook his head. "The normal so-called justice system has nothing on Ethan. He didn't kill those people. At least not directly. Anything he's done is out of your reach."

"TEA will handle him," LaShaun put in. "Jonah and Cee-Cee will make sure their criminal justice division will—"

"What? Have a trial? Put him in jail? He's got a whole network of dupes ready to follow him to hell. I'm about to do you all a favor and end this shit right here. Right now." Manny broke off with a startled gasp.

Esnard floated up from the gravel-like surface. Terrified, he gibbered in a combination of languages as his body rose higher. Esnard flailed his legs and arms as if trying to find something solid to climb. Manny watched him rise with an expression of shock. He looked at LaShaun, who gaped at the sight before them.

"What in God's name is going on?" Chase pulled LaShaun away as if ready to run and take her with him.

Jonah jogged forward. "I can't hold him out of reach much longer," he said, his voice raspy from the strain.

Manny whirled to face Jonah, who in turn shook his head to ward him off. LaShaun felt the pressure of energy when Manny pushed against Jonah. She joined in to reinforce Jonah and keep Esnard out of Manny's reach. Esnard groaned and soiled himself when the psychic tug of war twisted his body.

"Son, I've had more years than you to master this stuff. Besides, I'm more motivated." Manny wore a grim smile.

He thrust the knife just as Esnard drifted downward. Jonah let out a long, agonized growl. Esnard yelped when his body jerked hard. A ripple in the air enveloped them all. Manny's form shimmered, and he appeared suspended next to his brother. LaShaun watched in horror as the hunting knife sliced into Manny's prey. Esnard's mouth stretched wide into a circle, yet no sound came out. The front of his expensive shirt slit open. A bloody line appeared from his neck to his navel. Sound seemed to have been sucked from around them, as though an invisible hand had hit the mute button. The scene became a video in slow motion. LaShaun blinked, and things went back to normal.

With a shout, Chase leaped past her like a basketball player going for a slam dunk. He grabbed Manny's jacket with both hands and yanked. Chase and Manny went down into the murky bayou with a splash. Jonah fell to his knees panting hard. Esnard landed with a thump that shook the mining platform. He dangled half in and half out of the water, his head submerged. LaShaun collapsed onto all fours as deputies and TEA operatives converged on the scene. More shouts and movement. She crawled to the edge, ignoring the grit that scraped her hands. Only when Chase's head broke the surface, pulling Manny up in a chokehold, did she let go. She threw up into the water, felt a hand on her back, but didn't have the strength or will to look up.

"All is well, *ma petite*," a soothing, familiar contralto female voice said.

LaShaun let out a sob of relief at the scent of Cashmere Bouquet. She closed her eyes as loving arms cradled her. The voice hummed a Creole tune close to LaShaun's ear.

"Monmon Odette," she whispered. "I knew you'd come one day."

Chapter 19

LaShaun opened her eyes against the soft light of dawn coming through fabric to her left. She felt the silky comfort of her own sheets. Home sweet home. Fragrant herbs, rosemary, mint, and sage calmed her. Ellie's face popped into view.

"She's waking up, Auntie Rose," Ellie chirped over one shoulder. Then she frowned at her mother. "You've been naughty, out there fighting like a warrior when you got a baby inside you."

"Huh?" LaShaun pushed to sit up against the pillows piled at her back.

"That's enough for now, little lady," Chase rumbled. He playfully ruffled Ellie's mop of coiled hair pulled into a puff on the top of her head. "Go help Miss Rose fix Mama a snack."

"No, no, no. Please don't even mention any food." LaShaun swallowed hard against the queasiness rising in her throat. The baby flipped as if in agreement, which made her feel worse. "Oh, please take a nap, little one."

"Be back." Ellie bounced off with a giggle.

Chase sat on the side of the bed. He massaged her temples. "Your obstetrician is very annoyed with you. 'What part of take it easy didn't she understand?' A direct quote."

"She said the days of pregnant women sitting around knitting for nine months are long gone. Women compete in sports, operate businesses, juggle a house full of kids. All while pregnant." LaShaun's rebellious spirit returned.

"Which is not the same as getting into a fight with two psychopathic killers. Another quote." Chase's grin faded as he placed a hand on her stomach. "The good news is you're both okay. The baby's heartbeat is strong. He's in the right position."

LaShaun blinked back tears and sighed. Then she lifted an eyebrow at him. "*She*."

"You know what, I don't care. As long as you're both healthy." Chase gave LaShaun a lingering, tender kiss. Then he stood. "I have to go in to work, but if you want me to stay..."

"I'm fine. Mama's little helper is here to keep me in line. And sounds like Miss Rose came to the rescue as well, huh?" LaShaun smiled at the atmosphere of affection wrapped around their home.

"Yep, I didn't want to freak out your Aunt Shirleen. She's not entirely comfortable with the magic stuff. Besides, Miss Rose knew already. Oh, and your other sorceress pals, the twins, are out getting us groceries. I tried to stop them," Chase added when LaShaun started to speak.

Justine and Pauline Dupart, middle-aged ladies who'd become her adopted aunties, no doubt had been called in by Miss Rose. They rode hard for each other when trouble arrived, especially of the supernatural kind.

LaShaun laughed. "You might as well accept it and get on with your day. By the time those three leave we'll be well taken care of for weeks, maybe months."

"Guess you're right. I promised to be back by lunchtime." Chase didn't move despite his words. He gazed at LaShaun. "We have each other, our babies, our friends. I never understood more how precious that is."

"Yes, it is," LaShaun said. She smiled when he blew a kiss and left.

Miss Rose arrived with a tray moments after Chase was gone. She set it on a small table in the seating area of their master suite. Then she stood straight, hands folded before her. "Well, he's finally convinced I can take care of you. I should say so."

"Don't mind him. He's still a bit jumpy after last night," LaShaun said and waved away a glass of tea.

Miss Rose frowned, but didn't insist. She sighed, sat down, and munched on a biscuit in silence for a few seconds. "Cee-Cee and Jonah want to debrief on the craziness that went down in Devil's Swamp. Seems the legends about it being a place where bad things happen are true."

"I think Esnard knew about its history. You never did tell me the details," LaShaun said.

"According to the old journals I have, in French, mind you, and written in the 1700s, a group of pirates raided a slave ship. They were taking the Africans through the swamp. Headed for the slave market in New Orleans. Human cargo worth a lot of money. Plenty made their fortunes on the backs of human beings." Miss Rose clicked her tongue in disgust.

"Rousselle family journals mention slavery as well," LaShaun said, the good vibes of earlier gone at the dismal subject. The bright sunshine outside her window appeared to get weaker.

"So, a rival group of cutthroats decided to raid the raiders. They outnumbered the first group, so they won. Then they celebrated by getting drunk. They raped the women, the men, and even three children who had survived the Middle Passage. Stories say the local native peoples and others could hear the screams of agony for miles. Then a demon appeared. Some versions claim it was Satan himself. Anyway, he said, 'I haven't had a good drink of blood wine for too long. Slaughter them, and I'll reward you.' The pirates lusted for gold more anything, so they agreed. The stories say the swamp water is so dark because the blood of twenty slaves still flows there. And some say Satan still shows up to take a drink now and then."

"May their souls rest with God and the angels," LaShaun said. She and Miss Rose recited a prayer for the dead in Louisiana Creole French.

Miss Rose stood. "Enough of sadness."

"Does the legend say what happened to the slavers?" LaShaun asked.

"No, cher. A few became rich plantation owners," Miss Rose replied. She dabbed her lips with a napkin and stuck it in her pocket.

"Oh." LaShaun frowned.

"They died young, though. The rest of that murderous crew, well, they died. One by one. Not easy deaths, either." Miss Rose wore a hard smile.

LaShaun nodded, then looked at her sharply. "Wait a minute. If the legends don't say, how do you know what happened to them?"

"The ancestors. But that's a story for another day." Miss Rose cocked her head to one side.

Cee-Cee appeared with a wide grin. "How's the patient?"

"Don't start with the invalid talk." LaShaun threw back the covers and got out of bed to accept Cee-Cee's hug. She smoothed down her soft pink yoga-style pajamas.

"Hey, is she decent? Scratch that, I know she ain't. I mean is she dressed?" Jonah called from just outside the door and strolled in.

"You didn't wait for an answer." LaShaun slapped his shoulder and then wrapped both arms around him. "Good to see you in one piece."

Jonah held on tight. "I saw you go down and... I'm glad you're okay."

"Me too." LaShaun grinned when Jonah blushed at his show of emotion.

"Garland Esnard turning out to be Ethan Young, brother to the Blood River Ripper, is a hell of a story.

That Schaffer guy is over the moon." Cee-Cee plopped down and helped herself to the last biscuit.

"Geez. I was hoping he was long gone," LaShaun huffed with annoyance.

"Don't worry. We clamped down on the real details. So he's happily making up his own." Cee-Cee grinned. "But we've made it so bland, and his version is so outlandish, that 'Ghost Team USA' ratings are crap."

"I'll drink to *that*," LaShaun said and drank from a glass of orange juice Miss Rose had brought. She sank into the second chair of the seating area. "I'm so ready to hear about Esnard, aka Ethan Young."

Cee-Cee dusted crumbs from her fingers using a napkin and sat up. "Obviously Orin Young, the late unlamented daddy psycho, lied. Ethan didn't die. He managed to get away from Orin and left the state. Fell in with a white supremacist group in Kansas. Moved on to Michigan and got involved in organized crime. He double-crossed a Detroit gangster, stole a huge amount of money from him. Became a federal informant and re-invented himself again courtesy of the government."

"So, he's a white nationalist on top of every other disgusting thing. Sheesh." Jonah sat on the floor next to the chair LaShaun took.

Cee-Cee shook her head. "He's whatever he needs to be to get what he wants. Dude has no allegiance except to himself. Our working theory is he helped stir up shit between the two TEA factions. Maybe so he could rise to the top."

"I think you're right. But..." LaShaun felt the flush of warmth again. Then the faint echo of a girlish giggle inside her head made her blink. "He intended to be the hero who brought all sides together and become the next president of TEA's global council. Then he'd forge a secret alliance with Legion, and eventually combine the two. Think of the power he'd have."

Silence stretched between the three after LaShaun's voice died away. She closed her eyes as a floating sensation engulfed her. Her mind expanded until she had an aerial view of a landscape. Then as if a rubber band snapped, the image vanished. When LaShaun opened her eyes, Cee-Cee and Jonah were staring at her wide-eyed. They exchanged a look, then gazed at her again.

"Whoa, that's some vision. If you're right... Damn, we've got some heavy-duty work to do." Cee-Cee pulled out her cell phone. She started tapping fast as she talked. Ignoring all else, she became absorbed in sending messages.

"Shit," Jonah breathed. "Did you inhale monazite or some of the stuff got in your mouth? Maybe it can be absorbed through the skin; or maybe—"

LaShaun and Jonah stared at each other for a few seconds. Both sprang to their feet at the same time. "Ellie," they yelled together and scurried to the kitchen.

****

Ellie left for school under great protest. LaShaun reminded her to be good if she wanted a trip to the

Lafayette Children's Museum. Miss Rose insisted on tidying up before she left. Once Justine and Pauline arrived loaded with groceries, all three set out to make the house sparkle. They even watered the potted plants. By the time they finished, LaShaun would have few chores for at least a week. Again, though she tried arguing with them, the ladies laid out a delicious lunch. Jonah and Cee-Cee had established themselves in LaShaun's library. They were in a confidential video conference with top TEA officials.

True to his word, Chase came home just before one o'clock. His truck pulled in just as Miss Rose set the table with hot roast beef po-boys, potato chips, and sweet tea. Beau settled into his comfy doggie bed in the family room, content to lounge for a change.

"We gonna get gone," Justine said after they all greeted him.

"Yeah, I promised my daughter-in-law I'd pick up my grandson," her sister Pauline added, glancing at her watch. They left after checking to make sure they didn't need to do anything else.

Miss Rose made LaShaun and Chase sit down while she saw them out. Then she returned and sat at the kitchen island with them. She poured herself a glass of sweet tea and sighed.

"Well, well, well. Orin Young lied. No surprise there. But I can't get over how we didn't tumble to it," Miss Rose said.

"We were a bit preoccupied with demons and murders for the last ten years," LaShaun quipped.

"Somebody says their son died, you don't think he's making it up. Not that Orin Young was the typical father," Chase said with a grunt. He started to dig into the food, but stopped when LaShaun slapped his hand. "Hey!"

"Tell us what's going on, then eat," LaShaun said.

Chase laughed, then looked at both women when they didn't join him. "Y'all serious?"

"Did Ethan talk about him and Orin, like why his daddy lied? I mean, I don't get why he just disappeared." Miss Rose leaned forward eagerly.

"What about Manny? You could say him cutting his brother was self-defense. Is he in jail?"

Chase waved his hands as they shot more questions at him. "Whoa, whoa. Let me get my bearings. A ton of stuff went down in the last few hours."

"Sorry, dear. You catch your breath a minute. Then you can answer," Miss Rose said as she poured him a glass of sweet tea.

"Gee, thanks," Chase said as LaShaun squirmed in her seat. "Delicious, Miss Rose."

"You're gonna be wearing that tea in a minute if you don't start talking," LaShaun retorted.

"Okay, okay. Garland Esnard, or Ethan Young, isn't talking without his lawyer. Not that he's in any shape to be interviewed. Y'all did a number on him."

"Good," LaShaun said with a savage grin.

"TEA is providing him with an attorney." Chase nodded when LaShaun's mouth fell open.

"I can't believe it," she blurted and stared at Miss Rose.

"Makes sense," the older woman said. "They want him back in their hands quick. The best way for that to happen is to settle up down here. My guess is he'll be there within a week of y'all cutting him loose." Miss Rose sipped her tea calmly as LaShaun and Chase gazed at her in wonder.

"How do you know all that?" LaShaun managed to say finally.

"I was on the sub-council for a few years back in the day. I attended plenty of meetings. But that's a story for another day. Go on, son." Miss Rose smiled at them and drank more tea.

Chase recovered after a few minutes. "Uh, yeah, so... Anyways, we can't charge him with a crime. He's not implicated in the murders of Mathieu Baptiste or the undercover TEA guy. No evidence he did anything to Alison Hargrove either. Him being out at the mining site late at night is odd, but not a crime. The company won't even press trespassing charges."

"But he stole a huge quantity of a valuable mineral," LaShaun replied.

"The company operations manager didn't tell us that," Chase said.

Miss Rose nodded. "See? Thinks he's gotten away with something. Bet he's planning to disappear again."

"TEA is on to him, so good luck with *that*," LaShaun said with a snort.

Cee-Cee and Jonah strode back in full of purpose. Cee-Cee held the keys to their Land Rover in one hand. Jonah wore his back pack. They engaged in a brief whispered exchange before they got closer.

"We're leaving for real this time," Jonah said with a grin.

"A lot of heavy lifting is on my calendar.," Cee-Cee said. She stroked Beau's back when he walked over to her.

"I gotta get back to Regional in Dallas. Loads of forensic stuff to review as part of our criminal investigation. Oh, and thanks for the help, Chase." Jonah gave him a collegial slap on the back. They shook hands and grinned at each other.

"Well?" LaShaun looked at them both.

"Jonah was thinking two steps ahead last night. He had me put the state police on alert. One of their helicopters stopped the copter that lifted that load from Devil's Swamp," Chase said.

"Yeah, intercepted 'em and forced them to land at the Lafayette Regional Airport. They also had a load of cocaine and crystal meth on board," Jonah added.

"Then why aren't you going to charge Esnard, I mean Young?" LaShaun said to Chase.

"Because the woman and man lawyered up, but not before saying Esnard had nothing to do with it." Chase shrugged.

"TEA sent lawyers for them, too?" LaShaun looked at Cee-Cee and then Jonah.

"Nope. They hired their own legal team," Jonah replied. "The important thing is we got the monazite back and secured."

"Yeah, Dave and M.J. agreed to return the mineral to the mining company. We got pictures. The helicopter crew will be charged with distribution of drugs. They don't seem to be worried, though," Chase said.

"They're willing to take one for the team. Whichever team that is," LaShaun murmured with a frown.

"Exactly. But we're going to sort out this mess," Jonah said with the confidence and energy of youth.

"I pray you're right, son. I really do. Evil takes root like a weed and sprouts up all over." Miss Rose wore a less-certain expression, born of more years in troubled world. She stood, took off the apron she wore, and folded it neatly. "Time for me to go. My husband thinks he can't do without me. He's right."

They laughed with her as she told more jokes about her beloved other half. After another fifteen minutes of affectionate farewells, LaShaun and Chase were alone. They stood on the back porch, arms around each other. Beau barked once and bounded outside to run in the sunshine. Chase rubbed LaShaun's back as they watched him. The neat lawn and woods at its edge made a peaceful picture.

"You sure you feelin' okay, babe?" He kissed her right cheek.

"We're both fine." LaShaun started and looked up at him. "You didn't tell me about Manny."

"He's in custody. A hearing is scheduled on his parole status, but the report will include that he was protecting you. Of course, explaining how he knew to show up at Devil's Swamp is the tricky part," Chase said.

"He saw his brother, and despite the years and plastic surgery he recognized him. Esnard was on a TEA video conference when Manny happened to be with us."

"Happened to be with y'all, huh? Not like I didn't warn you to avoid the guy." Chase raised both dark eyebrows at her.

"Anyway, he put it together and tried to *help*. You could say he acted in self-defense, or—" LaShaun snapped her fingers. "Like you said, to save lives."

"Esnard was unarmed, and Manny had a big knife," Chase pointed out.

"Maybe he managed to take it from Esnard. Or maybe his brother got cut on a piece of mining equipment when he fell." LaShaun looked pleased with her own explanations.

Chase turned LaShaun until she faced him. He put both hands on her shoulders. "Stay out of any defense of Manny. He's not interested in you investigating for him anymore. And no, I didn't threaten or pressure him to stay away from you."

LaShaun pulled Chase close again. She gazed out at their forest, comparing her happiness to Manny's loneliness. She'd felt his kind of isolation before, shunned by most. Different in a way few understood.

"I know," LaShaun said. "Manny met his past in Ethan. He's not giving up on creating a decent life."

"What? LaShaun—"

"He didn't kill the woman he was convicted of murdering, but he has killed. There's no evidence left. I don't even know who the victim was or the circumstances. But I do know that Manny is going to try and make amends somehow." LaShaun could almost feel the weight of shame he carried.

"Not sure that's enough for the victim or her family, whoever they are," Chase said. "But three law enforcement agencies threw resources at investigating him for years. Like you said, no evidence. The court will decide if he goes back in or stays out."

"He'll go back for a couple of years, then get released again with added conditions," LaShaun said.

"The fortune teller has spoken. What about Ellie?"

"Hmm?" LaShaun blinked at him.

"Something is different since they fed her that mineral. I can't put my finger on it though." Chase frowned in concentration. "She gets an intense look sometimes and... I don't know."

"I think the monazite has enhanced her ability to read, project, predicts thoughts. A lot," LaShaun said. She massaged his arm when Chase winced. "Maybe it won't turn out so bad. I mean, she's not acting unbalanced or anything."

He dropped his hand and looked at her. "I hear a 'but' coming."

"We should let the doctors at TEA examine and monitor her. Just for a while at least," LaShaun added quickly when he clenched his teeth for a second.

"One visit with us close by and then we'll decide if they can do more," Chase countered.

"Sounds reasonable. And hey, she's at school. No calls about weird stuff happening. Back to normal." LaShaun continued to massage his muscular bicep. She felt tension ease in him.

"We can concentrate on us as a family, no drama. Not until you go into labor that is. Can't wait to have my two babies runnin' around." Chase's expression brightened at the prospect. "Speaking of which, I better get back to fixing up the nursery. I got the wallpaper done. Now I'll get with my dad to finish building the crib."

"That's wonderful, sweetie. Oh!" She put a hand on the slight bulge of her tummy.

"You okay?" Chase pulled her into his arms, concern wrinkling his brow again.

"I think we're having a soccer player," LaShaun replied with a laugh.

She smoothed a hand over his forehead to banish the frown lines. Chase went back to describing his baby preparations with even more excitement. LaShaun nodded as he talked. Meanwhile, Ellie's mischievous giggles echoed in her head across the miles between them. The baby poked LaShaun as if adding its say.

Mix knowledge of voodoo, Louisiana politics and forensic social work, and you get a snapshot of author Lynn Emery. Lynn has written twenty-eight novels so far, one of which inspired the BET made-for-television movie AFTER ALL based on her romantic suspense novel of the same name.

Her romantic suspense titles have been nominated for and won several awards, including Best Multicultural Mainstream Novel by Romantic Times Magazine.

Learn more at
www.lynnemery.com
www.facebook.com/lynn.emery.author

Books
by
Lynn Emery

"A gifted storyteller." Baton Rouge Advocate

"Ms. Emery writes with style and class." Romance Reviews Today

"Romance and mystery as deep as the undercurrents of the Louisiana bayou." Bookpage Magazine

LaShaun Rousselle Mystery Series

A Darker Shade of Midnight
Between Dusk and Dawn
Only By Moonlight
Into the Mist
Third Sight Into Darkness
Devil's Swamp

Joliet Sisters Mystery Series

Smooth Operator
Hunting Spirits
Dead Wrong
Dead Ahead

Triple Trouble Mystery Series

Best Enemies
Devilish Details
Pretty Dangerous

Single Title Romantic Suspense

After All
Night Magic
Sweet Mystery
Soulful Strut
Good Woman Blues
Tell Me Something Good
Gotta Get Next To You
One Love
A Time To Love
Tender Touch
Happy New Year, Baby
All I Want For Christmas
Kiss Lonely Goodbye
All I Want Is Forever
✱The Lipstick Chronicles

✱ Multi-author anthology

Printed in Great Britain
by Amazon

81744021R00212